HAUNTERS
at the
HEARTH

HAUNTERS
at the
HEARTH

Eerie Tales for Christmas Nights

Edited by
TANYA KIRK

This collection first published in 2022 by
The British Library
96 Euston Road
London NW1 2DB

Every effort has been made to trace copyright holders and to obtain their
permission for the use of copyright material. The publisher apologises
for any errors or omissions and would be pleased to be notified of any
corrections to be incorporated in reprints or future editions.

Cataloguing in Publication Data
A catalogue record for this publication is available from the British Library

ISBN 978 0 7123 5427 1
e-ISBN 978 0 7123 6815 5

Original frontispiece illustration from *The Robin Redbreast
Picture Book*, George Routledge and Sons, 1873.

Cover design by Mauricio Villamayor with illustration by Mag Ruhig
Text design and typesetting by Tetragon, London
Printed in England by CPI Group (UK) Ltd, Croydon, CRO 4YY

CONTENTS

INTRODUCTION

Christmas has long been portrayed as an idealised time when we gather together and enjoy the pleasures of hearty food, entertainments and a blazing fire in the hearth. The oral tradition of using this cosy time of year to share ghostly tales is long-established, but the written tradition really took off in the second half of the nineteenth century—credited to a rise in literacy, changing print technologies and an increased circulation of popular fiction periodicals. One reason why ghost stories are so enjoyable at Christmas is that they subvert any comfortable domestic familiarity. Homely everyday objects and settings are rendered unfamiliar and uncanny. We feel pleasantly unsettled.

The eighteen stories in this fourth collection of weird Christmas tales are drawn from across the spectral spectrum. The earliest dates from 1864, the first golden age of the Christmas ghost story, and the latest is from 110 years later, when belief in the paranormal had been overtaken by hard science, but our enjoyment of supernatural stories had not lessened. Here you will find well-respected writers known for their ghost tales, such as Amelia B. Edwards, W. W. Jacobs and Celia Fremlin. However there are also stories by authors better-known for an entirely different style of fiction—D. H. Lawrence, James Hadley Chase, and Winston Graham, for example. I've also included tales by two writers about whom we know little or nothing at all—namely E. S. Knights and George Denby. The subject matter of the stories is similarly wide-ranging, encompassing timeslips; ghostly retribution; portal fantasy; sinister carol singers; a possessed pantomime costume; body horror at a Christmas tree farm; and a Black Mass. It's one of the great joys of editing collections of festive ghost stories to see the different inventively eerie ways in which authors use the genre's traditional boundaries.

Should you find yourself sitting by an open fire this Christmas, look into the flames and perhaps you will see a spooky shape or two, flickering there...

TANYA KIRK

Lead Curator, Printed Heritage Collections 1601–1900

A NOTE FROM THE PUBLISHER

The original short stories reprinted in the British Library Tales of the Weird series were written and published in a period ranging across the nineteenth and twentieth centuries. There are many elements of these stories which continue to entertain modern readers; however, in some cases there are also uses of language, instances of stereotyping and some attitudes expressed by narrators or characters which may not be endorsed by the publishing standards of today. We acknowledge therefore that some elements in the stories selected for reprinting may continue to make uncomfortable reading for some of our audience. With this series British Library Publishing aims to offer a new readership a chance to read some of the rare material of the British Library's collections in an affordable paperback format, to enjoy their merits and to look back into the worlds of the past two centuries as portrayed by their writers. It is not possible to separate these stories from the history of their writing and as such the following stories are presented as they were originally published with minor edits only, made for consistency of style and sense. We welcome feedback from our readers, which can be sent to the following address:

British Library Publishing
The British Library
96 Euston Road
London, NW1 2DB
United Kingdom

THE PHANTOM COACH

Amelia B. Edwards

First published in *All the Year Round*, Christmas 1864

Amelia Ann Blanford Edwards (1831–1892) was a polymath. As a child she wrote stories and poems which she illustrated herself. She decided to aim for a career in music and learned the organ, then returned to the idea of being a writer, and in later life became an influential Egyptologist. She was also an active supporter of women's suffrage. Today Edwards is known more for her contributions to archaeology than her stories, as she campaigned for more ethical methods in which historic sites were preserved rather than plundered. However, she also published novels, children's books, poetry and travelogues, and was a regular contributor to Christmas periodicals, writing a number of ghost stories for them. This story first appeared in *All the Year Round*, a weekly periodical edited and co-owned by Charles Dickens. The magazine had already carried the first appearances in print of Dickens' novels *A Tale of Two Cities* and *Great Expectations*, as well as other significant Victorian serialised novels by Wilkie Collins and Elizabeth Gaskell.

This is a fairly traditional but menacingly atmospheric ghost story, in a similar vein to Dickens' much-anthologised tale 'The Signal-Man' which first appeared in the same magazine two years later. 'The Phantom Coach' speaks to the conflict between science and the spiritual world, which would become a major theme in supernatural fiction in the later nineteenth and early twentieth centuries.

The circumstances I am about to relate to you have truth to recommend them. They happened to myself, and my recollection of them is as vivid as if they had taken place only yesterday. Twenty years, however, have gone by since that night. During those twenty years I have told the story to but one other person. I tell it now with a reluctance which I find it difficult to overcome. All I entreat, meanwhile, is that you will abstain from forcing your own conclusions upon me. I want nothing explained away. I desire no arguments. My mind on this subject is quite made up, and, having the testimony of my own senses to rely upon, I prefer to abide by it.

Well! It was just twenty years ago, and within a day or two of the end of the grouse season. I had been out all day with my gun, and had had no sport to speak of. The wind was due east; the month, December; the place, a bleak wide moor in the far north of England. And I had lost my way. It was not a pleasant place in which to lose one's way, with the first feathery flakes of a coming snowstorm just fluttering down upon the heather, and the leaden evening closing in all around. I shaded my eyes with my hand, and stared anxiously into the gathering darkness, where the purple moorland melted into a range of low hills, some ten or twelve miles distant. Not the faintest smoke-wreath, not the tiniest cultivated patch, or fence, or sheep-track, met my eyes in any direction. There was nothing for it but to walk on, and take my chance of finding what shelter I could, by the way. So I shouldered my gun again, and pushed wearily forward; for I had been on foot since an hour after daybreak, and had eaten nothing since breakfast.

Meanwhile, the snow began to come down with ominous steadiness, and the wind fell. After this, the cold became more intense, and the night came rapidly up. As for me, my prospects darkened with the darkening sky, and my heart grew heavy as I thought how my young wife was already watching for me through the window of our little inn parlour, and thought of all the suffering in store for her throughout this weary night. We had been married four months, and, having spent our autumn in the Highlands, were now lodging in a remote little village situated just on the verge of the great English moorlands. We were very much in love, and, of course, very happy. This morning, when we parted, she had implored me to return before dusk, and I had promised her that I would. What would I not have given to have kept my word!

Even now, weary as I was, I felt that with a supper, an hour's rest, and a guide, I might still get back to her before midnight, if only guide and shelter could be found.

And all this time, the snow fell and the night thickened. I stopped and shouted every now and then, but my shouts seemed only to make the silence deeper. Then a vague sense of uneasiness came upon me, and I began to remember stories of travellers who had walked on and on in the falling snow until, wearied out, they were fain to lie down and sleep their lives away. Would it be possible, I asked myself, to keep on thus through all the long dark night? Would there not come a time when my limbs must fail, and my resolution give way? When I, too, must sleep the sleep of death. Death! I shuddered. How hard to die just now, when life lay all so bright before me! How hard for my darling, whose whole loving heart but that thought was not to be borne! To banish it, I shouted again, louder and longer, and then listened eagerly. Was my shout answered, or did I only fancy that I heard a far-off cry? I halloed again, and again the echo followed. Then a wavering speck of light came suddenly out of the dark, shifting, disappearing, growing momentarily nearer and brighter. Running towards it at full speed, I found myself, to my great joy, face to face with an old man and a lantern.

"Thank God!" was the exclamation that burst involuntarily from my lips.

Blinking and frowning, he lifted his lantern and peered into my face.

"What for?" growled he, sulkily.

"Well—for you. I began to fear I should be lost in the snow."

"Eh, then, folks do get cast away hereabouts fra' time to time, an' what's to hinder you from bein' cast away likewise, if the Lord's so minded?"

"If the Lord is so minded that you and I shall be lost together, friend, we must submit," I replied; "but I don't mean to be lost without you. How far am I now from Dwolding?"

"A gude twenty mile, more or less."

"And the nearest village?"

"The nearest village is Wyke, an' that's twelve mile t'other side."

"Where do you live, then?"

"Out yonder," said he, with a vague jerk of the lantern.

"You're going home, I presume?"

"Maybe I am."

"Then I'm going with you."

The old man shook his head, and rubbed his nose reflectively with the handle of the lantern.

"It ain't o' no use," growled he. "He 'ont let you in—not he."

"We'll see about that," I replied, briskly. "Who is He?"

"The master."

"Who is the master?"

"That's nowt to you," was the unceremonious reply.

"Well, well; you lead the way, and I'll engage that the master shall give me shelter and a supper tonight."

"Eh, you can try him!" muttered my reluctant guide; and, still shaking his head, he hobbled, gnome-like, away through the falling snow. A large mass loomed up presently out of the darkness, and a huge dog rushed out, barking furiously.

"Is this the house?" I asked.

"Ay, it's the house. Down, Bey!" And he fumbled in his pocket for the key.

I drew up close behind him, prepared to lose no chance of entrance, and saw in the little circle of light shed by the lantern that the door was heavily studded with iron nails, like the door of a prison. In another minute he had turned the key and I had pushed past him into the house.

Once inside, I looked round with curiosity, and found myself in a great raftered hall, which served, apparently, a variety of uses. One end was piled to the roof with corn, like a barn. The other was stored with flour-sacks, agricultural implements, casks, and all kinds of miscellaneous lumber; while from the beams overhead hung rows of hams, flitches, and bunches of dried herbs for winter use. In the centre of the floor stood some huge object gauntly dressed in a dingy wrapping-cloth, and reaching half way to the rafters. Lifting a corner of this cloth, I saw, to my surprise, a telescope of very considerable size, mounted on a rude movable platform, with four small wheels. The tube was made of painted wood, bound round with bands of metal rudely fashioned; the speculum, so far as I could estimate its size in the dim light, measured at least fifteen inches in diameter. While I was yet examining the instrument, and asking myself whether it was not the work of some self-taught optician, a bell rang sharply.

"That's for you," said my guide, with a malicious grin. "Yonder's his room."

He pointed to a low black door at the opposite side of the hall. I crossed over, rapped somewhat loudly, and went in, without waiting for an invitation. A huge, white-haired old man rose from a table covered with books and papers, and confronted me sternly.

"Who are you?" said he. "How came you here? What do you want?"

"James Murray, barrister-at-law. On foot across the moor. Meat, drink, and sleep."

He bent his bushy brows into a portentous frown.

"Mine is not a house of entertainment," he said, haughtily. "Jacob, how dared you admit this stranger?"

"I didn't admit him," grumbled the old man. "He followed me over the muir, and shouldered his way in before me. I'm no match for six foot two."

"And pray, sir, by what right have you forced an entrance into my house?"

"The same by which I should have clung to your boat, if I were drowning. The right of self-preservation."

"Self-preservation?"

"There's an inch of snow on the ground already," I replied, briefly; "and it would be deep enough to cover my body before daybreak."

He strode to the window, pulled aside a heavy black curtain, and looked out.

"It is true," he said. "You can stay, if you choose, till morning. Jacob, serve the supper."

With this he waved me to a seat, resumed his own, and became at once absorbed in the studies from which I had disturbed him.

I placed my gun in a corner, drew a chair to the hearth, and examined my quarters at leisure. Smaller and less incongruous in its arrangements than the hall, this room contained, nevertheless, much to awaken my curiosity. The floor was carpetless. The whitewashed walls were in parts scrawled over with strange diagrams, and in others covered with shelves crowded with philosophical instruments, the uses of many of which were unknown to me. On one side of the fireplace, stood a bookcase filled with dingy folios; on the other, a small organ, fantastically decorated with painted carvings of mediæval saints and devils. Through the half-opened door of a cupboard at the further end of the room, I saw a long array of geological specimens, surgical preparations, crucibles, retorts, and jars of chemicals; while on the mantelshelf beside me, amid a number of small objects, stood a model of the solar system, a small galvanic battery, and a microscope. Every chair had its burden. Every corner was heaped high with books. The very floor was littered over with maps, casts, papers, tracings, and learned lumber of all conceivable kinds.

I stared about me with an amazement increased by every fresh object upon which my eyes chanced to rest. So strange a room I had never seen; yet seemed it stranger still, to find such a room in a lone farmhouse amid those wild and solitary moors! Over and over again, I looked from my host to his surroundings, and from his surroundings back to my host, asking myself who and what he could be? His head was singularly fine; but it was more the head of a poet than of a philosopher. Broad in the temples, prominent over the eyes, and clothed with a rough profusion of perfectly white hair, it had all the ideality and much of the ruggedness that characterises the head of Louis von Beethoven. There were the same deep lines about the mouth, and the same stern furrows in the brow. There was the same concentration of expression. While I was yet observing him, the door opened, and Jacob brought in the supper. His master then closed his book, rose, and with more courtesy of manner than he had yet shown, invited me to the table.

A dish of ham and eggs, a loaf of brown bread, and a bottle of admirable sherry, were placed before me.

"I have but the homeliest farmhouse fare to offer you, sir," said my entertainer. "Your appetite, I trust, will make up for the deficiencies of our larder."

I had already fallen upon the viands, and now protested, with the enthusiasm of a starving sportsman, that I had never eaten anything so delicious.

He bowed stiffly, and sat down to his own supper, which consisted, primitively, of a jug of milk and a basin of porridge. We ate in silence, and, when we had done, Jacob removed the tray. I then drew my chair back to the fireside. My host, somewhat to my surprise, did the same, and turning abruptly towards me, said:

"Sir, I have lived here in strict retirement for three-and-twenty years. During that time, I have not seen as many strange faces, and I have not read a single newspaper. You are the first stranger who has crossed my threshold for more than four years. Will you favour me with a few words of information respecting that outer world from which I have parted company so long?"

"Pray interrogate me," I replied. "I am heartily at your service."

He bent his head in acknowledgment; leaned forward, with his elbows resting on his knees and his chin supported in the palms of his hands; stared fixedly into the fire; and proceeded to question me.

His inquiries related chiefly to scientific matters, with the later progress of which, as applied to the practical purposes of life, he was almost wholly unacquainted. No student of science myself, I replied as well as my slight information permitted; but the task was far from easy, and I was much relieved when, passing from interrogation to discussion, he began pouring forth his own conclusions upon the facts which I had been attempting to place before him. He talked, and I listened spellbound. He talked till I believe he almost forgot my presence, and only thought aloud. I had never heard anything like it then; I have never heard anything like it since. Familiar with all systems of all philosophies, subtle in analysis, bold in generalisation, he poured forth his thoughts in an uninterrupted stream, and, still leaning forward in the same moody attitude with his eyes fixed upon the fire, wandered from topic to topic, from speculation to speculation, like an inspired dreamer. From practical science to mental philosophy; from electricity in the wire to electricity in the nerve; from Watts to Mesmer, from Mesmer to Reichenbach, from Reichenbach to Swedenborg, Spinoza, Condillac, Descartes, Berkeley, Aristotle, Plato, and the Magi and mystics of the East, were transitions which, however bewildering in their variety and scope, seemed easy and harmonious upon his lips as sequences in music. By-and-by—I forget now by what link of conjecture or illustration—he passed on to that field which lies beyond the boundary line of even conjectural philosophy, and reaches no man knows whither. He spoke of the soul and its aspirations; of the spirit and its powers; of second sight; of prophecy; of those phenomena which, under the names of ghosts, spectres, and supernatural appearances, have been denied by the sceptics and attested by the credulous, of all ages.

"The world," he said, "grows hourly more and more sceptical of all that lies beyond its own narrow radius; and our men of science foster the fatal tendency. They condemn as fable all that resists experiment. They reject as false all that cannot be brought to the test of the laboratory or the dissecting-room. Against what superstition have they waged so long and obstinate a war, as against the belief in apparitions? And yet what superstition has maintained its hold upon the minds of men so long and so firmly? Show me any fact in physics, in history, in archæology, which is supported by testimony so wide and so various. Attested by all races of men, in all ages, and in all climates, by the soberest sages of antiquity, by the rudest savage of today, by the Christian, the Pagan, the Pantheist, the Materialist, this phenomenon is treated as a nursery tale by the philosophers of our century. Circumstantial evidence weighs with them as a feather in the balance. The comparison of causes with effects, however valuable in physical science, is put aside as worthless and unreliable. The evidence of competent witnesses, however conclusive in a court of justice, counts for nothing. He who pauses before he pronounces, is condemned as a trifler. He who believes, is a dreamer or a fool."

He spoke with bitterness, and, having said thus, relapsed for some minutes into silence. Presently he raised his head from his hands, and added, with an altered voice and manner, "I, sir, paused, investigated, believed, and was not ashamed to state my convictions to the world. I, too, was branded as a visionary, held up to ridicule by my contemporaries, and hooted from that field of science in which I had laboured with honour during all the best years of my life. These things happened just three-and-twenty years ago. Since then, I have lived as you see me living now, and the world has forgotten me, as I have forgotten the world. You have my history."

"It is a very sad one," I murmured, scarcely knowing what to answer.

"It is a very common one," he replied. "I have only suffered for the truth, as many a better and wiser man has suffered before me."

He rose, as if desirous of ending the conversation, and went over to the window.

"It has ceased snowing," he observed, as he dropped the curtain, and came back to the fireside.

"Ceased!" I exclaimed, starting eagerly to my feet. "Oh, if it were only possible—but no! it is hopeless. Even if I could find my way across the moor, I could not walk twenty miles tonight."

"Walk twenty miles tonight!" repeated my host. "What are you thinking of?"

"Of my wife," I replied, impatiently. "Of my young wife, who does not know that I have lost my way, and who is at this moment breaking her heart with suspense and terror."

"Where is she?"

"At Dwolding, twenty miles away."

"At Dwolding," he echoed, thoughtfully. "Yes, the distance, it is true, is twenty miles; but—are you so very anxious to save the next six or eight hours?"

"So very, very anxious, that I would give ten guineas at this moment for a guide and a horse."

"Your wish can be gratified at a less costly rate," said he, smiling. "The night mail from the north, which changes horses at Dwolding, passes within five miles of this spot, and will be due at a certain cross-road in about an hour and a quarter. If Jacob were to go with you across the moor, and put you into the old coach-road, you could find your way, I suppose, to where it joins the new one?"

"Easily—gladly."

He smiled again, rang the bell, gave the old servant his directions, and, taking a bottle of whisky and a wineglass from the cupboard in which he kept his chemicals, said:

"The snow lies deep, and it will be difficult walking tonight on the moor. A glass of usquebaugh before you start?"

I would have declined the spirit, but he pressed it on me, and I drank it. It went down my throat like liquid flame, and almost took my breath away.

"It is strong," he said; "but it will help to keep out the cold. And now you have no moments to spare. Good night!"

I thanked him for his hospitality, and would have shaken hands, but that he had turned away before I could finish my sentence. In another minute I had traversed the hall, Jacob had locked the outer door behind me, and we were out on the wide white moor.

Although the wind had fallen, it was still bitterly cold. Not a star glimmered in the black vault overhead. Not a sound, save the rapid crunching of the snow beneath our feet, disturbed the heavy stillness of the night. Jacob, not too well pleased with his mission, shambled on before in sullen silence, his lantern in his hand, and his shadow at his feet. I followed, with my gun over my shoulder, as little inclined for conversation as himself. My thoughts were full of my late host. His voice yet rang in my ears. His eloquence yet held my imagination captive. I remember to this day, with surprise, how my over-excited brain retained whole sentences and parts of sentences, troops of brilliant images, and fragments of splendid reasoning, in the very words in which he had uttered them. Musing thus over what I had heard, and striving to recall a lost link here and there, I strode on at the heels of my guide, absorbed and unobservant. Presently—at the end, as it seemed to me, of only a few minutes—he came to a sudden halt, and said:

"Yon's your road. Keep the stone fence to your right hand, and you can't fail of the way."

"This, then, is the old coach-road?"

"Ay, 'tis the old coach-road."

"And how far do I go, before I reach the cross-roads?"

"Nigh upon three mile."

I pulled out my purse, and he became more communicative.

"The road's a fair road enough," said he, "for foot passengers; but 'twas over steep and narrow for the northern traffic. You'll mind where the parapet's broken away, close again the sign-post. It's never been mended since the accident."

"What accident?"

"Eh, the night mail pitched right over into the valley below— a gude fifty feet an' more—just at the worst bit o' road in the whole county."

"Horrible! Were many lives lost?"

"All. Four were found dead, and t'other two died next morning."

"How long is it since this happened?"

"Just nine year."

"Near the sign-post, you say? I will bear it in mind. Good night."

"Gude night, sir, and thankee." Jacob pocketed his half-crown, made a faint pretence of touching his hat, and trudged back by the way he had come.

I watched the light of his lantern till it quite disappeared, and then turned to pursue my way alone. This was no longer matter of the slightest difficulty, for, despite the dead darkness overhead, the line of stone fence showed distinctly enough against the pale gleam of the snow. How silent it seemed now, with only my footsteps to listen to; how silent and how solitary! A strange disagreeable sense of loneliness stole over me. I walked faster. I hummed a fragment of a tune. I cast up enormous sums in my head, and accumulated them at compound interest. I did my best, in short, to forget the startling speculations to which I had but just been listening, and, to some extent, I succeeded.

Meanwhile the night air seemed to become colder and colder, and though I walked fast I found it impossible to keep myself warm. My feet were like ice. I lost sensation in my hands, and grasped my gun mechanically. I even breathed with difficulty, as though, instead of traversing a quiet north country highway, I were scaling the uppermost heights of some gigantic Alp. This last symptom became presently so distressing, that I was forced to stop for a few minutes, and lean against the stone fence. As I did so, I chanced to look back up the road, and there, to my infinite relief, I saw a distant point of light, like the gleam of an approaching lantern. I at first concluded that Jacob had retraced his steps and followed me; but even as the conjecture presented itself, a second light flashed into sight—a light evidently parallel with the first, and approaching at the same rate of motion. It needed no second thought to show me that these must be the carriage-lamps of some private vehicle, though it seemed strange that any private vehicle should take a road professedly disused and dangerous.

There could be no doubt, however, of the fact, for the lamps grew larger and brighter every moment, and I even fancied I could already see the dark outline of the carriage between them. It was coming up very fast, and quite noiselessly, the snow being nearly a foot deep under the wheels.

And now the body of the vehicle became distinctly visible behind the lamps. It looked strangely lofty. A sudden suspicion flashed upon me. Was it possible that I had passed the cross-roads in the dark without observing the sign-post, and could this be the very coach which I had come to meet?

No need to ask myself that question a second time, for here it came round the bend of the road, guard and driver, one outside passenger, and four steaming greys, all wrapped in a soft haze of light, through which the lamps blazed out, like a pair of fiery meteors.

I jumped forward, waved my hat, and shouted. The mail came down at full speed, and passed me. For a moment I feared that I had not been seen or heard, but it was only for a moment. The coachman pulled up; the guard, muffled to the eyes in capes and comforters, and apparently sound asleep in the rumble, neither answered my hail nor made the slightest effort to dismount; the outside passenger did not even turn his head. I opened the door for myself, and looked in. There were but three travellers inside, so I stepped in, shut the door, slipped into the vacant corner, and congratulated myself on my good fortune.

The atmosphere of the coach seemed, if possible, colder than that of the outer air, and was pervaded by a singularly damp and disagreeable smell. I looked round at my fellow-passengers. They were all three, men, and all silent. They did not seem to be asleep, but each leaned back in his corner of the vehicle, as if absorbed in his own reflections. I attempted to open a conversation.

"How intensely cold it is tonight," I said, addressing my opposite neighbour.

He lifted his head, looked at me, but made no reply.

"The winter," I added, "seems to have begun in earnest."

Although the corner in which he sat was so dim that I could distinguish none of his features very clearly, I saw that his eyes were still turned full upon me. And yet he answered never a word.

At any other time I should have felt, and perhaps expressed, some annoyance, but at the moment I felt too ill to do either. The icy coldness of the night air had struck a chill to my very marrow, and the strange smell inside the coach was affecting me with an intolerable nausea. I shivered from head to foot, and, turning to my left-hand neighbour, asked if he had any objection to an open window?

He neither spoke nor stirred.

I repeated the question somewhat more loudly, but with the same result. Then I lost patience, and let the sash down. As I did so, the leather strap broke in my hand, and I observed that the glass was covered with a thick coat of mildew, the accumulation, apparently, of years. My attention being thus drawn to the condition of the coach, I examined it more narrowly, and saw by the uncertain light of the outer lamps that it was in the last stage of dilapidation. Every part of it was not only out of repair, but in a condition of decay. The sashes splintered at a touch. The leather fittings were crusted over with mould, and literally rotting from the woodwork. The floor was almost breaking away beneath my feet. The whole machine, in short, was foul with damp, and had evidently been dragged from some outhouse in which it had been mouldering away for years, to do another day or two of duty on the road.

I turned to the third passenger, whom I had not yet addressed, and hazarded one more remark.

"This coach," I said, "is in a deplorable condition. The regular mail, I suppose, is under repair?"

He moved his head slowly, and looked me in the face, without speaking a word. I shall never forget that look while I live. I turned cold at heart under it. I turn cold at heart even now when I recall it. His eyes glowed with a fiery unnatural lustre. His face was livid as the face of a corpse. His bloodless lips were drawn back as if in the agony of death, and showed the gleaming teeth between.

The words that I was about to utter died upon my lips, and a strange horror—a dreadful horror—came upon me. My sight had by this time become used to the gloom of the coach, and I could see with tolerable distinctness. I turned to my opposite neighbour. He, too, was looking at me, with the same startling pallor in his face, and the same stony glitter in his eyes. I passed my hand across my brow. I turned to the passenger on the seat beside my own, and saw—oh Heaven! how shall I describe what I saw? I saw that he was no living man—that none of them were living men, like myself! A pale phosphorescent light—the light of putrefaction—played upon their awful faces; upon their hair, dank with the dews of the grave; upon their clothes, earth-stained and dropping to pieces; upon their hands, which were as the hands of corpses long buried. Only their eyes, their terrible eyes, were living; and those eyes were all turned menacingly upon me!

A shriek of terror, a wild unintelligible cry for help and mercy; burst from my lips as I flung myself against the door, and strove in vain to open it.

In that single instant, brief and vivid as a landscape beheld in the flash of summer lightning, I saw the moon shining down through a rift of stormy cloud—the ghastly sign-post rearing its warning finger by the wayside—the broken parapet—the plunging horses—the black gulf below. Then, the coach reeled like a ship at sea. Then, came a mighty crash—a sense of crushing pain—and then, darkness.

It seemed as if years had gone by when I awoke one morning from a deep sleep, and found my wife watching by my bedside. I will pass over the scene that ensued, and give you, in half a dozen words, the tale she told me with tears of thanksgiving. I had fallen over a precipice, close against the junction of the old coach-road and the new, and had only been saved from certain death by lighting upon a deep snowdrift that had accumulated at the foot of the rock beneath. In this snowdrift I was discovered at daybreak, by a couple of shepherds, who carried me to the nearest shelter, and brought a surgeon to my aid. The surgeon found me in a state of raving delirium, with a broken arm and a compound fracture of the skull. The letters in my pocket-book showed my name and address; my wife was summoned to nurse me; and, thanks to youth and a fine constitution, I came out of danger at last. The place of my fall, I need scarcely say, was precisely that at which a frightful accident had happened to the north mail nine years before.

I never told my wife the fearful events which I have just related to you. I told the surgeon who attended me; but he treated the whole adventure as a mere dream born of the fever in my brain. We discussed the question over and over again, until we found that we could discuss it with temper no longer, and then we dropped it. Others may form what conclusions they please—I know that twenty years ago I was the fourth inside passenger in that Phantom Coach.

JERRY BUNDLER

W. W. Jacobs

First published in *The Windsor Magazine*, December 1897

William Wymark Jacobs (1863–1943) was born in Wapping in East London. His father managed the South Devon wharf, and W. W. (as he was known) spent a lot of time around the London docks as a child. Aged sixteen he got a job as a clerk, working for various employers until 1899, by which point he was earning enough as an author to write full time. Like many other writers of the late nineteenth century he started off penning short stories that he submitted to magazines. An early appreciator of his work was Jerome K. Jerome, who as the editor of *The Idler* accepted several of Jacobs' stories. Nautical and dockland settings often featured in his work, but today he is best-remembered for his classic ghost story 'The Monkey's Paw' (1902).

'Jerry Bundler' is a traditional tale which uses some familiar ghost story tropes to great effect. Jacobs dramatized the tale in 1899 (as *The Ghost of Jerry Bundler*) and it was performed at St. James' Theatre in London, being revived three years later for a further run.

It wanted a few nights to Christmas, a festival for which the small market town of Torchester was making extensive preparations. The narrow streets which had been thronged with people were now almost deserted; the cheap-jack from London, with the remnant of breath left him after his evening's exertions, was making feeble attempts to blow out his naphtha lamp, and the last shops open were rapidly closing for the night.

In the comfortable coffee-room of the old Boar's Head, half a dozen guests, principally commercial travellers, sat talking by the light of the fire. The talk had drifted from trade to politics, from politics to religion, and so by easy stages to the supernatural. Three ghost stories, never known to fail before, had fallen flat; there was too much noise outside, too much light within. The fourth story was told by an old hand with more success; the streets were quiet, and he had turned the gas out. In the flickering light of the fire, as it shone on the glasses and danced with shadows on the walls, the story proved so enthralling that George, the waiter, whose presence had been forgotten, created a very disagreeable sensation by suddenly starting up from a dark corner and gliding silently from the room. "That's what I call a good story," said one of the men, sipping his hot whisky. "Of course it's an old idea that spirits like to get into the company of human beings. A man told me once that he travelled down the Great Western with a ghost and hadn't the slightest suspicion of it until the inspector came for tickets. My friend said the way that ghost tried to keep up appearances by feeling for it in all its pockets and looking on the floor was quite touching. Ultimately it gave it up and with a faint groan vanished through the ventilator."

"That'll do, Hirst," said another man.

"It's not a subject for jesting," said a little old gentleman who had been an attentive listener. "I've never seen an apparition myself, but I know people who have, and I consider that they form a very interesting link between us and the afterlife. There's a ghost story connected with this house, you know."

"Never heard of it," said another speaker, "and I've been here some years now."

"It dates back a long time now," said the old gentleman. "You've heard about Jerry Bundler, George?"

"Well, I've just 'eard odds and ends, sir," said the old waiter, "but I never put much count to 'em. There was one chap 'ere what said 'e saw it, and the gov'ner sacked 'im prompt."

"My father was a native of this town," said the old gentleman, "and knew the story well. He was a truthful man and a steady churchgoer, but I've heard him declare that once in his life he saw the appearance of Jerry Bundler in this house."

"And who was this Bundler?" inquired a voice.

"A London thief, pickpocket, highwayman—anything he could turn his dishonest hand to," replied the old gentleman; "and he was run to earth in this house one Christmas week some eighty years ago. He took his last supper in this very room, and after he had gone up to bed a couple of Bow Street runners, who had followed him from London but lost the scent a bit, went upstairs with the landlord and tried the door. It was stout oak, and fast, so one went into the yard, and by means of a short ladder got onto the window-sill, while the other stayed outside the door. Those below in the yard saw the man crouching on the sill, and then there was a sudden smash of glass, and with a cry he fell in a heap on the stones at their feet. Then in the moonlight they saw the white face of the pickpocket peeping over the sill, and while some stayed in the yard, others ran into the house and helped the other man to break the door in. It was difficult to obtain an entrance even then, for it was barred with heavy furniture, but they got in at last, and the first thing that met their eyes was the body of Jerry dangling from the top of the bed by his own handkerchief."

"Which bedroom was it?" asked two or three voices together.

The narrator shook his head. "That I can't tell you; but the story goes that Jerry still haunts this house, and my father used to declare positively that the last time he slept here the ghost of Jerry Bundler lowered itself from the top of his bed and tried to strangle him."

"That'll do," said an uneasy voice. "I wish you'd thought to ask your father which bedroom it was."

"What for?" inquired the old gentleman.

"Well, I should take care not to sleep in it, that's all," said the voice, shortly.

"There's nothing to fear," said the other. "I don't believe for a moment that ghosts could really hurt one. In fact my father used to confess that it was only the unpleasantness of the thing that upset him, and that for all practical purposes Jerry's fingers might have been made of cottonwool for all the harm they could do."

"That's all very fine," said the last speaker again; "a ghost story is a ghost story, sir; but when a gentleman tells a tale of a ghost in the house in which one is going to sleep, I call it most ungentlemanly!"

"Pooh! nonsense!" said the old gentleman, rising; "ghosts can't hurt you. For my own part, I should rather like to see one. Good night, gentlemen."

"Good night," said the others. "And I only hope Jerry'll pay you a visit," added the nervous man as the door closed.

"Bring some more whisky, George," said a stout commercial; "I want keeping up when the talk turns this way."

"Shall I light the gas, Mr. Malcolm?" said George.

"No; the fire's very comfortable," said the traveller. "Now, gentlemen, any of you know any more?"

"I think we've had enough," said another man; "we shall be thinking we see spirits next, and we're not all like the old gentleman who's just gone."

"Old humbug!" said Hirst. "I should like to put him to the test. Suppose I dress up as Jerry Bundler and go and give him a chance of displaying his courage?"

"Bravo!" said Malcolm, huskily, drowning one or two faint "Noes." "Just for the joke, gentlemen."

"No, no! Drop it, Hirst," said another man.

"Only for the joke," said Hirst, somewhat eagerly. "I've got some things upstairs in which I am going to play in *The Rivals*—knee-breeches, buckles, and all that sort of thing. It's a rare chance. If you'll wait a bit I'll give you a full-dress rehearsal, entitled, 'Jerry Bundler; or, The Nocturnal Strangler.'"

"You won't frighten us," said the commercial, with a husky laugh.

"I don't know that," said Hirst, sharply; "it's a question of acting, that's all. I'm pretty good, ain't I, Somers?"

"Oh, you're all right—for an amateur," said his friend, with a laugh.

"I'll bet you a level sov. you don't frighten me," said the stout traveller.

"Done!" said Hirst. "I'll take the bet to frighten you first and the old gentleman afterwards. These gentlemen shall be the judges."

"You won't frighten us, sir," said another man, "because we're prepared for you; but you'd better leave the old man alone. It's dangerous play."

"Well, I'll try you first," said Hirst, springing up. "No gas, mind."

He ran lightly upstairs to his room, leaving the others, most of whom had been drinking somewhat freely, to wrangle about his proceedings. It ended in two of them going to bed.

"He's crazy on acting," said Somers, lighting his pipe. "Thinks he's the equal of anybody almost. It doesn't matter with us, but I won't let him go to the old man. And he won't mind so long as he gets an opportunity of acting to us."

"Well, I hope he'll hurry up," said Malcolm, yawning; "it's after twelve now."

Nearly half an hour passed. Malcolm drew his watch from his pocket and was busy winding it, when George, the waiter, who had been sent on an errand to the bar, burst suddenly into the room and rushed towards them.

"'E's comin', gentlemen," he said breathlessly.

"Why, you're frightened, George," said the stout commercial, with a chuckle.

"It was the suddenness of it," said George, sheepishly; "and besides, I didn't look for seein' 'im in the bar. There's only a

37

glimmer of light there, and 'e was sitting on the floor behind the bar. I nearly trod on 'im."

"Oh, you'll never make a man, George," said Malcolm.

"Well, it took me unawares," said the waiter. "Not that I'd have gone to the bar by myself if I'd known 'e was there, and I don't believe you would either, sir."

"Nonsense!" said Malcolm. "I'll go and fetch him in."

"You don't know what it's like, sir," said George, catching him by the sleeve. "It ain't fit to look at by yourself, it ain't, indeed. It's got the— What's that?"

They all started at the sound of a smothered cry from the staircase and the sound of somebody running hurriedly along the passage. Before anybody could speak, the door flew open and a figure bursting into the room flung itself gasping and shivering upon them.

"What is it? What's the matter?" demanded Malcolm. "Why, it's Mr. Hirst." He shook him roughly and then held some spirit to his lips. Hirst drank it greedily and with a sharp intake of his breath gripped him by the arm.

"Light the gas, George," said Malcolm.

The waiter obeyed hastily. Hirst, a ludicrous but pitiable figure in knee-breeches and coat, a large wig all awry and his face a mess of grease paint, clung to him, trembling.

"Now, what's the matter?" asked Malcolm.

"I've seen it," said Hirst, with a hysterical sob. "O Lord, I'll never play the fool again, never!"

"Seen what?" said the others.

"Him—it—the ghost—anything!" said Hirst, wildly.

"Rot!" said Malcolm, uneasily.

"I was coming down the stairs," said Hirst. "Just capering down—as I thought—it ought to do. I felt a tap—"

He broke off suddenly and peered nervously through the open door into the passage.

"I thought I saw it again," he whispered.

"Look—at the foot of the stairs. Can you see anything?"

"No, there's nothing there," said Malcolm, whose own voice shook a little. "Go on. You felt a tap on your shoulder—"

"I turned round and saw it—a little wicked head and a white dead face. Pah!"

"That's what I saw in the bar," said George. "'Orrid it was—devilish!"

Hirst shuddered, and, still retaining his nervous grip of Malcolm's sleeve, dropped into a chair.

"Well, it's a most unaccountable thing," said the dumbfounded Malcolm, turning round to the others. "It's the last time I come to this house."

"I leave tomorrow," said George. "I wouldn't go down to that bar again by myself, no, not for fifty pounds!"

"It's talking about the thing that's caused it, I expect," said one of the men; "we've all been talking about this and having it in our minds. Practically we've been forming a spiritualistic circle without knowing it."

"Hang the old gentleman!" said Malcolm, heartily. "Upon my soul, I'm half afraid to go to bed. It's odd they should both think they saw something."

"I saw it as plain as I see you, sir," said George, solemnly. "P'raps if you keep your eyes turned up the passage you'll see it for yourself."

They followed the direction of his finger, but saw nothing, although one of them fancied that a head peeped round the corner of the wall.

"Who'll come down to the bar?" said Malcolm, looking round.

"You can go, if you like," said one of the others, with a faint laugh; "we'll wait here for you."

The stout traveller walked towards the door and took a few steps up the passage. Then he stopped. All was quite silent, and he walked slowly to the end and looked down fearfully towards the glass partition which shut off the bar. Three times he made as though to go to it; then he turned back, and, glancing over his shoulder, came hurriedly back to the room.

"Did you see it, sir?" whispered George.

"Don't know," said Malcolm, shortly. "I fancied I saw something, but it might have been fancy. I'm in the mood to see anything just now. How are you feeling now, sir?"

"Oh, I feel a bit better now," said Hirst, somewhat brusquely, as all eyes were turned upon him.

"I dare say you think I'm easily scared, but you didn't see it."

"Not at all," said Malcolm, smiling faintly despite himself.

"I'm going to bed," said Hirst, noticing the smile and resenting it. "Will you share my room with me, Somers?"

"I will with pleasure," said his friend, "provided you don't mind sleeping with the gas on full all night."

He rose from his seat, and bidding the company a friendly good-night, left the room with his crestfallen friend. The others saw them to the foot of the stairs, and having heard their door close, returned to the coffee-room.

"Well, I suppose the bet's off?" said the stout commercial, poking the fire and then standing with his legs apart on the hearthrug; "though, as far as I can see, I won it. I never saw a man so scared in all my life. Sort of poetic justice about it, isn't there?"

"Never mind about poetry or justice," said one of his listeners; "who's going to sleep with me?"

"I will," said Malcolm, affably.

"And I suppose we share a room together, Mr. Leek?" said the third man, turning to the fourth.

"No, thank you," said the other, briskly; "I don't believe in ghosts. If anything comes into my room I shall shoot it."

"That won't hurt a spirit, Leek," said Malcolm, decisively.

"Well the noise'll be like company to me," said Leek, "and it'll wake the house too. But if you're nervous, sir," he added, with a grin, to the man who had suggested sharing his room, "George'll be only too pleased to sleep on the door-mat inside your room, I know."

"That I will, sir," said George, fervently; "and if you gentlemen would only come down with me to the bar to put the gas out, I could never be sufficiently grateful."

They went out in a body, with the exception of Leek, peering carefully before them as they went. George turned the light out in the bar and they returned unmolested to the coffee-room, and, avoiding the sardonic smile of Leek, prepared to separate for the night.

"Give me the candle while you put the gas out, George," said the traveller.

The waiter handed it to him and extinguished the gas, and at the same moment all distinctly heard a step in the passage outside. It stopped at the door, and as they watched with bated breath, the door creaked and slowly opened. Malcolm fell back open-mouthed, as a white, leering face, with sunken eyeballs and close-cropped bullet head, appeared at the opening.

For a few seconds the creature stood regarding them, blinking in a strange fashion at the candle. Then, with a sidling movement, it came a little way into the room and stood there as if bewildered.

Not a man spoke or moved, but all watched with a horrible fascination as the creature removed its dirty neckcloth and its head rolled on its shoulder. For a minute it paused, and then, holding the rag before it, moved towards Malcolm.

The candle went out suddenly with a flash and a bang. There was a smell of powder, and something writhing in the darkness on the floor. A faint, choking cough, and then silence. Malcolm was the first to speak. "Matches," he said, in a strange voice. George struck one. Then he leapt at the gas and a burner flamed from the match. Malcolm touched the thing on the floor with his foot and found it soft. He looked at his companions. They mouthed inquiries at him, but he shook his head. He lit the candle, and, kneeling down, examined the silent thing on the floor. Then he rose swiftly, and dipping his handkerchief in the water-jug, bent down again and grimly wiped the white face. Then he sprang back with a cry of incredulous horror, pointing at it. Leek's pistol fell to the floor and he shut out the sight with his hands, but the others, crowding forward, gazed spell-bound at the dead face of Hirst.

Before a word was spoken the door opened and Somers hastily entered the room. His eyes fell on the floor. "Good God!" he cried. "You didn't—"

Nobody spoke.

"I told him not to," he said, in a suffocating voice. "I told him not to. I told him—"

He leaned against the wall, deathly sick, put his arms out feebly, and fell fainting into the traveller's arms.

BONE TO HIS BONE

E. G. Swain

First published in *The Stoneground Ghost Tales:*
Compiled from the Recollections of the Reverend Roland Batchel,
Vicar of the Parish (London, 1912)

Edmund Gill Swain (1861–1938) was a close friend of the great antiquarian ghost story pioneer M.R. James, attending many of James' Christmas ghost story readings and also working with him to stage amateur theatricals. He was a contemporary of James at Cambridge, and they both later worked at King's College: Swain as the chaplain, and James as the Dean. The two remained good friends after Swain left Cambridge in 1905, having been appointed vicar of Stanground, a village near Peterborough. In 1912, Swain published *The Stoneground Ghost Tales*, a series of connected ghost stories inspired by his new parish, and featuring a fictionalised version of himself: Mr. Batchel, the rector of Stoneground.

   Swain shared James' antiquarian interests, and had an enthusiasm for archaeology, which is evident in this story. He did not hold absolutely to James' guidance for a successful ghost story though. In the preface to his 1911 collection, *More Ghost Stories*, James wrote, 'The ghost should be malevolent or odious: amiable and helpful apparitions are all very well in fairy tales or in local legends, but I have no use for them in a fictitious ghost story.' Although admittedly 'Bone to his Bone' is not as frightening as the best of James, the subtle understanding between ghost and vicar makes this story special.

William Whitehead, Fellow of Emmanuel College, in the University of Cambridge, became Vicar of Stoneground in the year 1731. The annals of his incumbency were doubtless short and simple: they have not survived. In his day were no newspapers to collect gossip, no parish magazines to record the simple events of parochial life. One event, however, of greater moment then than now, is recorded in two places. Vicar Whitehead failed in health after twenty-three years of work, and journeyed to Bath in what his monument calls "the vain hope of being restored". The duration of his visit is unknown; it is reasonable to suppose that he made his journey in the summer, it is certain that by the month of November his physician told him to lay aside all hope of recovery.

Then it was that the thoughts of the patient turned to the comfortable straggling vicarage he had left at Stoneground, in which he had hoped to end his days. He prayed that his successor might be as happy there as he had been himself. Setting his affairs in order, as became one who had but a short time to live, he executed a will, bequeathing to the Vicars of Stoneground, for ever, the close of ground he had recently purchased because it lay next the vicarage garden. And by a codicil, he added to the bequest his library of books. Within a few days, William Whitehead was gathered to his fathers.

A mural tablet in the north aisle of the church, records, in Latin, his services and his bequests, his two marriages, and his fruitless journey to Bath. The house he loved, but never again saw, was taken down forty years later, and re-built by Vicar James Devie. The garden, with Vicar Whitehead's "close of ground" and other adjacent lands, was opened out and planted, somewhat before 1850, by Vicar Robert Towerson. The aspect of everything has changed. But in a convenient chamber on the first floor of the present vicarage the library of Vicar Whitehead stands very much as he used it and loved it, and as he bequeathed it to his successors "for ever".

The books there are arranged as he arranged and ticketed them. Little slips of paper, sometimes bearing interesting fragments of writing, still mark his places. His marginal comments still give life to pages from which all other interest has faded, and he would have but a dull imagination who could sit in the chamber amidst these books without ever being carried back 180 years into the past, to the time when the newest of them left the printer's hands.

Of those into whose possession the books have come, some have doubtless loved them more, and some less; some, perhaps, have left them severely alone. But neither those who loved them, nor those who loved them not, have lost them, and they passed, some century and a half after William Whitehead's death, into the hands of Mr. Batchel, who loved them as a father loves his children. He lived alone, and had few domestic cares to distract his mind. He was able, therefore, to enjoy to the full what Vicar Whitehead had enjoyed so long before him. During many a long summer evening would he sit poring over long-forgotten books; and since the chamber, otherwise called the library, faced the south, he could also spend sunny winter mornings there without discomfort. Writing at a small table, or reading as he stood at a tall desk, he would browse amongst the books like an ox in a pleasant pasture.

There were other times also, at which Mr. Batchel would use the books. Not being a sound sleeper (for book-loving men seldom are), he elected to use as a bedroom one of the two chambers which opened at either side into the library. The arrangement enabled him to beguile many a sleepless hour amongst the books, and in view of these nocturnal visits he kept a candle standing in a sconce above the desk, and matches always ready to his hand.

There was one disadvantage in this close proximity of his bed to the library. Owing, apparently, to some defect in the fittings of the room, which, having no mechanical tastes, Mr. Batchel had never investigated, there could be heard, in the stillness of the night, exactly such sounds as might arise from a person moving about amongst the books. Visitors using the other adjacent room would often remark at breakfast, that they had heard their host in the library at one or two o'clock in the morning, when, in fact, he had not left his bed. Invariably Mr. Batchel allowed them to suppose that he had been where they thought him. He disliked idle controversy, and was unwilling to afford an opening for supernatural talk. Knowing well enough the sounds by which his guests had been deceived, he wanted no other explanation of them than his own, though it was of too vague a character to count as an explanation. He conjectured that the window-sashes, or the doors, or "something", were defective, and was too phleg-matic and too unpractical to make any investigation. The matter gave him no concern.

Persons whose sleep is uncertain are apt to have their worst nights when they would like their best. The consciousness of a special need for rest seems to bring enough mental disturbance to forbid it. So on Christmas Eve, in the year 1907, Mr. Batchel, who would have liked to sleep well, in view of the labours of Christmas Day, lay hopelessly wide awake. He exhausted all the known devices for courting sleep, and, at the end, found himself wider awake than ever. A brilliant moon shone into his room, for he hated window-blinds. There was a light wind blowing, and the sounds in the library were more than usually suggestive of a person moving about. He almost determined to have the sashes "seen to", although he could seldom be induced to have anything "seen to". He disliked changes, even for the better, and would submit to great inconvenience rather than have things altered with which he had become familiar.

As he revolved these matters in his mind, he heard the clocks strike the hour of midnight, and having now lost all hope of falling asleep, he rose from his bed, got into a large dressing gown which hung in readiness for such occasions, and passed into the library, with the intention of reading himself sleepy, if he could.

The moon, by this time, had passed out of the south, and the library seemed all the darker by contrast with the moonlit chamber he had left. He could see nothing but two blue-grey rectangles formed by the windows against the sky, the furniture of the room being altogether invisible. Groping along to where the table stood, Mr. Batchel felt over its surface for the matches which usually lay there; he found, however, that the table was cleared of everything. He raised his right hand, therefore, in order to feel his way to a shelf where the matches were sometimes mislaid, and at that moment, whilst his hand was in mid-air, the matchbox was gently put into it!

Such an incident could hardly fail to disturb even a phlegmatic person, and Mr. Batchel cried "Who's this?" somewhat nervously. There was no answer. He struck a match, looked hastily round the room, and found it empty, as usual. There was everything, that is to say, that he was accustomed to see, but no other person than himself.

It is not quite accurate, however, to say that everything was in its usual state. Upon the tall desk lay a quarto volume that he had certainly not placed there. It was his quite invariable practice to replace his books upon the shelves after using them, and what we may call his library habits were precise and methodical. A book out of place like this, was not only an offence against good order, but a sign that his privacy had been intruded upon. With some surprise, therefore, he lit the candle standing ready in the sconce, and proceeded to examine the book, not sorry, in the disturbed condition in which he was, to have an occupation found for him.

The book proved to be one with which he was unfamiliar, and this made it certain that some other hand than his had removed it from its place. Its title was *The Compleat Gard'ner* of M. de la Quintinye made English by John Evelyn Esquire. It was not a work in which Mr. Batchel felt any great interest. It consisted of divers reflections on various parts of husbandry, doubtless entertaining enough, but too deliberate and discursive for practical purposes. He had certainly never used the book, and growing restless now in mind, said to himself that some boy having the freedom of the house, had taken it down from its place in the hope of finding pictures.

But even whilst he made this explanation he felt its weakness. To begin with, the desk was too high for a boy. The improbability that any boy would place a book there was equalled by the improbability that he would leave it there. To discover its uninviting character would be the work only of a moment, and no boy would have brought it so far from its shelf.

Mr. Batchel had, however, come to read, and habit was too strong with him to be wholly set aside. Leaving *The Compleat Gard'ner* on the desk, he turned round to the shelves to find some more congenial reading.

Hardly had he done this when he was startled by a sharp rap upon the desk behind him, followed by a rustling of paper. He turned quickly about and saw the quarto lying open. In obedience to the instinct of the moment, he at once sought a natural cause for what he saw. Only a wind, and that of the strongest, could have opened the book, and laid back its heavy cover; and though he accepted, for a brief moment, that explanation, he was too candid to retain it longer. The wind out of doors was very light. The window-sash was closed and latched, and, to decide the matter finally, the book had its back, and not its edges, turned towards the only quarter from which a wind could strike.

Mr. Batchel approached the desk again and stood over the book. With increasing perturbation of mind (for he still thought of the matchbox) he looked upon the open page. Without much reason beyond that he felt constrained to do something, he read the words of the half completed sentence at the turn of the page—

"at dead of night he left the house and passed into the solitude of the garden."

But he read no more, nor did he give himself the trouble of discovering whose midnight wandering was being described, although the habit was singularly like one of his own. He was in no condition for reading, and turning his back upon the volume he slowly paced the length of the chamber, "wondering at that which had come to pass".

He reached the opposite end of the chamber and was in the act of turning, when again he heard the rustling of paper, and by the time he had faced round, saw the leaves of the book again turning over. In a moment the volume lay at rest, open in another place, and there was no further movement as he approached it. To make sure that he had not been deceived, he read again the words as they entered the page. The author was following a not uncommon practice of the time, and throwing common speech into forms suggested by Holy Writ: "So dig," it said, "that ye may obtain."

This passage, which to Mr. Batchel seemed reprehensible in its levity, excited at once his interest and his disapproval. He was prepared to read more, but this time was not allowed. Before his eye could pass beyond the passage already cited, the leaves of the book slowly turned again, and presented but a termination of five words and a colophon.

The words were, "to the North, an Ilex". These three passages, in which he saw no meaning and no connection, began to entangle themselves together in Mr. Batchel's mind. He found himself repeating them in different orders, now beginning with one, and now with another. Any further attempt at reading he felt to be impossible, and he was in no mind for any more experiences of the unaccountable. Sleep was, of course, further from him than ever, if that were conceivable. What he did, therefore, was to blow out the candle, to return to his moonlit bedroom, and put on more clothing, and then to pass downstairs with the object of going out of doors.

It was not unusual with Mr. Batchel to walk about his garden at night-time. This form of exercise had often, after a wakeful hour, sent him back to his bed refreshed and ready for sleep. The convenient access to the garden at such times lay through his study, whose French windows opened on to a short flight of steps, and upon these he now paused for a moment to admire the snow-like appearance of the lawns, bathed as they were in the moonlight. As he paused, he heard the city clocks strike the half-hour after midnight, and he could not forbear repeating aloud—

"At dead of night he left the house, and passed into the solitude of the garden."

It was solitary enough. At intervals the screech of an owl, and now and then the noise of a train, seemed to emphasise the solitude by drawing attention to it and then leaving it in possession of the night. Mr. Batchel found himself wondering and conjecturing what Vicar Whitehead, who had acquired the close of land to secure quiet and privacy for a garden, would have thought of the railways to the west and north. He turned his face northwards, whence a whistle had just sounded, and saw a tree beautifully outlined against the sky. His breath caught at the sight. Not because the tree was unfamiliar. Mr. Batchel knew all his trees. But what he had seen was "to the north, an Ilex".

Mr. Batchel knew not what to make of it all. He had walked into the garden hundreds of times and as often seen the Ilex, but the words out of the *Compleat Gard'ner* seemed to be pursuing him in a way that made him almost afraid. His temperament, however, as has been said already, was phlegmatic. It was commonly said, and Mr. Batchel approved the verdict, whilst he condemned its inexactness, that "his nerves were made of fiddle-string", so he braced himself afresh and set upon his walk round the silent garden, which he was accustomed to begin in a northerly direction, and was now too proud to change. He usually passed the Ilex at the beginning of his perambulation, and so would pass it now.

He did not pass it. A small discovery, as he reached it, annoyed and disturbed him. His gardener, as careful and punctilious as himself, never failed to house all his tools at the end of a day's work. Yet there, under the Ilex, standing upright in moonlight brilliant enough to cast a shadow of it, was a spade.

Mr. Batchel's second thought was one of relief. After his extraordinary experiences in the library (he hardly knew now whether they had been real or not) something quite commonplace would act sedatively, and he determined to carry the spade to the tool-house.

The soil was quite dry, and the surface even a little frozen, so Mr. Batchel left the path, walked up to the spade, and would have drawn it towards him. But it was as if he had made the attempt upon the trunk of the Ilex itself. The spade would not be moved. Then, first with one hand, and then with both, he tried to raise it, and still it stood firm. Mr. Batchel, of course, attributed this to the frost, slight as it was. Wondering at the spade's being there, and annoyed at its being frozen, he was about to leave it and continue his walk, when the remaining words of the *Compleat Gard'ner* seemed rather to utter themselves, than to await his will—

"So dig, that ye may obtain."

Mr. Batchel's power of independent action now deserted him. He took the spade, which no longer resisted, and began to dig. "Five spadefuls and no more," he said aloud. "This is all foolishness."

Four spadefuls of earth he then raised and spread out before him in the moonlight. There was nothing unusual to be seen. Nor did Mr. Batchel decide what he would look for, whether coins, jewels, documents in canisters, or weapons. In point of fact, he dug against what he deemed his better judgment, and expected nothing. He spread before him the fifth and last spadeful of earth, not quite without result, but with no result that was at all sensational. The earth contained a bone. Mr. Batchel's knowledge of anatomy was sufficient to show him that it was a human bone. He identified it, even by moonlight, as the *radius,* a bone of the forearm, as he removed the earth from it, with his thumb.

Such a discovery might be thought worthy of more than the very ordinary interest Mr. Batchel showed. As a matter of fact, the presence of a human bone was easily to be accounted for. Recent excavations within the church had caused the upturning of numberless bones, which had been collected and reverently buried. But an earth-stained bone is also easily overlooked, and this *radius* had obviously found its way into the garden with some of the earth brought out of the church.

Mr. Batchel was glad, rather than regretful at this termination to his adventure. He was once more provided with something to do. The re-interment of such bones as this had been his constant care, and he decided at once to restore the bone to consecrated earth. The time seemed opportune. The eyes of the curious were closed in sleep, he himself was still alert and wakeful. The spade remained by his side and the bone in his hand. So he betook himself, there and then, to the churchyard. By the still generous light of the moon, he found a place where the earth yielded to his spade, and within a few minutes the bone was laid decently to earth, some 18 inches deep.

The city clocks struck one as he finished. The whole world seemed asleep, and Mr. Batchel slowly returned to the garden with his spade. As he hung it in its accustomed place he felt stealing over him the welcome desire to sleep. He walked quietly on to the house and ascended to his room. It was now dark: the moon had passed on and left the room in shadow. He lit a candle, and before undressing passed into the library. He had an irresistible curiosity to see the passages in John Evelyn's book which had so strangely adapted themselves to the events of the past hour.

In the library a last surprise awaited him. The desk upon which the book had lain was empty. *The Compleat Gard'ner* stood in its place on the shelf. And then Mr. Batchel knew that he had handled a bone of William Whitehead, and that in response to his own entreaty.

OBERON ROAD

A. M. Burrage

First published in *The London Magazine*, December 1924

Alfred McLelland Burrage (1889–1956) came from a family dependent on the magazine industry. Both his father and his uncle were writers of adventure stories for periodicals aimed at boys. His father died when Alfred was still at school and he quickly began submitting his own stories to magazines, probably in an attempt to keep the family solvent. In 1915, Burrage attested under the Derby Scheme—which means that he volunteered to enlist as a soldier if called upon. He did fight in World War I, continuing to send stories home for publication, although this was awkward as mail was censored and understandably the army was not keen on having to get through sheaves of pages of fiction in addition to conventional letters. His works were mainly either romance and adventure hybrids, or ghost stories. This tale gives a glimpse of a fantastical world hidden in the dull suburbia of commuterland between the wars.

I am sorry to have to begin this true tale by breaking one of the written laws of the short story. My numerous Guides to Young Authors, compiled by gentlemen of great but undiscovered literary ability, assure me that I should begin with a striking incident or some pregnant dialogue, and never—no, never—with a long and prosy character sketch.

Well, no doubt they are right, but they were never set the task of writing this particular story. If you don't like my way of doing it, you had best say *au revoir*, and turn over a few pages, and perhaps we may meet again more auspiciously a month or so hence. For, honestly, I don't know how to begin this tale about Michael Cubitt without telling you all that ought essentially to be known about the man.

Michael Cubitt—you who are still reading—was a man of forty-two, or maybe forty-three, and he lived in the very worst suburb in the south-east of London. He lived there for two reasons—because he had settled there as a mere boy and hated changes, and because it was cheaper than most other suburbs. For he was very fond of money, and it would seem that his affection was reciprocated, since he had plenty. Not fond of money for money's sake, mind you, but because he wanted to make sure when he grew old of having a fire by which to warm his thin hands. He had already made sure of that fire; his money was safely and skilfully invested; but good and bad habits are alike tenacious.

Cubitt was a lawyer, a partner in a City firm with an enormous practice. He had begun in the same firm as a clerk, and had prudently bought his articles with part of the one thousand pounds which Aunt Martha left him. He was thin and spare, sallow and bloodless, and his humour—what there was of it—was sardonic. He had no friends and no enemies, because so far as could be discovered, he had never done anybody a bad or a good turn.

His landlady in Fenton Road, who had been ministering to him for more than twenty years, would not have lost him for anything, but at the same time she rather disliked him. For, as she told Mrs. Perkins next door, although he paid regular and gave no trouble, there was something about him that wasn't quite 'uman.

Subject to railway strikes and minor alterations in the timetable, he went up by the same train every morning, and came back by the same train every evening. His only recreations seemed to consist of reading heavy books on conveyancing, and working out chess problems which are to be found in the more intellectual kind of newspapers. He had no apparent vices and no apparent virtues. Nobody but himself knew exactly what he got out of life.

He was not even fond of fresh air, and the only exercise he took was in walking from Fenton Road to the station, and from the station back again to Fenton Road.

Fenton Road was only two or three hundred yards from the station as the crow flies, but it was actually near half a mile by road, by reason of one having to walk round three sides of a square. The streets were old-fashioned and badly planned, and Cubitt was shocked and dismayed when he came to reckon up how much boot leather he had been compelled to waste in consequence. If you wanted to go from the station to the place of his abode, you had to cross the road, turn to the right, and walk about a furlong until you came to Norman Avenue; there you turned to the left, walked down Norman Avenue for the best part of a quarter of a mile, and turned to the left again. This brought you into Fenton Road, and Cubitt's lodgings were about two hundred yards up on the left. He hated Norman Avenue cordially, and when the weather was damp, and the road was up—as it was that Christmas time—he hated it worse than ever.

It was three or four evenings before Christmas, and the weather was wet and muggy and depressing, and the only snow to be seen was on the covers of the magazines, when Michael Cubitt departed from custom so far as to speak to a stranger. What made him do it he didn't know. He was in a bad temper because of the approaching holidays, when he wouldn't know what to do with his time, and because it was raining in streaks, and because Norman Avenue was "up", and there would be no walking on the road, and he would be jostled by young fools who insist on walking abreast, and his eyes would be imperilled by the rib-ends of innumerable umbrellas. But, in spite of all this, he actually vouchsafed an answer when the only other occupant of his compartment laid aside an evening paper and suddenly addressed him.

"A lot of rain," said the stranger casually.

Cubitt regarded him with a long, comprehensive glance. A queer-looking fellow, this man who sat opposite him. He was tall and thin and wore his clothes as if they grew upon him, like the fur of an animal. His mouth was long and straight, almost ludicrously like a receptacle for letters, his forehead high and narrow, and his eyes small, dark, beady, and full of meaningless laughter. But it was his ears which interested Cubitt most. These were long and large and had no lobes to them, and at the tops they were distinctly pointed. He caught himself wondering if they were the ears of a criminal; at least they were the ears of no normal person.

"Wretched weather," Cubitt grunted.

"Oh, I like it," said the other, grinning, "it makes the toadstools grow."

Cubitt frowned slightly over what he considered to be a pleasantry which was either feeble or beyond his understanding.

"And, of course," he grunted, "they've taken Norman Avenue up, and the pavements will be all over wet clay which the navvies have trodden there, and I shan't be able to move for people with shopping baskets and umbrellas. I don't know what the L.C.C. is thinking of—taking up the roads at this time of the year."

The stranger had one eye closed as if in contemplation of something, but the other, turned upon Cubitt, grew suddenly very bright and friendly.

"You live in Judge Park?" he asked.

"Yes, Fenton Road," said Cubitt, wondering at the same time what made him so communicative.

"Ah, I know Judge Park. I'm going there myself tonight. I've got something to give to a good policeman who gave a poor man sixpence yesterday instead of running him in for being without a home."

"Oh!" said Cubitt shortly, not greatly interested.

"So," added the stranger, making his eyes snap merrily, "when you see him standing up in the rain, holding up some traffic with one hand, and beckoning other traffic forward with the other, you'll know he won't really be there at all. He'll be back in a hayfield down Shropshire way."

It was at this point that Cubitt wished he had brought an evening paper to retire behind, for he now surmised that his companion was a lunatic; and although he did not suppose him to be dangerous, he was very glad that Judge Park was the next station.

"But why go through Norman Avenue at all?" demanded the stranger, altering his tone.

"Because it's the shortest way to Fenton Road. It's the only way unless I turn to the left outside the station, and lose a quarter of a mile, and on a night like this."

"Nonsense! There's a much shorter way. Why don't you go through Oberon Road?"

"Oberon Road? I've never heard of it."

"Cross the road outside the station," said the stranger glibly, "turn to your right, and it's the first turning on your left."

"But that's Norman Avenue."

"No, it isn't. It's Oberon Road—a long way before you get to Norman Avenue."

Cubitt scowled because he hated to be contradicted.

"I tell you, sir," he said, "that there isn't any turning on the left until you come to Norman Avenue. It's all solid houses, and I ought to know because I've gone home that way every week-day evening for the last twenty-odd years."

"Oberon Road is there," said the stranger, "only you haven't noticed it."

"But it's impossible!" Cubitt exclaimed, wondering why he was taking the trouble to argue with a madman. "Do you mean that it runs parallel with Norman Avenue and leads into Fenton Road?"

"It leads almost anywhere, and it doesn't run parallel to any road in the world that I've ever heard of."

Cubitt was glad that the electric train stopped just then with all the abruptness peculiar to its kind, and to see Judge Park on the station lamps, although the light of them revealed straight diagonal lines of rain. He was first out of the compartment, because he had no liking for his queer companion.

"Good night," he grunted over his shoulder.

"Oberon Road," returned the other. "The first on your left before you get to Norman Avenue."

Cubitt joined the swarm of people collecting around the barrier, showed his season ticket, and went out as usual through the booking office. He did not wait under shelter to put up his umbrella, but opened it as he hurried across the road. He hurried not only because it was wet, but because he did not want to be overtaken by the madman who had been talking to him in the train. A very queer fellow, that! Fancy trying to tell him, Michael Cubitt, about a road on the left before one came to Norman Avenue! Why, it was all one solid unbroken line of villas and blocks of flats. Certainly there ought to have been a road cut through. It was scandalous that the people of Fenton Road should be compelled to go so far out of their way to and from the station. And if there had been such a road, as if he, Cubitt, wouldn't have known of it, seeing that he had gone that way every day for twenty-odd years.

So thought Cubitt as, with head down, he hurried forward under his umbrella. But he had not gone many yards ere he was brought up sharply and his thoughts rudely scattered. The pavement before him suddenly ended, as if he had reached the entrance to a side road. The kerb on his right hand made a sweep to the left, enclosing him in an arc of a circle. At his feet was a gutter down which a muddy stream was flowing, to sing and splutter in a grating on the corner. Surely, he thought with a start, this couldn't be Norman Avenue already.

He lifted his gaze and knew immediately that it was not Norman Avenue.

He knew the houses on the corners too well to be mistaken. One of them was called Hazlehurst, and the other, being a place of public entertainment, was known as the Black Swan. And here were two villas which he could have sworn had hitherto been unbroken links in a long chain. He looked up, and there, painted on a board alongside one of the villas, was Oberon Road, as plain as a pikestaff!

So it was true after all, and Cubitt stood staring, holding his open umbrella down and letting the rain fall upon his head and shoulders.

"Well, I'm damned!" said Michael Cubitt, and you must understand that it was very rarely indeed that he was guilty of such an exclamation. Well, there was Oberon Road, an undoubted fact, and inviting him to take the short cut which he had so often desired. If it ran straight, he reflected, it ought to bring him out into Fenton Road close to his lodgings. And yet he hesitated. There was something eerie about it all. How was it possible that he could have been so blind as not to see this road before? He could have sworn that it wasn't there in the morning. And how could they have made a road all in a few hours?

He looked up and down Station Road. That at least was normal.

Commonplace people were moving up and down, brushing against him as he stood there. A laden motor-bus ploughed by, spurting up liquid mud. On the other side of Station Road a youth was playing a mouth-organ, and another youth was wringing his mouth awry to do a like injustice to the King's English and a popular sentimental song. And these commonplace sights and sounds heartened Michael Cubitt. Absurd to have such vague, unquiet fancies when the world about him seemed to be as normal and as ugly as ever.

In a moment or two Cubitt made up his mind. He wheeled to the left and strode boldly up the pavement of Oberon Road.

At first Oberon Road was just like any other suburban road, except that it was unlit; and as Cubitt drew farther and farther away from the main thoroughfare the darkness grew deeper, until at last he could not see his hands which grasped the umbrella. And by and by the sounds of traffic and distant voices died away, and Cubitt walked in darkness and silence. And a great awe came upon him.

But after a little while the darkness lifted. The rain clouds above him parted, and the moon looked through, like a shining face peering between curtains. And the light grew stronger and stronger, until it was as bright sunlight, and Cubitt looked around him and uttered a little gasp of amazement and delight.

For Oberon Road was such a road as he had never seen before in any suburb or in any fair city. The houses were small, but they were a delight to the eye; some were thatched and some were gabled, after the Elizabethan style, and some were plastered and showed rough old timber; for all of them looked old. And all were set in delightful gardens of flowers and fair lawns and wooded spaces in which one knew there were little hidden arbours. And strangely enough it was not winter here, and the weather was warm and fair without being hot, as in the early days of a fine

May. And Cubitt, who had never before coveted anything that was lovely for its own sake, and had been content to stay on in his dingy lodgings to save expenses, caught himself thinking: "I must certainly buy a house in Oberon Road, whatever it costs."

In the front garden of one of these houses sat a girl who was lovelier than moonlight, who rocked a cradle with her foot, and sang a love song to the strumming of a guitar which she held in her white hands. So Cubitt went up to the gate, and lifted his bowler hat, and asked her if she knew of a house for sale or to be let, or failing that, would it be possible to get lodgings? And the girl stared at him curiously, and ceased singing, and shook her head.

"I really cannot tell you," she said, "I should inquire at the estate office."

"And where is that?" he asked.

"Farther along. I would gladly come and show you, but Jack may be here at any minute, and it would never do for us to be absent when he came."

"And who is Jack?" Cubitt asked.

"He is a failure, and unsuccessful poet; and when he has money he drinks; and when he has drunk he comes here for a little while. It is wrong of him to drink, but that is all understood and forgiven because he has suffered much. And because he was once kind and generous and brave, and beautiful in mind and body, they let him come here sometimes. No, I must not on any account be absent when Jack comes."

"I see," said Cubitt, who did not see at all. And lifting his bowler hat to her he passed on; and almost ran into Jenkins, one of his clerks, who was hurrying past in flannels, carrying a tennis racket.

"Why, Jenkins," he exclaimed, "fancy seeing you here!"

"Considering I live here, sir, it's really not so strange after all. That is to say, I live here sometimes. But I mustn't stop, sir, because I am going to play tennis with the dearest girl in the world. And one day, as soon as I can afford it, we are going to get married."

"One moment, Jenkins. I want to know if I can get a house."

"I really mustn't stop, sir. You see, I didn't expect to meet you here. And, really, I get so little time for tennis."

It was then that Cubitt remembered that Jenkins had been lamed in the War, and was no longer able to play the game which had once been a passion with him. And he passed on, wondering, to see at a garden gate a boy with a cricket bat under his arm, and a familiar blazer hanging loose over his shoulders. He recognised the boy at once and greeted him with a shout of surprise, and the boy laughingly welcomed him, addressing him as Cupid.

Now Cupid was the name by which Cubitt had been called at school.

"If it isn't young Harvey!" Cubitt exclaimed. "And what are you doing there with that cricket bat?"

"I am going to get some practice," said young Harvey gravely, "because, as you know, I am going to play for Middlesex when I grow up, and I must keep my hand in. But I never thought I should see you again, Cupid. And how funny and old and queer you look! And you do look silly with that umbrella!"

"Do you live here always, Harvey?" Cubitt asked wistfully. "Or do you only come here sometimes?"

"Why, I live here always," said young Harvey. And then Cubitt remembered that young Harvey had died when a boy of fourteen, and fear smote him again.

"Well," he stammered, "I hope you will do very well for Middlesex."

"Yes," said the boy gravely, "we shall have a very good team when I begin to play. What with myself and Stoddart and Trott and J.T. Hearne. And they say that new man Warner is very good. So you won't mind if I run off and get some practice, will you?"

So Cubitt watched him run away, and then, carrying his bewilderment like a load, walked on up the sunlit road between the fair houses and the fair gardens. For the moon which had first made light for him had given place to the sun, and his own shadow was the only ugly thing that he could see.

And along the road he met many, who were all very beautiful and very young, youths and young girls. For the most part they walked in pairs, and these couples had no eyes for anybody else but just each other. And Cubitt read in their eyes such love for each other that his heart smote him with a pain which he had not suffered for more than twenty years, and had not thought ever to feel again.

It seemed to him that he had not walked very far ere he came to a house which was more beautiful than all the others; and why it was more beautiful he could not say, except that it gave more delight to his eyes. It was made of old red brick, with high rectangular windows, and a great wistaria in full bloom, with branches like a vine's, almost covered the face of it. Between the gate and the front door was a broad flagged path with moss and grass growing between the stones, and dividing two green lawns, on the left of which was a sundial.

And while he stood yearning after this little place of delight the door burst open and a little girl ran down the flagged path

69

towards him. She was fair-haired and blue-eyed, and her frock was blue to match her eyes, and she wore a little white house-wifely apron. And he knew her at once for Gladys, a little girl with whom he had played at being sweethearts when he was a small boy and whom he was once firmly determined to marry when he grew up.

This Gladys burst open the gate and ran straight into his arms and kissed him laughingly and violently, with a straight pursed-up mouth, as children kiss.

"Why, Gladys," he said, "if I had not just decided that I must give up being surprised, I should fall dead with amazement."

"Dead?" she repeated wonderingly. "What is 'dead'?"

"And is this your house, my dear?" he asked quickly, for her question troubled him.

"And yours, too. Don't you remember it is just the house we decided we must have after we were married? And you were to have a real gun instead of one that only fired peas? And I was to have real babies instead of dolls?"

"My house?" he repeated. "Our house?"

"Only, of course, you can't come and live in it like that. There's a regulation against it. For something has happened to you, and you're not a nice boy with inky fingers and a bag of sweets in your pocket any more. You're a funny old gentleman with an umbrella and a bowler hat. And you can only come here as the little boy you once were. But I know you're my Michael, all the same."

Cubitt clasped the child to him rather wearily and began to whisper to her:

"My dear, tell me how I am to help being what I am. If this is my house it is unfair that I may not come and live in it. And how am I to be once more the boy who used to play with you in fields on which the builders have made houses since?"

"Perhaps," said Gladys, "you have not paid for our house. And it is only as little Michael that you can live in it. Why, all your old toys are in the attic, where they have been waiting for you all these years. And I have been wanting so much to hear you recite 'Hohenlinden' again."

"But what am I to do about it?" he asked hopelessly.

"If I were you," she said, "I should go and see them at the estate office."

"Is that it, over there?" he asked.

"No. Where you are pointing now is the shed where Father Christmas keeps his sledge. You can see the reindeer grazing just beside it. He is a jolly old gentleman is Father Christmas, and often comes in to see me. No, that is the estate office—farther up the road, where I am pointing now."

"My dear," said Cubitt, still holding her in his arms, "I do not understand it. I do not understand anything. I only know that I, who thought I had never loved anything nor could love anything save myself, now love you better than anything else in life. I say this to you, who am an oldish man while you are still a child. And if I can win back to the boyhood which seemed to have been stolen from me while I slept, I may yet share with you the house which once we built together out of a dream."

So said Cubitt, and she kissed him again with a little happy laugh and pursed-up mouth. Then Cubitt strode down the road to the estate office. The estate office was like any other estate office, but its surroundings invested it with a kind of beauty. Cubitt tapped at the door, and a voice bade him come in, and he entered to confront a very beautiful young man with white folded wings who sat behind a roll-top desk. And a little to his left was another young man, not so beautiful, and with smaller wings, who pored over a ledger. Now it was well that Cubitt was determined to be surprised at nothing, for truly a house agent with wings is an unusual sight; and one would more expect to see a man of that calling decorated with horns and a tail. But Cubitt swallowed his surprise, even when he heard himself addressed courteously by name.

"Good-day, Mr. Cubitt, and what can I do for you?"

"I want a house," said Cubitt slowly and distinctly.

"A house? What sort of house? We have only small houses here, for those who require great mansions do not come to Oberon Road."

"It is a small house that I want," said Cubitt. "That one with the wisteria and the sundial in front."

"The sundial is merely a superfluous decoration, Mr. Cubitt, because here it is always noon. But do you mean the house where Gladys lives?"

"That is the house. I understand that it is my house, too."

"Yours?" He turned sharply to his clerk. "Look it up, please, will you?"

And the clerk turned over several pages of the ledger and presently said, "The house was built for Mr. Cubitt, but he has not paid for it."

"There you are, you see!" said the agent severely. "And you don't think we're going to have middle-aged men with umbrellas living in Oberon Road, do you?"

Then Cubitt, controlling his voice with difficulty, said, "I can pay for my house. You have only to say how much. For I have a great deal of money invested in gilt-edged securities, which I could realise in an hour."

"I do not know the price, Mr. Cubitt," said the clear, hard voice. "But I do not think that you can pay it now."

"But—young Harvey never had any money!"

"Oh, yes, he did. He had a great deal. He had sixpence once, his week's pocket-money. And he gave it to a woman on the road who carried a baby which was starving because she was starving. And Jenkins bought his house here with a mouthful of water which he gave to a wounded man on Paschendael, when he himself was wounded. It was his last drop of water, for none dared drink from the shell-holes; so he too paid a great price for his house, Mr. Cubitt. And that girl whom you first saw here, she also paid a great price, for she gave all she had to an outcast; and that was tears, and sympathy, and a message of hope."

"Do you mean that she gave them to the drunken poet she spoke of?" said Cubitt, with just a hint of outraged virtue in his tone, "I wonder you have such an undesirable tenant. But perhaps he paid dearly for his villa."

"He did, Mr. Cubitt. He ruined himself to save a friend, and he was never strong enough to begin again. Some men are like that, Mr. Cubitt. We do not admire drunkards; but when his brain is drugged with spirits he creeps here sometimes for little blessed half hours, and because he has paid for his house we have not the heart to turn him out."

"Ah, the poor fellow!" said Cubitt, suddenly melting.

The agent regarded him out of kinder eyes.

"How did you get here, Mr. Cubitt?" he asked; and Cubitt told him.

"This is one of Dandalon's tricks," said the clerk curtly. "He's always trying to be funny. It's about time you told him about it."

"And yet," said the agent thoughtfully, "I do not altogether blame Dandalon. For I have just perceived symptoms in Mr. Cubitt which bid me hope that we may yet do business together."

"Ah, do you think so?" cried Cubitt, his face brightening. "But tell me—oh, tell me—how much must I pay? Is it all that I have?"

"No," said the agent, his voice growing very gentle, "not all that you have; but all that you think you cannot spare. And you must give all your heart with it, and try at the same time not to think of the little house which you may be buying."

"I will! I will!" Cubitt cried, very close to tears.

"Ah, well, then, perhaps we shall see you again not as you are today, and it may be that we shall become better acquainted."

The agent spread his wings a little to help him rise to his feet; and he moved towards Cubitt, which was also towards the door, as a signal that the interview was at an end.

"Goodbye," said Cubitt, brokenly.

The agent held the door open for him.

"Goodbye for the present—Michael," he said kindly, and he gave Cubitt the least little push between the shoulders.

And Cubitt stepped outside; not on to the fair road from which he had entered the office, but into the rain and darkness of the main thoroughfare of Judge Park.

Now I am afraid I know how the late Mr. Dickens would have finished off this story. He would have made Cubitt straightway empty his pockets into the hands of the first tramp, and found some snow to enable him to pelt an errand boy out of sheer good nature. And Cubitt would have raised everybody's wages at the office next morning, and bought the prize turkey for the old charwoman whose oven wasn't big enough to cook it, and invited himself to the junior clerks' Christmas party and made an idiot of himself by dancing there.

But Cubitt did nothing to qualify himself for an asylum, although a change was soon apparent in him. He started giving, and perhaps the agent, hearing of these things, smiled, knowing how desperately it hurt Cubitt to give. And because it hurt him, this was counted in Cubitt's favour. And really I believe the man tried hard to be sorry for those to whom he gave. And that also was counted for grace.

More than that, besides being kind to others, the man began to be kinder to himself. He wore better clothes, and changed his lodgings—to the bitter indignation of his landlady—and sometimes stood himself a bottle of wine with his lunch, and thus gradually became a human being. And these things also were entered on his credit side.

And strangest of all he sought out Gladys again, and found her not only a spinster but extremely unwilling to remain one. She was now a fine woman of forty-one, and looked not a day over thirty-nine, at which age time ceases for all self-respecting women. So he married her; and this again was not counted against him, since he was well old enough to know his own mind. It was on their return from the honeymoon that Cubitt had a queer aberration. They were just getting into a taxicab to drive to their new home, and Cubitt was thinking deeply of something—very likely wondering if fourpence were enough for a tip, or whether he oughtn't to spring sixpence.

"Drive us to Oberon Road, please," he said.

The man didn't know where it was. But I think he may have taken them there, all the same.

THE LAST LAUGH

D. H. Lawrence

First appeared in *The New Decameron* volume IV (Oxford, 1925)

David Herbert Lawrence (1885–1930) was born in Eastwood near Nottingham, the son of a miner and a lace-maker—these being the area's most prominent industries at that time. After initially leaving school and taking a job as a clerk, he re-entered education and this time did well, winning a scholarship and training to become a teacher. His first novel, *The White Peacock*, was published in 1911 when he was 25 years old. He would go on to a successful but controversial career as a novelist, with works including *Sons and Lovers* (1913), *The Rainbow* (1915), *Women in Love* (1920), and most notoriously, *Lady Chatterley's Lover* (1928). Lawrence's frank depiction of sexuality, including same-sex attraction, was scandalous for the time, and in his own lifetime the literary establishment did not always value his talent.

The New Decameron, in which this tale first appeared, is a collection of interlinked stories, intended as a re-interpretation of Boccaccio's *Decameron* for the 20th century. In place of Boccaccio's original frame narrative, which featured a group of people sheltering from the Black Death in a villa outside Florence, this new version instead consists of stories told by the party of men and women travelling under the guidance of Mr. Hector Turpin of Turpin's Temperamental Tours. Published over six volumes from 1919–1929, the collection included contributions from writers such as Storm Jameson and Dorothy L. Sayers.

Lawrence's story appeared as 'The tale of the lady of fashion', and picks up the themes of bodily sensation and disability that appeared in his novels.

Like 'Oberon Road', this story describes a London turned from familiar to strange, and explores the question of whether we can trust our perceptions.

There was a little snow on the ground, and the church clock had just struck midnight. Hampstead in the night of winter for once was looking pretty, with clean, white earth and lamps for moon, and dark sky above the lamps.

A confused little sound of voices, a gleam of hidden yellow light. And then the garden door of a tall, dark Georgian house suddenly opened, and three people confusedly emerged. A girl in a dark-blue coat and fur turban, very erect; a fellow with a little dispatch case, slouching; a thin man with a red beard, bare-headed, peering out of the gateway down the hill that swung in a curve downward toward London.

"Look at it! A new world!" cried the man in the beard ironically, as he stood on the step and peered out.

"No, Lorenzo! It's only whitewash!" cried the young man in the overcoat. His voice was handsome, resonant, plangent, with a weary, sardonic touch.

As he turned back, his face was dark in shadow.

The girl with the erect, alert head, like a bird, turned back to the two men.

"What was that?" she asked, in her quick, quiet voice.

"Lorenzo says it's a new world. I say it's only whitewash," cried the man in the street.

She stood still and lifted her woolly, gloved finger. She was deaf and was taking it in.

Yes, she had got it. She gave a quick, chuckling laugh, glanced very quickly at the man in the bowler hat, then back at the man in the stucco gateway, who was grinning like a satyr and waving good-by.

"Good-by, Lorenzo!" came the resonant, weary cry of the man in the bowler hat.

"Good-by!" came the sharp, night-bird call of the girl.

The green gate slammed, then the inner door. The two were alone in the street, save for the policeman at the corner. The road curved steeply downhill.

"You'd better mind how you *step*!" shouted the man in the bowler hat, leaning near the erect, sharp girl, and slouching in his walk. She paused a moment, to make sure what he had said.

"Don't mind me, I'm quite all right. Mind yourself!" she said quickly. At that very moment he gave a wild lurch on the slippery snow, but managed to save himself from falling. She watched him, on tiptoes of alertness. His bowler hat bounced away in the thin snow. They were under a lamp near the curve. As he ducked for his hat he showed a bald spot, just like a tonsure, among his dark, thin, rather curly hair. And when he looked up at her, with his thick, black brows sardonically arched, and his rather hooked nose self-derisive, jamming his hat on again, he seemed like a satanic young priest. His face had beautiful lines, like a faun, and a doubtful, martyred expression. A sort of faun on the cross, with all the malice of the complication.

"Did you hurt yourself?" she asked, in her quick, cool, unemotional way.

"No!" he shouted derisively.

"Give me the machine, won't you?" she said, holding out her woolly hand. "I believe I'm safer."

"Do you *want* it?" he shouted.

"Yes, I'm sure I'm safer."

He handed her the little brown dispatch case, which was really a Marconi listening machine for her deafness. She marched erect as ever. He shoved his hands deep in his overcoat pockets and slouched along beside her, as if he wouldn't make his legs firm. The road curved down in front of them, clean and pale with snow under the lamps. A motor car came churning up. A few dark figures slipped away into the dark recesses of the houses, like fishes among rocks above a sea bed of white sand. On the left was a tuft of trees sloping upward into the dark.

He kept looking around, pushing out his finely shaped chin and his hooked nose as if he were listening for something. He could still hear the motor car climbing on to the Heath. Below was the yellow, foul-smelling glare of the Hampstead tube station. On the right the trees.

The girl, with her alert, pink-and-white face, looked at him sharply, inquisitively. She had an odd, nymphlike inquisitiveness, sometimes like a bird, sometimes a squirrel, sometimes a rabbit; never quite like a woman. At last he stood still, as if he would go no farther. There was a curious, baffled grin on his smooth, cream-coloured face.

"James," he said loudly to her, leaning toward her ear. "Do you hear somebody *laughing*?"

"Laughing?" she retorted quickly. "Who's laughing?"

"I don't know. *Somebody!*" he shouted, showing his teeth at her in a very odd way.

"No, I hear nobody," she announced.

"But it's most *extraordinary*!" he cried, his voice slurring up and down. "Put on your machine."

"Put it on?" she retorted. "What for?"

"To see if you can *hear* it," he cried.

"Hear what?"

"The *laughing*. Somebody laughing. It's most *extraordinary*."

She gave her odd little chuckle and handed him her machine. He held it while she opened the lid and attached the wires, putting the band over her head and the receivers at her ears, like a wireless operator. Crumbs of snow fell down the cold darkness. She switched on; little yellow lights in glass tubes shone in the machine. She was connected, she was listening. He stood with his head ducked, his hands shoved down in his overcoat pockets.

Suddenly he lifted his face and gave the weirdest, slightly neighing laugh, uncovering his strong, spaced teeth and arching his black brows, and watching her with queer, gleaming, goatlike eyes.

She seemed a little dismayed.

"There!" he said. "Didn't you hear it?"

"I heard *you*!" she said, in a tone which conveyed that *that* was enough.

"But didn't you hear *it*?" he cried, unfurling his lips oddly again.

"No!" she said.

He looked at her vindictively, and stood again with ducked head. She remained erect, her fur hat in her hand, her fine bobbed hair banded with the machine band and catching crumbs of snow, her odd, bright-eyed, deaf nymph's face lifted with blank listening.

"There!" he cried, suddenly jerking up his gleaming face. "You mean to tell me you can't—" He was looking at her almost diabolically. But something else was too strong for him. His face wreathed with a startling, peculiar smile, seeming to gleam, and suddenly the most extraordinary laugh came bursting out of him, like an animal laughing. It was a strange, neighing sound, amazing in her ears. She was startled, and switched her machine quieter.

A large form loomed up: a tall, clean-shaven young policeman.

"A radio?" he asked laconically.

"No, it's my machine. I'm deaf!" said Miss James quickly and distinctly. She was not the daughter of a peer for nothing.

The man in the bowler hat lifted his face and glared at the fresh-faced young policeman with a peculiar white glare in his eyes.

"Look here!" he said distinctly. "Did you hear some one laughing?"

"Laughing! I hear you, sir."

"No, *not* me." He gave an impatient jerk of his arm, and lifted his face again. His smooth, creamy face seemed to gleam, there were subtle curves of derisive triumph in all its lines. He was careful not to look directly at the young policeman. "The most extraordinary laughter I ever heard," he added, and the same touch of derisive exultation sounded in his tones.

The policeman looked down on him cogitatingly.

"It's perfectly all right," said Miss James coolly. "He's not drunk. He just hears something that we don't hear."

"Drunk!" echoed the man in the bowler hat, in profoundly amused derision. "If I were merely drunk—" And off he went again in the wild, neighing, animal laughter, while his averted face seemed to flash.

At the sound of the laughter something roused in the blood of the girl and of the policeman. They stood nearer to one another, so that their sleeves touched and they looked wonderingly across at the man in the bowler hat. He lifted his black brows at them.

"Do you mean to say you heard nothing?" he asked.

"Only you," said Miss James.

"Only you, sir!" echoed the policeman.

"What was it like?" asked Miss James.

"Ask me to *describe* it!" retorted the young man, in extreme contempt. "It's the most marvellous sound in the world."

And truly he seemed wrapped up in a new mystery.

"Where does it come from?" asked Miss James, very practical.

"*Apparently*," he answered in contempt, "from over there." And he pointed to the trees and bushes inside the railings over the road.

"Well, let's go and see!" she said. "I can carry my machine and go on listening."

The man seemed relieved to get rid of the burden. He shoved his hands in his pockets again and sloped off across the road. The policeman, a queer look flickering on his fresh young face, put his hand round the girl's arm carefully and subtly, to help her. She did not lean at all on the support of the big hand, but she was interested, so she did not resent it. Having held herself all her life intensely aloof from physical contact, and never having let any man touch her, she now, with a certain nymphlike voluptuousness, allowed the large hand of the young policeman to support her as they followed the quick, wolflike figure of the other man across the road uphill. And she could feel the presence of the young policeman, through all the thickness of his dark-blue uniform, as something young and alert and bright.

When they came up to the man in the bowler hat, he was standing with his head ducked, his ears pricked, listening beside the iron rail inside which grew big, black holly trees tufted with snow, and old, ribbed, silent English elms.

The policeman and the girl stood waiting. She was peering into the bushes with the sharp eyes of a deaf nymph, deaf to the world's noises. The man in the bowler hat listened intensely. A lorry rolled downhill, making the earth tremble.

"There!" cried the girl, as the lorry rumbled darkly past. And she glanced round with flashing eyes at her policeman, her fresh, soft face gleaming with startled life. She glanced straight into the puzzled, amused eyes of the young policeman. He was just enjoying himself.

"Don't you see?" she said, rather imperiously.

"What is it, miss?" answered the policeman.

"I mustn't point," she said. "Look where I look."

And she looked away with brilliant eyes, into the dark holly bushes. She must see something, for she smiled faintly, with subtle satisfaction, and she tossed her erect head in all the pride of vindication. The policeman looked at her instead of into the bushes. There was a certain brilliance of triumph and vindication in all the poise of her slim body.

"I always knew I should see him," she said triumphantly to herself.

"Whom do you see?" shouted the man in the bowler hat.

"Don't you see him, too?" she asked, turning round her soft, arch, nymphlike face anxiously. She was anxious for the little man to see.

"No, I see nothing. What do you see, James?" cried the man in the bowler hat, insisting.

"A man."

"Where?"

"There. Among the holly bushes."

"Is he there now?"

"No! He's gone."

"What sort of a man?"

"I don't know."

"What did he look like?"

"I can't tell you."

But at that instant the man in the bowler hat turned suddenly, and the arch, triumphant look flew to his face.

"Why, he must be *there*!" he cried, pointing up the grove. "Don't you hear him laughing? He must be behind those trees."

And his voice, with curious delight, broke into a laugh again, as he stood and stamped his feet on the snow, and danced to his own laughter, ducking his head. Then he turned away and ran swiftly up the avenue lined with old trees.

He slowed down as a door at the end of a garden path, white with untouched snow, suddenly opened, and a woman in a long-fringed black shawl stood in the light. She peered out into the night. Then she came down to the low garden gate. Crumbs of snow still fell. She had dark hair and a tall, dark comb.

"Did you knock at my door?" she asked of the man in the bowler hat.

"I? No!"

"Somebody knocked at my door."

"Did they? Are you sure? They can't have done. There are no footmarks in the snow."

"Nor are there!" she said. "But somebody knocked and called something."

"That's very curious," said the man. "Were you expecting some one?"

"No. Not exactly expecting any one. Except that one is always expecting Somebody, you know." In the dimness of the snow-lit night he could see her making big, dark eyes at him.

"Was it some one laughing?" he said.

"No. It was no one laughing, exactly. Some one knocked, and I ran to open, hoping as one always hopes, you know—"

"What?"

"Oh—that something wonderful is going to happen."

He was standing close to the low gate. She stood on the opposite side. Her hair was dark, her face seemed dusky, as she looked up at him with her dark, meaningful eyes.

"Did you wish some one would come?" he asked.

"Very much," she replied, in her plangent voice.

He bent down, unlatching the gate. As he did so the woman in the black shawl turned and, glancing over her shoulder, hurried back to the house, walking unevenly in the snow, on her high-heeled shoes. The man hurried after her, hastening like a hound to catch up.

Meanwhile the girl and the policeman had come up. The girl stood still when she saw the man in the bowler hat going up the garden walk after the woman in the black shawl with the fringe.

"Is he going in?" she asked quickly.

"Looks like it, doesn't it?" said the policeman.

"Does he know that woman?"

"I can't say. I should say he soon will," replied the policeman.

"But who is she?"

"I couldn't say who she is."

The two dark, confused figures entered the lighted doorway, then the door closed on them.

"He's gone," said the girl outside on the snow. She hastily began to pull off the band of her telephone receiver, and switched off her machine. The tubes of secret light disappeared, she packed up the little leather case. Then, pulling on her soft fur cap, she stood once more ready.

The slightly martial look which her long, dark-blue, military-seeming coat gave her was intensified, while the slightly anxious, bewildered look of her face had gone. She seemed to stretch herself, to stretch her limbs free. And the inert look had left her full, soft cheeks. Her cheeks were alive with the glimmer of pride and a new, dangerous surety.

She looked quickly at the tall young policeman. He was clean-shaven, fresh-faced, smiling oddly under his helmet, waiting in subtle patience a few yards away. She saw that he was a decent young man, one of the waiting sort.

The second of ancient fear was followed at once in her by a blithe, unaccustomed sense of power.

"Well!" she said. "I should say it's no use waiting." She spoke decisively.

"You don't have to wait for him, do you?" asked the policeman.

"Not at all. He's much better where he is." She laughed an odd, brief laugh. Then glancing over her shoulder, she set off down the hill, carrying her little case. Her feet felt light, her legs felt long and strong. She glanced over her shoulder again. The young policeman was following her, and she laughed to herself. Her limbs felt so lithe and so strong, if she wished she could easily run faster than he. If she wished, she could easily kill him, even with her hands.

So it seemed to her. But why kill him? He was a decent young fellow. She had in front of her eyes the dark face among the holly bushes, with the brilliant, mocking eyes. Her breast felt full of power, and her legs felt long and strong and wild. She was surprised herself at the sensation of triumph and of rosy anger. Her hands felt keen on her wrists. She who had always declared she had not a muscle in her body! Even now, it was not muscle, it was a sort of flame.

Suddenly it began to snow heavily, with fierce, frozen puffs of wind. The snow was small, in frozen grains, and hit sharp on her face. It seemed to whirl round her as if she herself were whirling in a cloud. But she did not mind. There was a flame in her, her limbs felt flamey and strong, amid the whirl.

And the whirling, snowy air seemed full of presences, full of strange, unheard noises. She was used to the sensation of noises taking place which she could not hear. This sensation became very strong. She felt something was happening in the wild air.

The London air was no longer heavy and clammy, saturated with ghosts of the unwilling dead. A new, clean tempest swept down from the pole, and there were noises.

Voices were calling. In spite of her deafness she could hear some one, several voices, calling and whistling, as if many people were hallooing through the air:

"He's come back! Aha! He's come back!"

There was a wild, whistling, jubilant sound of voices in the storm of snow. Then obscured lightning winked through the snow in the air.

"Is that thunder and lightning?" she asked of the young police-man, as she stood still, waiting for his form to emerge through the veil of whirling snow.

"Seems like it to me," he said.

And at that very moment the lightning blinked again, and the dark, laughing face was near her face, it almost touched her cheek.

She started back, but a flame of delight went over her.

"There!" she said. "Did you see that?"

"It lightened," said the policeman. She was looking at him almost angrily. But then the clean, fresh animal look of his skin, and the tame-animal look in his frightened eyes amused her; she laughed her low, triumphant laugh. He was obviously afraid, like a frightened dog that sees something uncanny.

The storm suddenly whistled louder, more violently, and, with a strange noise like castanets, she seemed to hear voices clapping and crying:

"He is here! He's come back!"

She nodded her head gravely.

The policeman and she moved on side by side. She lived alone in a little stucco house in a side street down the hill. There was a church and a grove of trees, and then the little old row of houses. The wind blew fiercely, thick with snow. Now and again a taxi went by with its lights showing weirdly. But the world seemed empty, uninhabited save by snow and voices.

As the girl and the policeman turned past the grove of trees near the church, a great whirl of wind and snow made them stand still, and in the wild confusion they heard a whirling of sharp, delighted voices, something like seagulls, crying:

"He's here! He's here!"

"Well, I'm jolly glad he's back," said the girl calmly.

"What's that?" said the nervous policeman, hovering near the girl.

The wind let them move forward. As they passed along the railings it seemed to them the doors of the church were open, and the windows were out, and the snow and the voices were blowing in a wild career all through the church.

"How extraordinary that they left the church open!" said the girl.

The policeman stood still. He could not reply.

And as they stood they listened to the wind and the church full of whirling voices all calling confusedly.

"*Now* I hear the laughing," she said suddenly.

It came from the church: a sound of low, subtle, endless laughter, a strange, naked sound.

"Now I hear it!" she said.

But the policeman did not speak. He stood cowed, listening to the strange noises in the church.

The wind must have blown out one of the windows, for they could see the snow whirling in volleys through the black gap, and whirling inside the church like a dim light. There came a sudden crash, followed by a burst of chuckling, naked laughter. The snow seemed to make a queer light inside the building, like ghosts moving, big and tall.

There was more laughter, and a tearing sound. On the wind, pieces of paper, leaves of books, came whirling among the snow through the dark window. Then a white thing, soaring like a crazy bird, rose up on the wind as if it had wings, and lodged on a black tree outside, struggling. It was the altar cloth.

There came a bit of gay, trilling music. The wind was running over the organ pipes like Pan pipes, quickly up and down. Snatches of wild, gay, trilling music, and bursts of the naked, low laughter.

"Really!" said the girl. "This is most extraordinary. Do you hear the music and the people laughing?"

"Yes, I hear somebody on the organ!" said the policeman.

"And do you get the puff of warm wind? Smelling of spring. Almond blossom, that's what it is! A most marvellous scent of almond blossom. Isn't it an extraordinary thing!"

She went on triumphantly past the church, and came to the row of little old houses. She entered her own gate in the little railed entrance.

"Here I am!" she said finally. "I'm home now. Thank you very much for coming with me."

She looked at the young policeman. His whole body was white as a wall with snow, and in the vague light of the arc lamp from the street his face was humble and frightened.

"Can I come in and warm myself a bit?" he asked humbly. She knew it was fear rather than cold that froze him. He was in mortal fear.

"Well!" she said. "Stay down in the sitting room if you like. But don't come upstairs, because I am alone in the house. You can make up the fire in the sitting room, and you can go when you are warm."

She left him on the big, low couch before the fire, his face bluish and blank with fear. He rolled his blue eyes after her as she left the room. But she went up to her bedroom, and fastened her door.

In the morning she was in her studio upstairs in her little house, looking at her own paintings and laughing to herself. Her canaries were talking and shrilly whistling in the sunshine that followed the storm. The cold snow outside was still clean, and the white glare in the air gave the effect of much stronger sunshine than actually existed.

She was looking at her own paintings, and chuckling to herself over their comicalness. Suddenly they struck her as absolutely absurd. She quite enjoyed looking at them, they seemed to her so grotesque. Especially her self-portrait, with its nice brown hair and its slightly opened rabbit mouth and its baffled, uncertain rabbit eyes. She looked at the painted face and laughed in a long, rippling laugh, till the yellow canaries like faded daffodils almost went mad in an effort to sing louder. The girl's long, rippling laugh sounded through the house uncannily.

The housekeeper, a rather sad-faced young woman of a superior sort—nearly all people in England are of the superior sort, superiority being an English ailment—came in with an inquiring and rather disapproving look.

"Did you call, Miss James?" she asked loudly.

"No. No, I didn't call. Don't shout, I can hear quite well," replied the girl.

The housekeeper looked at her again.

"You knew there was a young man in the sitting room?" she said.

"No. Really!" cried the girl. "What, the young policeman? I'd forgotten all about him. He came in in the storm to warm himself. Hasn't he gone?"

"No, Miss James."

"How extraordinary of him! What time is it? Quarter to nine! Why didn't he go when he was warm? I must go and see him, I suppose."

"He says he's lame," said the housekeeper censoriously and loudly.

"Lame! That's extraordinary. He certainly wasn't last night. But don't shout. I can hear quite well."

"Is Mr. Marchbanks coming in to breakfast, Miss James?" said the housekeeper, more and more censorious.

"I couldn't say. But I'll come down as soon as mine is ready. I'll be down in a minute, anyhow, to see the policeman. Extraordinary that he is still here."

She sat down before her window, in the sun, to think a while. She could see the snow outside, the bare, purplish trees. The air all seemed rare and different. Suddenly the world had become quite different, as if some skin or integument had broken, as if the old, mouldering London sky had crackled and rolled back, like an old skin, shrivelled, leaving an absolutely new blue heaven.

"It really is extraordinary!" she said to herself. "I certainly saw that man's face. What a wonderful face it was!

"I shall never forget it. Such laughter! He laughs longest who laughs last. He certainly will have the last laugh. I like him for that: he will laugh last. Must be some one really extraordinary! How very nice to be the one to laugh last. He certainly will. What a wonderful being! I suppose I must call him a being. He's not a person exactly.

"But how wonderful of him to come back and alter all the world immediately! *Isn't* that extraordinary. I wonder if he'll have altered Marchbanks. Of course, Marchbanks never saw him. But he heard him. Wouldn't that do as well, I wonder! I *wonder*!"

She went off into a muse about Marchbanks. She and he were such friends. They had been friends like that for almost two years. Never lovers. Never that at all. But *friends*.

And after all, she had been in love with him: in her head. This seemed now so funny to her: that she had been, in her head, so much in love with him. After all, life was too absurd.

Because now she saw herself and him as such a funny pair. He so funnily taking life terribly seriously, especially his own life. And she so ridiculously *determined* to save him from himself. Oh, how absurd! *Determined* to save him from himself, and wildly in love with him in the effort. The determination to save him from himself!

Absurd! Absurd! Absurd! Since she had seen the man laughing among the holly bushes—*such* extraordinary, wonderful laughter—she had seen her own ridiculousness. Really, what fantastic silliness, saving a man from himself! Saving anybody. What fantastic silliness! How much more amusing and lively to let a man go to perdition in his own way. Perdition was more amusing than salvation anyhow, and a much better place for most men to go to.

She had never been in love with any man, and only spuriously in love with Marchbanks. She saw it quite plainly now. After all, what nonsense it all was, this being-in-love business. Thank goodness she had never made the humiliating mistake.

No, the man among the holly bushes had made her see it all so plainly: the ridiculousness of being in love, the *infra dig* business of chasing a man or being chased by a man.

"Is love really so absurd and *infra dig*?" she said aloud to herself.

"Why of course!" came a deep, laughing voice.

She started round, but nobody was to be seen.

"I expect it's that man again!" she said to herself. "It really *is* remarkable, you know. I consider it's a remarkable thing that I never really wanted a man—*any* man. And there I am over thirty. It *is* curious. Whether it's something wrong with me, or right with me, I can't say. I don't know till I've proved it. But I believe, if that man kept on laughing, something would happen to me."

She smelt the curious smell of almond blossom in the room, and heard the distant laugh again.

"I do wonder why Marchbanks went with that woman last night. Whatever could he want of her?—or she him? So strange, as if they both had made up their minds to something! How extraordinarily puzzling life is! So messy, it all seems.

"Why does nobody ever laugh in life like that man. He *did* seem so wonderful. So scornful! And so proud! And so real! With those laughing, scornful, amazing eyes, just laughing and disappearing again. I can't imagine him chasing any woman, thank goodness. It's all so messy. My policeman would be messy if one would let him: like a dog. I do dislike dogs, really I do. And men do seem so doggy!"

But even while she mused, she began to laugh again to herself with a long, low chuckle. How wonderful of that man to come and laugh like that and make the sky crack and shrivel like an old skin. Wasn't he wonderful! Wouldn't it be wonderful if he just touched her. Even touched her. She felt, if he touched her, she herself would emerge new and tender out of an old, hard skin. She was gazing abstractedly out of the window.

"There he comes, just now," she said abruptly. But she meant Marchbanks, not the laughing man.

There he came, his hands still shoved down in his overcoat pockets, his head still rather furtively ducked, in the bowler hat, and his legs still rather shambling. He came hurrying across the road, not looking up, deep in thought, no doubt. Thinking profoundly, with agonies of agitation, no doubt about his last night's experience. It made her laugh.

She, watching from the window above, burst into a long laugh, and the canaries went off their heads again.

He was in the hall below. His resonant voice was calling, rather imperiously:

"James! Are you coming down?"

"No," she called. "You come up."

He came up two at a time, as if his feet were a bit savage with the stairs for obstructing him.

In the doorway he stood staring at her with a vacant, sardonic look, his grey eyes moving with a queer light And she looked back at him with a curious, rather haughty carelessness.

"Don't you want your breakfast?" she asked. It was his custom to come and take breakfast with her each morning.

"No," he answered loudly. "I went to a tea shop."

"Don't shout," she said. "I can hear you quite well."

He looked at her with mockery and a touch of malice.

"I believe you always could," he said, still loudly.

"Well, anyway, I can now, so you needn't shout," she replied.

And again his grey eyes, with the queer, greyish phosphorescent gleam in them, lingered malignantly on her face.

"Don't look at me," she said calmly. "I know all about everything."

He burst into a pouf of malicious laughter.

"Why, what's the matter!" he said curiously. "What have you been doing?"

"I don't quite know. Why? Are you going to call me to account?"

"Did you hear that laughing?"

"Oh, yes. And many more things. And saw things, too."

"Have you seen the paper?"

"No. Don't shout, I can hear."

"There's been a great storm, blew out the windows and doors of the church outside here, and pretty well wrecked the place."

"I saw it. A leaf of the church Bible blew right in my face—from the Book of Job." She gave a low laugh.

"But what else did you see?" he cried loudly.

"I saw *him*."

"Who?"

"Ah, that I can't say."

"But what was he like?"

"That I can't tell you. I don't really know."

"But you must know. Did your policeman see him, too?"

"No, I don't suppose he did. My policeman!" And she went off into a long ripple of laughter. "He is by no means mine. But I *must* go downstairs and see him."

"It's certainly made you very strange," Marchbanks said. "You've got no *soul*, you know."

"Oh, thank goodness for that!" she cried. "My policeman has one. I'm sure. My *policeman*!" And she went off again into a long peal of laughter, the canaries pealing shrill accompaniment.

"What's the matter with you?" he said.

"Having no soul. I never had one really. It was always fobbed off on me. Soul was the only thing there was between you and me. Thank goodness it's gone. Haven't you lost yours? The one that seemed to worry you, like a decayed tooth?"

"But what are you *talking* about?" he cried.

"I don't know," she said. "It's all so extraordinary. But look here, I *must* go down and see my policeman. He's downstairs in the sitting room. You'd better come with me."

They went down together. The policeman, in his waistcoat and shirt sleeves, was lying on the sofa, with a very long face.

"Look here!" said Miss James to him. "Is it true you're lame?"

"It is true. That's why I'm here. I can't walk," said the fair-haired young man as tears came to his eyes.

"But how did it happen? You weren't lame last night," she said.

"I don't know how it happened—but when I woke up and tried to stand up, I couldn't do it." The tears ran down his distressed face.

"How very extraordinary!" she said. "What can we do about it?"

"Which foot is it?" asked Marchbanks. "Let us have a look at it."

"I don't like to," said the poor devil.

"You'd better," said Miss James.

He slowly pulled off his stocking, and showed his white left foot curiously clubbed, like the weird paw of some animal. When he looked at it himself, he sobbed.

And as he sobbed, the girl heard again the low, exulting laughter. But she paid no heed to it, gazing curiously at the weeping young policeman.

"Does it hurt?" she asked.

"It does if I try to walk on it," wept the young man.

"I'll tell you what," she said. "We'll telephone for a doctor, and he can take you home in a taxi."

The young fellow shamefacedly wiped his eyes.

"But have you no idea how it happened?" asked Marchbanks anxiously.

"I haven't myself," said the young fellow.

At that moment the girl heard the low, eternal laugh right in her ear. She started, but could see nothing.

She started round again as Marchbanks gave a strange, yelping cry, like a shot animal. His white face was drawn, distorted in a curious grin, that was chiefly agony but partly wild recognition. He was staring with fixed eyes at something. And in the rolling agony of his eyes was the horrible grin of a man who realises he has made a final, and this time fatal, fool of himself.

"Why," he yelped in a high voice, "I knew it was he!" And with a queer, shuddering laugh he pitched forward on the carpet and lay writhing for a moment on the floor. Then he lay still, in a weird, distorted position, like a man struck by lightning.

Miss James stared with round, staring brown eyes.

"Is he dead?" she asked quickly.

The young policeman was trembling so that he could hardly speak. She could hear his teeth chattering.

"Seems like it," he stammered.

There was a faint smell of almond blossom in the air.

DR. BROWNING'S BUS

E. S. Knights

First appeared in *Horrors: A Collection of Uneasy Tales* (1933)

E. S. Knights is a rather more mysterious figure than most of the other authors in this book. It's probable that he was Edward Spurgeon Knights (1909–1984) who also wrote *Essex Folk: Tales from Village, Farm and Marsh* (1935), a history of vanishing rural life in the county in a similar vein to Ronald Blythe's *Akenfield* (1969).

'Dr. Browning's Bus' appeared as the first story in the collection *Horrors* (1933), edited by Charles Birkin and with a dust jacket that warned 'You are advised <u>not</u> to read these tales at night.' The story may have been in part inspired by Amelia B. Edwards' 'The Phantom Coach', re-worked for 1930s modernism and with an Essex setting.

Dr. Herbert Browning was the type of man who is known to many people, yet few could claim to know him at all intimately. Of a somewhat retiring nature, he had all his life failed to make friendships, which to others seemed to come so easily. He was a man of middle height and of sturdy build, with a slight tendency to stoop. His kindly face was crowned with a thatch of untidy hair which fifty-seven years had turned an iron grey. The pale eyes were the far-seeing eyes of a mystic rather than the calculating eyes of a professional man who had seen many battles of life and death, and with their light of sympathy and understanding had watched many set forth on their voyage into the unknown.

On finding himself at the age of fifty-four in possession of a sufficiency of this world's goods, Dr. Browning had parted with his large suburban practice, and had retired to Eastman's Farm, a small country property left him by a distant relative.

Eastman's Farm was an old rambling country house in the heart of Essex. It was not a farm in the proper sense of the word, but only so in name, from its once having been used as a farm in the days when it formed part of the manorial property. A lord of the manor had sold it into private hands many years before Dr. Browning became the owner, and its various owners before him had cared for the place and turned it into a country residence, but as in most rural districts its old name had clung fast.

The farm lay some three-quarters of a mile out of the nearest village of Denholm. The main road left the village going down a steep hill towards the west. A quarter of a mile out of the village a narrow lane branched off from the main road and wandered down between high banks and towering elm trees which in the autumn cast a thick carpet of brown leaves, while the cold winds heralding winter whistled through the bare branches. Down, always down, ran the little lane, past the woods and ploughed fields and the little stone church which had seen the Norman invaders, had heard feverish prayers at various times of wars and pestilence, and had received in due course the past generations of peaceful villagers. A little way past the church the lane took a sharp turn to the left and then branched into two ways, one leading into the woods, and the other to the entrance of Eastman's Farm.

The house itself was ancient and sprawling, hiding behind tall trees like guardian spirits by an holy place. In bright sunshine the house was a pleasant enough place, with its warm red-tiled roof above half-timbered walls. Inside, the old rooms downstairs branched off from a central brick-floored hall, from which the visitor caught a glimpse of ancient oak panelling and small diamond-paned windows, with here and there a splash of colour where the light flashed through odd panes of old stained glass. Such was the home of Dr. Browning. A charming place on a bright summer day, but guests were not so anxious to stay or even to visit when the winter set in. The place then had an air as of something more than human, of a dark brooding, as if not all was as quiet as the secluded spot would at first suggest, while in the long dark evenings when the cold wind moaned outside and the doors shook in their places and the timbers of the old house creaked, while outside the trees bowed to the gale and their long, dripping branches like the limp fingers of dead men scattered ice cold sweat as they laboured in the ever-driving wind—then the aspect was indeed changed, and men shuddered at the thought of such an abode.

As with many other such places, curious tales hung round Eastman's Farm. Old village wives told of a brutal farmer who had lived there with only an ancient dame to "do for him." One day after a fearful storm they were both found dead in front of the house with no suggestion of how they met their end, and ever since it was firmly believed that their unhappy spirits visited the farm during a storm.

Dr. Browning laughed at such tales, but not so old Mrs. Larkin, his housekeeper, who dreaded the approach of a storm, and at the first sign fled to the kitchen and lit as many lamps and candles as she could get into the room, in order to frighten away the "things," as she called them, should they venture near the house. On one stormy evening Dr. Browning found Mrs. Larkin sitting in the middle of seven lamps and nine candles, with an expression on her face of apprehension of the unknown, mingled with indignation at being found surrounded by evidence of her fears.

Dr. Browning closed the book he had been reading with a snap and looked at his watch, "Nearly six o'clock," he murmured to himself, as he replaced his watch. He did not like the prospect of leaving the cheerfully blazing log fire and the warmth and peace of his study for the cold and wet outside. He had promised to go and see old Biddy Jenkins, as she was called, who lived in a little cottage at the foot of the hill leading into the village.

For many weeks she had been ill, and was not expected to last long. The Vicar had asked him as a favour if he would call and do anything he could to ease the woman's last hours.

Dr. Browning rose from his chair and walked to the windows and pulled the curtains aside, and looked out into the darkness.

The rain beat down, and the wind blew round the house in great gusts which shook the trees in the garden, casting showers of spray on to the lawn beneath. Beyond the hedge huge dark masses marked where tall elms bent in the wind, and all round were signs of dark, wet and cold.

Readjusting the curtains, Dr. Browning opened his study door and passed into the hall.

"Well, Mrs. Larkin, a fine night for 'Farmer,'" he said, as he saw the worthy lady coming downstairs.

"Ah, sir," she said. "Ye mustn't talk like that, for I be real frit o' he."

Laughing at the old woman's fears, Dr. Browning asked where his rubber knee-boots were.

"Sir," gasped Mrs. Larkin, "you aint agoin' out o' a night like this, and such a mind too, be ye?"

"I must," said the doctor, "I have promised to see old Biddy Jenkins, and I must go."

With an uneasy shake of the head the old woman walked away, returning within a few moments with the doctor's boots in her hand. Having put on his boots and buttoned up his coat, the doctor undid the door.

With a trembling voice, Mrs. Larkin said: "You—you'll not be too late, sir, will you? I be wunnerful feared o' these nights."

"No, no," said Dr. Browning, with a smile on his face, "I'll not be late, Mrs. Larkin; tell the 'farmer' to wait till I come back."

Going out and slamming the door behind him, the doctor strode down the path to the gate. Here, removed from the shelter of the house, the wind caught him with its full force and nearly dashed him off his feet. Stumbling along in the intense dark up the lane, the doctor almost regretted having left the warmth and comfort of his study. The rain lashed at him in all its fury, finding every point of vantage. It trickled up his sleeves if he raised his hand to adjust his scarf, and ran down his neck if he failed to do so. The wind tried every trick to remove his hat, and tore at his coat in an endeavour to take it off his back. Long rank grasses like dank beards of old, old men hung from the high banks, and brushed his coat, and boughs above his head creaked in the gale. A curious snuffling noise repeated from time to time came from behind the hedge on his left, and caused a cold shiver to run down his back. Mentally shaking himself he realised that it was probably a cow trying to find a little shelter from the storm behind the hedge.

Struggling along in the wind and rain he said, half out aloud: "It's a good thing my heart's all right, or, at any rate, I think it is."

Nearing the end of the lane leading into the main road he saw the lights of a bus coining slowly along in the direction of the village. Running as best he could up the last rise in the lane, he held his hand out for the bus to stop. Jumping on to the step as it came alongside, he made his way to the front seat and sat down, glad of a respite in which to regain his breath after the pull up the lane.

After a moment or two it occurred to him that it was unusual for a bus at this time of the evening; the last bus to the village was at four o'clock in the afternoon. "Probably a late bus for something on in the village," he told himself, but then he thought a special would not have stopped for him. Looking round the dimly lighted interior he saw that there were three other occupants, a man and two women, sitting close by the door. Of a conductor he could see no sign. Both the man and the two women had their heads bent so that he could not see their faces, and all seemed to be sitting perfectly still, as if asleep.

With a start he realised that he could hear no noise of the bus moving along, no window rattled, and there was absolutely no noise of the wheels on the wet road, and yet the thing was apparently moving. Dr. Browning laughed at himself, all the same, rather uneasily. "Evidently," he chid himself, "you are nearly as bad as Mrs. Larkin," but this did not, however, quieten him; even with the raging gale outside, he kept repeating, there should be some noise, some sense of motion.

Peering through the window he could just make out the tops of the hedges. "Yes, they were certainly moving along," as he could see from the gently undulating hedge-top—but inside the bus there was absolutely no sense of motion whatever.

By this time Dr. Browning was thoroughly uneasy. Was he daft, was he unwell, or merely suddenly a bit nervy? Knowing that they should be by this time near the foot of the hill leading to the village, he rose to leave the bus. As he walked past the man at the back of the bus he caught a glimpse of his face, and it was the most brutal and coarse face that he had ever seen.

Standing on the footboard with his fare in his hand he waited, half wondering what to do with it in the absence of a conductor. The bus seemed to be slowing down, and he knew that meant the hill outside the village, so pocketing the coin he made ready to jump off. Just as he stepped off the bus the woman sitting nearest the door turned her face full towards him, and with a cry of surprise he fell off the step. The face was the face of Biddy Jenkins.

Realising that he was wet, stiff and cold, Dr. Browning found himself lying at the bottom of the bank bordering the road to the village, and not 100 yards from the lane leading to his home. His first thought was of how long he had been there; looking at his watch he saw that it was ten o'clock. With a wave of returning conscience came back the memory of the walk up the dark lane, and the journey on the bus, and lastly, the face of Biddy Jenkins. He certainly could not go to her cottage now in the state he was in—there was only one thing to do, and that was to find his way home as best he could. Wet through, and with his face and hands bleeding from scratches, Dr. Browning struggled to his feet. His head ached abominably, but he struggled up the bank and down the road into the lane leading to Eastman's Farm. Downhill the going was better; the rain had ceased, and the wind was not quite so strong as when he set out, also a moon shone out fitfully from the ragged clouds.

He did not quite know how he got home, but get there he did. Opening the door to his knock, Mrs. Larkin screamed when she saw the state he was in.

"It's all right, Mrs. Larkin," he gasped. "I fell down the bank on the main road." Murmuring commiseration and looking askance at the mud on his clothes, Mrs. Larkin recounted her fears of the evening concerning the ghostly "Farmer," and her being alone in the house. After washing his face and hands in some water which the woman brought him, he sent her away and went into his study, where he mixed himself a stiff glass of brandy, and settled in front of the fire to "get calm," as he told himself, and to think over the curious events of the evening.

He was uneasy about the bus; it was strange, deucedly strange, and then the faces, and of all faces, that of Biddy Jenkins. When he saw her the day before she was desperately ill and with no hope of recovery, and yet he himself had seen her that very evening on a bus.

"Come in," he called, in response to a knock on the door.

Mrs. Larkin's head appeared round the corner, and she said: "They sent a message up from old Biddy's arter you'd gorne, sir; she died jest arter six this evening."

"Annie, come here," called Mrs. Larkin to her niece, who had recently come to help her aunt at Eastman's Farm. "What was that the doctor said to you when you took his tea in, said he was a-goin' out did he, and a night like this too?"

"Yes, aunt," said her niece, her mouth full of half-eaten bread and jam.

"I can't understand what he wants to go out for on a night like this, raining and blowing as it is; he ain't been hisself lately, not since that night over a month agoo, and it was jest such a night as this when he went out and came back all covered with mud and his face all bleeding—looked as if he'd seen suthin' he did, give me such a turn when I opened the door. That was why I wrote to your mother and said as I wanted you to come here, I couldn't stay in the house alone no longer."

"Is he mad, do you think, aunt?" questioned her niece with a frightened look.

"Mad, girl, no," replied her aunt, "the doctor ain't mad, but ever since that night I was telling you of, he has been somehow different to what he was affor. He never used to talk to hisself for one thing, and how he goes on talking to hisself for hours on end. He give me such a start last evening when I went in with his supper," continued Mrs. Larkin. "Just as I opened the door he said, and quite loud, mind you: 'Biddy Jenkins was in the bus with the "Farmer."' I nearly dropped the tray. He must a' seen as I looked queer, for he said all hurried-like: 'It's all right, Mrs. Larkin, I—I was talking to myself, set the tray here on the table, there's a good soul, and then go away.'

"You remember, gal, I told you about the 'Farmer,' didn't I? Well, don't you goo outside the house on a night like this, else you may see suthin' as you don't want to see. Perhaps the doctor see him," added the woman, with a shudder.

"No, aunt," said her niece, giving a fearful look towards the door, "I don't want to go out, and I don't want to see 'he.'"

The conversation lapsed into silence, and the two looked into the heart of the brightly blazing fire, each lost in her own thoughts.

The opening of a door roused both from their reverie.

"That's the doctor agoin' out," said the older woman, "he's arter his hat and coat now."

Slow footsteps walked across the hall, and the front door opened and closed with a bang, Dr. Browning had gone out.

"What a night to go out," said the girl to her aunt; "it's pouring with rain, and there's a gale fit to wreck all the ships of the sea." Going to the window the girl pulled the heavy curtains aside and peered out into the darkness beyond. Suddenly with a gasping little cry which brought the older woman to her feet, she turned a white terror-stricken face from the window.

"Aunt, aunt," she gasped, "there is something, someone, moving in the shrubbery, it's—it's the 'Farmer.'"

"Girl, you're mad," said her aunt, dashing to the door and putting up a thick bar. "Don't make a sound, it can't be 'him,' there are no such things as ghosts," a sudden streak of bravery rising within her at a moment of stress, and feeling herself weak at showing fear before her niece.

Outside the wind moaned round and round the old house, somewhere above a door banged loudly, making both women start violently. A sudden heavier shower of rain lashed at the windows, while a crack and a rending noise outside told where some mighty tree had parted with one of its members in the hard fight which raged around it. How long they sat huddled before the fire they could not say. Each was afraid to speak, afraid to break the silence in the room, broken only by the solemn ticking of the small clock on the mantel-shelf. Both listened fearfully to the storm outside, the girl biting her nails and looking every now and then towards the window, as if afraid of that which at any moment might pierce the thick hangings, while the older woman hardly moved, keeping her gaze fixed on the fire; only the quick rising and falling of her bosom and the twitching of her hands told of the mental fight within.

A muffled bang at the front door made them both start to their feet, the girl uttering a little whimpering cry.

"That's the doctor back," said the older woman, "we must let him in."

Opening the door leading into the hall, and moving slowly towards the door with her niece following closely behind, Mrs. Larkin called: "Is that you, doctor?"

"Yes, yes," came a choking voice from the outside, which made them both stiffen with fright. "Undo the door quickly, for Heaven's sake."

Drawing back the latch, Mrs. Larkin swung the door open. It was Dr. Browning, white of face and soaked with wet, and with a thin stream of blood running from his right ear.

"Mrs. Larkin," he gasped, to the terrified woman, "the bus called for me, the 'Farmer' and Biddy Jenkins were inside," and with a great cry Dr. Browning fell dead across the doorstep.

WHITTINGTON'S CAT

Eleanor Smith

First appeared in *Satan's Circus* (Indianapolis, 1934)

Lady Eleanor Furneaux Smith (1902–1945) was born in Birkenhead in the north west of England, the daughter of barrister F. E. Smith, who later became a reactionary Conservative MP and was elevated to the peerage. Eleanor was his eldest daughter, and shared his reactionary politics, declaring herself in 1937 to be 'a warm adherent of General Franco's'. Associated with the 'Bright Young Things' of the 1920s, she initially worked as a society gossip columnist and film reviewer, but eventually moved into working in publicity for circus companies. This role inspired both her first novel, *Red Wagon* (1930) as well as the collection of short stories *Satan's Circus*. The latter book was first published in in the UK in 1932. The story reprinted here, 'Whittington's Cat', was added in 1934 when the book was reissued in the USA. In it, the cheery Christmas tradition of the pantomime becomes a source of horror and humiliation.

Martin was the name of the young man who went alone nearly every evening to the local pantomime. Usually, he sat in the dress circle, but sometimes he patronised the stalls, and he had even been seen on more than one occasion seated—still quite alone—in a stage box. The programme girls knew him by sight, and discussed him very frequently, for the regularity of his attendance made him appear something of an oddity in their eyes. Always, however, they decided that he must be in love either with the Principal Boy or with the Principal Girl. Very often, when they had nothing better to do, they had bets with one another as to which of the two had caught his eye. Unless, of course, this eye had fallen upon someone else—upon Columbine, for instance, or upon the Fairy Queen…

Martin himself was quite unconscious of their interest. Nor was he in love with anyone, with the possible exception of Marlene Dietrich. His reasons for visiting the Burford Hippodrome so constantly were, in fact, purely aesthetic—he was engaged in compiling a book that was to be entitled *Pantomime throughout the Ages*.

Why such a subject ever in the first place appealed to him is impossible to understand; he knew nothing of pantomime, nor was he acquainted with anyone likely to be of assistance to him in this direction; all he knew was that he felt the urge to write, and to write, what is more, upon this particular subject. Hence these nightly visits to the Burford Hippodrome.

Early that autumn, visiting a local curiosity shop, he had stumbled by chance upon a series of spangled prints representing characters from popular pantomimes; fascinated by the glitter and gaiety of these little pictures, he had bought the lot, and hung them in his bedroom; he was determined to reproduce them as illustrations to the book, and it is conceivable that his fondness for the collection may have influenced his choice of subject.

There was no particular reason why Martin should have bothered to write a book at all. He was rich, and had no need to work. In Burford and its neighbourhood he was considered a *parti*, and the eyes of those mothers whose daughters were marriageable rested very fondly and very frequently upon him.

His own mother had died when he was very young, and his father, a retired mill-owner, had left him pleasantly endowed upon departing this life about a year before the pantomime mania became manifest.

Life, then, for Martin, was comfortable if dull. He continued to inhabit the ancestral home, a large pleasant villa in a fashionable suburb of Burford, and his every want was ministered to by Mr. and Mrs. Renshaw, who were respectively manservant and cook, and who had attended to his father many years before. His life was perhaps inclined to be lonely. He was only twenty-five. Provincial society sometimes seemed tedious to him, and then he would toy with the idea of living in London, or cruising round the world, or spending a winter in Monte Carlo. But in the end he was always too timid, too conservative, to embark upon adventures so tremendous. Burford had, after all, been good enough for his father before him and for his grandfather before that, and he had a curious idea that he might, in London, find himself more lonely than was already the case. In Burford he knew everyone, everyone of Burford consequence, that is, and he dined out regularly, and was respected by the tradesmen, and made an impressive appearance each Sunday in his parish church.

He supposed that one day he would have to marry, and beget children, and carry on his family name, but whenever this idea occurred to him he felt slightly uncomfortable, for he had never, with the sole exception of the doctor's niece met anyone who in the least attracted him, and his own natural shyness made it difficult for him to appear at his ease in the society of women. He invariably decided, after such reflections, to live a life of great austerity, a life devoted uniquely to the pursuit of literature. Then he discovered the pantomime prints, and from that moment his destiny seemed assured.

Unfortunately, the famous book was by no means swift in materialising. He had always supposed that it would keep him occupied for at least five years, but whenever he came to ponder upon the magnitude of his task and his own ignorance of his subject, he decided that ten years might be an optimistic time-limit to put upon his labours.

And now every night he sat at the Burford Hippodrome to watch *Dick Whittington,* and it was really discouraging to realise how very little nearer he was even to beginning his book. So many trivial matters seemed to occupy his mind whenever he tried to concentrate upon the technique of pantomime. He could not help speculating, for instance, upon the adenoids of the Principal Girl, and wondering why she had never had them removed in childhood; it irritated him when the Principal Boy sang flat, which he very often did; and sometimes he suspected the Dame of being ever so slightly intoxicated.

That it would have been possible to scrape up an acquaint-ance with any of these people never once occurred to him; he would have been too timid, in any case, to take the first step, and actually he was interested in them not as people, nor as actors, but merely as the traditional characters of Christmas pantomime.

One frosty day, early in January, he informed Mrs. Renshaw that he would once again be dining at six o'clock.

"Yes, sir," she answered politely, but she seemed to hover in the doorway, and he was conscious that she had not yet finished with him. He was correct in this surmise; she coughed for a moment, and then asked, casually:

"The pantomime again, Mr. Martin?"

He was conscious that the Renshaws must think his behaviour absurd, and he therefore answered curtly, "Yes", hoping that that would be an end of the matter.

And it seemed to be, for Mrs. Renshaw changed the subject. She said: "I hope that cat didn't keep you awake last night, Mr. Martin?"

"What cat? I didn't hear anything..."

"There was one howling all night on the roof. Renshaw threw a shoe at it, and then it stopped for a bit."

"No, I didn't hear anything," Martin repeated.

He was bored with the subject, for he disliked cats at the best of times. He added, hoping to get rid of Mrs. Renshaw: "Six o'clock, then."

And this time she went.

That night, Martin sat in the front row of the dress circle to watch the tribulations of Dick, Alice Fitzwarren and the Emperor of Baghdad. During the performance something happened that he had always known would happen if he continued to haunt the Burford Hippodrome. His natural shyness made him long to avoid such an embarrassing encounter, yet to many men, less courageous perhaps than himself, what he dreaded would not have seemed so very terrible.

During a certain scene, Dick Whittington's Cat left the stage to climb up to one of the stage boxes, thence to swing itself along the circle, where it was wont to engage one or other of the spectators in badinage, much to the delight of the entire audience.

Now it was Martin's turn to be picked out, and the odd thing is that he had known this all night. He turned scarlet, gripping the rail with both hands, while the Cat scrambled straight towards him, and small boys nearly split their sides with laughter. Just opposite to him the Cat paused, balancing itself astride the circle; it thrust its mask close to him, and as he flinched away, the audience roared its delight at the embarrassment of this young ninny.

The Cat wore a suit of shaggy black hair. It seemed enormous, almost like a giant, as it peered towards him, and he could discover no human lineaments beneath the fiercely whiskered mask. Even as he recoiled he tried to force a ghastly smile, and then the Cat, approaching nearer still, whispered to him:

"Poor Tom's a-cold..."

Then it vanished, swinging away faster than it had come.

Martin felt self-conscious for the remainder of the evening. He decided that he would never again patronise the circle—he was too well known locally to endure such ridicule. He went home, made a few notes, and poured himself out a glass of beer. As he was finishing his drink, his eye fell upon the open notebook at his side. He read:

Origin of the Catskin

> This hairy, faun-like garb, the introduction into pantomime
> of the feline grotesque, is believed to date from the days of
> Daemonology, or Devil-Worship. The Cat…

He read the paragraph once more, shaking his head. It was, after all, entirely surmise. He shut the book and went to bed.

That night his sleep was inclined to be fitful, and once when he woke just before dawn, he could hear distinctly the miowling of that stray cat which had already disturbed the Renshaws. Too sleepy, too comfortable to care very much one way or the other, he buried his head in his pillows and soon dozed off once more. Then he dreamed, a vague, perplexing dream, during the course of which he sat once more in the Hippodrome circle, and the Pantomime Cat, thrusting its mask close to his face, muttered in his ear: "Poor Tom's a-cold."

When he woke in the morning he found that he himself was cold, the bedclothes having tumbled upon the floor during the course of his restless night. It was a clear frosty day, and there were ice-flowers trailing across his windowpane. He ate his breakfast with enjoyment and remembered that he was lunching with his oldest friend, the doctor who had brought him into the world.

Dr. Browning was a sharp-witted little man in appearance rather like a dried-up russet apple. He was something of a gourmet; he had a pretty niece named Gwen, and Martin always enjoyed lunching with him very much indeed.

Today they were alone; Gwen was spending Christmas with an aunt in London.

"Still haunting the pantomime, Martin?" the doctor asked quizzically.

"Yes. I go nearly every night."

"Do tell me what it is that fascinates you so much about that very shoddy show? Is she blonde, brunette, or auburn-haired?"

"I've told you, sir, about fifty times, that—"

"Oh, I know all about that famous book. And a very excellent excuse, if I may say so. I only wish I'd practised authorship instead of surgery."

While the doctor was engaged in his favourite pursuit of teasing Martin, something uncomfortable happened. The household cat, a large sluggish tabby, suddenly saw fit to spring from beneath the table where she was concealed, on to the guest's knee; with an exclamation of horror, Martin flung out his hand and threw poor Tabitha most violently from his lap, whereupon she gave a screech of anger and bolted from the room.

"I'm so sorry," Martin cried. He had jumped to his feet all prepared to brandish his napkin, to which he clung as though it were a sword.

"There's no need to be so rough!" rebuked the doctor, who was exceedingly fond of Tabitha, and who much disliked seeing her upset. "Nerves a bit jumpy, aren't they?"

"I'm so sorry," Martin said again.

He sat down, feeling incredibly foolish.

The doctor repeated his question.

"No," said Martin, in reply to this, "my nerves aren't in the least jumpy, really they're not. It's only—you know cats always give me the creeps. I know it sounds idiotic, but honestly it's the truth."

"Pantomimes—cats—what on earth next?" was the doctor's retort to these excuses. "God bless my soul, Martin, you're growing into an old maid before my very eyes! Why don't you get away from Burford for a bit—travel—see the world—meet other young people? Cats, indeed!"

And he snorted most violently, with the result that his guest felt sulky and resentful, and the lunch immediately turned into something of a failure.

None the less Martin went off to the pantomime once more that same evening.

He was sitting all alone in a box, musing as to the probable origin of Pantaloon, when the Frightful Thing occurred. And it was really very frightful indeed. On the stage, a transformation scene was in progress. Tinsel roses were melting into a gilded bower, peopled with dancing elves, when suddenly he felt a touch upon his neck. This touch was indescribably horrible—it was so soft, so furtive, so obviously the contact, not of a hand, but of a padded, cushiony paw. He turned, to see the Cat bending over him. In the darkness of the box the Cat's eyes gleamed emerald. In one second Martin realised the appalling truth—the Cat was no longer an actor in a shaggy suit, but a real Cat, a giant Cat, a Cat nearly six feet tall.

Martin sprang to his feet. He felt faint, but had no desire to cry out. The Cat said again, suggestively: "Poor Tom's a-cold." It put its paw upon his shoulder, patting him, obviously conciliatory, and with that sickening and velvety caress his will-power suddenly failed him. He had no longer any will of his own; it was all in one moment surrendered.

Swiftly it had passed, this will of his, like a dark wave, right away from him into the personality of the Cat.

He watched his companion dumbly, waiting to see what was wanted of him.

And it pointed, with one paw, at his overcoat, that hung upon a peg in the box, together with his hat and muffler. Vaguely he grasped what this gesture signified; it was desirous of escape, and it could only succeed in this project were it disguised in the outward lineaments of a human being.

He picked up his overcoat and held it out towards his companion. Slowly, snake-like, the Cat slid itself into the coat. It twined the muffler dexterously about its chin, so that the black mask was at least partly concealed; the felt hat it jammed forward upon its ears so that still more was hidden; then having regarded itself critically in the mirror at the back of the box, it motioned to Martin.

"Home," it commanded briefly.

And Martin, that was now no longer Martin so much as an animated puppet, a Robot taught only to obey, found himself opening the door of the box that his companion might precede him. The Cat strolled through this door with an air almost nonchalant; had it not been for a plume of black tail protruding beneath the overcoat, it might well have passed for some sober Burford citizen.

Outside it was snowing.

The air was thick with a cloud of drifting snowflakes, and the pavement was already powdered as though with icing sugar.

The Cat moved quietly by Martin's side.

Martin wondered whether this was some ghastly nightmare from which he would presently awake. Glancing behind him, fearful of curiosity, he observed with a curious detachment the footprints of the Cat, walking beside his own in the snow, round, padded, clear-cut, the prints not of a man but of the gigantic beast that it was. He shivered. They walked on in silence. Soon they had arrived at Martin's house, and he was obediently fumbling for his latchkey even while he prayed most desperately for escape.

How could he possibly introduce this fiend, this spectre, into the pleasant, humdrum security of his own home? For one second, then, his apathy changed into the fierce frightened rebellion of a wild thing, and then he turned to face the Cat, although his tongue clove to the roof of his mouth and his knees were shaking.

"You can't—"

But two eyes, like fixed and glaring emeralds, bore like searchlights into his own, and in one moment his defiance had withered away, so that he was once more the slave of this thing that his own imagination had created from an actor's motley. The Cat stepped over the threshold before him, and that he knew was a significant moment in the history of this strange adventure. From that instant he realised that the Cat was to be master of his home.

He shut the door behind him.

Very deliberately the Cat divested itself of overcoat, hat and muffler. It stretched itself, then, so that a ripple of movement slid through all its body, and he was reminded of the many dozing tabbies that he had seen stretch thus on the hearthrugs of his friends.

It said: "Supper?"

He could not in any way define its voice. He would have been unable to describe it. Was it husky, miowling, high-pitched, or gruff? Was it perhaps not so much a voice as the sinister reflection, perfectly comprehended by him, of the Cat's own immediate desires? The interpretative shadow of its dark mind? He did not know; all he knew was he himself moved, spoke, and thought in some hideous trance; he was passive obedience to the will of the Cat; he felt sick, and would have cut his own throat had he been so commanded.

"What sort of supper?"

And his own voice for the matter of that, sounded totally unfamiliar to him. A rusty creak that seemed to come from a long way away. If he pinched himself, perhaps he would awake from all that this nightmare meant... he pinched, but nothing happened. The nightmare was still there.

The Cat appeared to ponder.

"Some fish, some milk," it said, at length.

He tried to tell himself: "That's all right. Fish and milk—why, of course. It's just an ordinary cat. Nothing at all to worry about."

Aloud, he said: "Will you come into the dining-room?"

The Cat at once followed him into the respectability of this apartment, where Martin's father had so often stayed alone to drink his port. It sat down—at the head of the table. Its bushy tail stuck out from behind the chair. It said, and again he sensed a menacing inflection:

"Don't be long. Tom's hungry."

He found himself in the larder without knowing how he got there. He discovered some tinned sardines, half a lobster and a jug of milk. He hastened back into the dining-room.

The Cat ate—like other cats. Exactly like other cats. That, too, should have been reassuring, but it wasn't. When it had finished eating, it washed its face meticulously, licking its great paws first, again like other cats.

It looked at Martin.

"Where is poor Tom's room?"

He was not astonished by this question. He had known from the first moment his companion entered the front door that it was there to stay. He knew, too, that sleep for him would not be possible with such a presence in his home.

"I'll show you", he said, "the three spare rooms."

In silence they made a tour of the bedroom floor. On the threshold of each room the Cat hesitated, peered and shook its head. One room was too cold, another faced the wrong way, and the third looked damp.

"Show your room."

So that was it! He longed, at that moment, for some last remaining feeble flicker of defiance, or courage, or self-respect; he longed in vain; his will was still the will of the Cat. When it ordered, he must obey, since he could not cast off this hateful thrall.

"This is my room."

The Cat glanced at the great glowing fire, the soft comfortable bed, the warm curtains, all the luxury and security of this pleasant apartment.

It seemed to grin.

"This will do."

And in one moment, the detestable black furry form had glided into Martin's own bed, had insinuated itself beneath his silk eiderdown, had cushioned its whiskered head upon his own pillows. He was dispossessed; the Cat was most certainly master now.

He returned to the farthest spare room, where he made himself up a bed. The night passed slowly; he was too terrified to sleep, and, even had he wished to do so, the persistent yowling of cats on the roof outside would probably have interfered with his slumbers.

Mrs. Renshaw, the next morning, was disturbed by Martin at an unusually early hour. He looked ghastly, and demanded a cup of tea. He then said to her in hesitating accents:

"Mrs. Renshaw, I don't want either you or Renshaw to go near my room today."

Mrs. Renshaw seemed astonished.

He continued:

"I—the fact of the matter is that I met an old friend of mine last night. He—he's ill; he's got a bad chill, and what's more, he's in quarantine for—for scarlet fever. I'm going to nurse him myself, and I don't want anyone else to go near him."

Mrs. Renshaw continued to look astonished. She said, at length:

"But I've had the scarlet fever, Mr. Martin, and if there's any trouble—"

He interrupted her harshly.

"I shall look after my friend myself. I don't wish germs to be carried all over the house. And now, will you get some haddock for breakfast? Some haddock, and a glass of warm milk..."

"Whatever's happened to Martin?" Gwen Browning asked her uncle, about a week later.

The doctor glanced vaguely up from his crossword.

"I didn't know anything had happened to him. I haven't seen him for about a fortnight."

"That's just what I mean," said the girl. "He's never even been to see me since I got back from London. Shall I ring him up and ask him to supper?"

"Of course, my dear. Ask him by all means."

The doctor thought, not for the first time, how pleased he would be if Martin married his niece, and then at once forgot them both in the mysteries of his crossword.

"I don't think Mr. Martin can come to the telephone," Renshaw told Gwen shortly afterwards, in a cautious tone of voice.

"Why not? He's in, isn't he? I'll hold on."

"He's upstairs. He's engaged. Could you leave a message, Miss?"

Gwen gave her message, not without a slight feeling of rebuff. That afternoon, Renshaw rang her up to say that Martin was sorry he would be unable to come to supper—he was confined to the house with a bad cold.

"We'll ask him again in a day or two," commented the doctor. He added that Martin's cold did not surprise him—the weather was as treacherous as he ever remembered.

That same evening, just before dusk, as the doctor was returning home after his rounds, he heard from the kerb opposite to where he was walking the well-known wail of the cats'-meat man. He crossed the road immediately; he was always ready to give Tabitha a treat. He was, however, just too late. As he approached he heard the man say to another customer:

"That's the lot, sir. You've cleared me out for the day."

The customer turned, saw the doctor, and looked thoroughly dismayed. It was Martin, his pockets stuffed full of cats' meat.

"Thought you had a cold?" the doctor said, with brisk humour.

Martin hesitated. At length, he stammered: "I-I have."

The doctor suddenly noticed that even by twilight the boy looked drawn and ill.

"You ought to be indoors, you know."

"I'm just going home."

"Whatever possessed you to come out, with an east wind like this? Surely not just to buy cats' meat?"

And the doctor roared with laughter at his own joke.

"I'm going now," Martin muttered.

"Well, I'll walk with you to the corner."

They set off in silence.

"Come in and have supper, when you're feeling better. Gwen hasn't seen you since she went away."

"Is she well?" Martin asked listlessly.

"She's all right. But you've lost weight since I saw you last, Martin. Sure you wouldn't like me to look you up professionally?"

"Oh, no, indeed not," Martin protested, with such violence that the doctor was almost inclined to take offence. He was, however, good-natured; he felt sorry for the boy, and at length he tried another topic of conversation.

"You probably caught a chill at your beloved pantomime."

"I haven't been there for a week."

"By the way, talking of the pantomime, did you read about that odd theft down at the theatre, the other day?"

"No. What was it?"

"You remember Dick Whittington's Cat? But of course you do, as you went every night. Well, someone apparently stole the Cat costume from a dressing-room just before the show, and so the poor fellow who acts the Cat had to go on and play the part in his ordinary clothes. They got another costume down from London the next day, but the funny part is, they've never found the other one. Fancy you not seeing that!"

Here, to his great astonishment, the doctor found that he was addressing the air. Martin had vanished round the corner with a quite extraordinary celerity and with no word of farewell whatsoever.

"That boy's mad," the doctor told Gwen later, "stark, staring mad. Mooning about, looking like death, buying enough cats' meat to stock a Cats' Home, and treating me, *me,* who brought him into the world, with the most infernal puppy-dog impudence! Running away from me, I tell you! He's as mad as a hatter!"

Gwen said: "But Martin hates cats."

"He's mad, I tell you," the doctor repeated.

"But I tell you he hates them. He dreads them. He can't even be in the room with Tabitha."

"I don't wish to discuss the young cub any further."

But the doctor had by no means finished with Martin, although at the moment he really imagined that he had.

The next morning Renshaw arrived, while Gwen and her uncle were at breakfast, requesting the favour of an immediate interview.

"Show him in," said the doctor, "and give me another cup of tea, Gwen."

Gwen obeyed.

"Do you want to see the doctor alone?" she asked Renshaw, who appeared perturbed.

"No, Miss, not particularly. That is, what I have to say is private, but I'd be glad all the same, and so I'm sure would Mrs. Renshaw, if you'd listen to what I have to say, as well as Dr. Browning."

"Influenza, I suppose?" queried the doctor, eating toast and marmalade.

"Nobody's ill, sir, not at home. Not as far as we know, that is. But Mrs. Renshaw will be soon, if it isn't stopped."

The doctor began to show signs of interest.

"Suppose you sit down, Renshaw, and tell us quite slowly what's worrying you. Take your time—I'm in no particular hurry at the moment. It's Mr. Martin, I suppose?"

"In a way," Renshaw admitted cautiously.

He sat down as he was told, and began:

"More than a week ago Mr. Martin told us he had this friend sick in his own bedroom, and that we weren't to go inside the room or disturb him in any way. He said the gentleman was an old friend of his, and eccentric—didn't like servants, and would only eat food brought to him by Mr. Martin."

"Did you see this mysterious friend when he arrived?"

"No, sir. He came back with Mr. Martin late one night. We didn't know he was in the house until the next morning. We thought it queer, but we did just as Mr. Martin said. Mrs. Renshaw cooked for him, and Mr. Martin always took it up, and meanwhile Mr. Martin was sleeping in the spare room. At last I asked whether one of us mightn't go up to the gentleman, just to sweep, and make his bed."

He paused.

"Well?"

"Well, sir, Mr. Martin flew into the most dreadful passion. He turned pale, and shouted at me, and swore, and asked me if I didn't understand plain English. He said that if he ever found either of us messing about near that bedroom, he'd have to make different arrangements. I asked him, then, how long the gentleman was going to stay, and he flew up again. Said it was none of my business, and told me to get out of the room and not interfere."

"And then?" the doctor wanted to know.

"For the last few days Mr. Martin has looked as white as a sheet, and seems a regular bundle of nerves—quite unlike his usual self. He keeps on complaining, too, to Mrs. Renshaw, about the gentleman's food—says it isn't fit to eat, and the gentleman *must* be humoured. He's never complained about Mrs. Renshaw's cooking before, sir, nor has anyone else."

"What sort of food, by the way, is being sent up to the gentleman?" Dr. Browning asked.

"Fish, sir, mostly. Sometimes a little chicken, and any amount of milk. The odd thing is, sir, that—well, he must eat all the bones, for none ever come down on the tray. We can't quite make it out."

There was a pause. For the first time a vague sensation of apprehension obtruded itself into the pleasant room.

Then the doctor asked: "Anything else, Renshaw?"

The man glanced across at him, and then dropped his eyes. "Yes, sir, since you mention it. Something a bit queer. I don't scarcely expect you to believe it, although Mrs. Renshaw will bear me out."

"I think we'd better hear it," the doctor decided, in a kind tone of voice, "if I am to be of any help to you. What was this queer thing, eh?"

Renshaw licked his lips, smiled nervously, and began:

"Well, it was like this. The cats have been very bad round the house, lately, screeching all night. It hasn't been easy to sleep, with so much row. Last night I'd just dropped off when Mrs. Renshaw woke me up. She said she heard someone moving about downstairs. It was nearly two o'clock, so it worried us both. I listened and heard footsteps. I thought it was perhaps Mr. Martin, in a restless fit, but all the same, we couldn't very well leave it at that. We got out of bed and went downstairs, as quiet as we could. I had my electric torch."

He paused.

"Go on," encouraged the doctor. "What happened then?"

"There was nothing, sir, although we'd both heard footsteps. But all the same, there was something funny in the drawing-room—you know the great goldfish bowl that belonged to Mr.

Martin's mother? Well, there it was, standing in the middle of the floor, with a lot of water slopped out of it, and all the fish gone—every one."

"An odd thing to steal, goldfish!"

"That's not all, sir. As we tiptoed upstairs we determined to go past Mr. Martin's bedroom, to see if the strange gentleman was awake."

"Yes!" Gwen's voice was eager now.

"We did so, Miss. There was a thread of light under the door. We stopped a minute to listen."

He paused once more, averting his eyes.

"Well?"

"Dr. Browning, there's something in that room that's not human. I swear there is: I'm not easily scared."

"Go on, Renshaw."

"We stopped to listen, as I told you. We both heard it moving about. It wasn't walking—it was *padding*, like a great beast. And we heard it snarling, as though it was growling away to itself, and I tell you that noise made your blood run cold."

"Anything else?"

"No, sir. Only, while it was still growling, the cats outside started again, and then the Thing in the room became quiet. We went back to bed, and this morning, after we'd talked it over, we both decided I should come to you."

"A queer story," commented the doctor; "tell me, Mr. Martin has been nervous and irritable since the arrival of this mysterious guest, I think you said. Has he shown any other signs of being unlike himself?"

Renshaw said simply: "He seems afraid, sir." He added: "And he looks very bad."

The doctor jumped up.

"I'll come over with you now, Renshaw. Wait while I get my hat."

"Can I come, too?" Gwen wanted to know.

Her uncle looked doubtful.

"Oh, do let me! Perhaps—if he's ill—perhaps Martin might want me."

"All right, you can come. But hurry up."

They were silent, all three of them, as they walked across the busy streets of Burford towards Martin's home.

When they arrived at the house they were admitted by Mrs. Renshaw, who looked pale and anxious.

"Where's Mr. Martin?" asked the doctor.

"I don't know, sir. I haven't seen him since he took the gentleman's breakfast upstairs."

"How long ago was that?"

"It must be about an hour, sir."

"We'll go and see for ourselves," the doctor said to Renshaw. "Don't worry—I'll take all responsibility. Gwen, you go into the drawing-room and wait."

"But, Uncle—"

"Do as I tell you, there's a good girl. For all we know, there may be a lunatic at large upstairs. Come on, Renshaw, and bring a stout walking-stick from the umbrella stand there. I've got mine."

The house seemed very still as they walked upstairs. Only the guttural ticking of a grandfather clock disturbed the silence of the hall. They paused outside the bedroom, but all was quiet there, as well.

"If it's locked," whispered the doctor, "we must break it open. Are you ready?"

But the door was not locked. When the doctor turned the handle, it opened immediately, and they walked in without any difficulty whatsoever.

The room was in a strange condition. Sheets and blankets had been stripped off the bed and flung haphazard about the floor, which was still further cluttered up with piles of feathers, as though someone had been plucking chickens, gnawed bones, dirty plates, dishes, and empty glasses that had at one time probably contained milk. The windows were closed, and the room smelled of stale food. There was another odour, too, one more difficult to define—the strong, harsh stink of an animal's body.

At first sight, the room was empty.

Then the two men caught sight of something dark lying on the floor, at the foot of the bed.

"That's it," the doctor muttered.

Gingerly they approached the heap of black fur that lay coiled so still. A second afterwards the doctor burst out laughing. His laughter was rather forced.

"Fooled again," he said.

For the black object upon the floor was nothing more nor less than a shaggy suit, with mask attached, of the kind worn by actors impersonating animals in Christmas plays. For a moment all horror was removed; the hairy skin, the papier-mâché mask, brought back immediately reassuring memories of *Peter Pan*, of other pleasant, childish, homely amusements. The doctor picked up the suit and held it, dangling limply from his hand, nothing more nor less than an empty, grotesque, tousled cat's skin.

Then Renshaw, moving across to the other side of the bed, gave a sudden cry of fear and horror. The doctor dropped the cat's suit more abruptly than he had picked it up.

"Look, sir!"

On the floor near the fireplace Martin's body lay sprawled. It was concealed by the bed; that was why they had not seen it before.

The doctor knelt down and gently lifted the boy's head. It was then, as he afterwards said, that he himself, with all his fund of grim experience, felt physically sick. Martin's throat was bleeding profusely. It was lacerated, torn—a mass of fiendish, slashing, brutal wounds. The mark of the Beast; for such fury of destruction by tooth and claw no human being could ever have been responsible.

"Good God!" whispered Renshaw. "Is he dead?"

The doctor answered brusquely: "Get me a basin of water. Quickly, do you hear? *Quickly!*"

It was many, many weeks afterwards that Martin, still looking ghastly pale and with his neck swathed in bandages, lay back on his sofa and asked Dr. Browning if he might speak to him for a few minutes.

"It's about all this," he said. "I've never felt like mentioning it before, either to you or to Gwen, but I've got to face it one day, and I believe I'm feeling up to it at last. Won't you please sit down?"

The doctor obeyed. He looked worried; he had been dreading this moment.

"Well, Martin?"

"Well, doctor? Won't you tell me the truth? Did I go off my head for a time? Did I live like an animal and in the end try to commit suicide? Or did a real lunatic dress himself in that skin and take possession of my house?"

"What do you yourself really think?" the doctor asked him gravely.

"What do I think? My opinion has never changed—I think as I did then. I am still convinced, absolutely and completely convinced, that some frightening thing, materialising as a gigantic cat, took entire possession, not only of my house, but of my mind and of my soul. Hypnotism—it was more than that, far far more. I was the *will* of this creature, whatever it may have been. I existed only to do its bidding. Then, one day, I suppose it grew angry with me for some reason or other, or perhaps grew tired of being here, and it attacked me, before it disappeared. That sounds like a madman's explanation, doesn't it? But frankly, I have no other. Now tell me what you think."

The doctor lighted his pipe.

"I think you're very lucky to be alive."

"What else?"

"I'll tell you, Martin, since you want to know. What I've got to say is unethical and the world would probably laugh me out of the medical profession if it heard me talking to you, but I'll chance that." He took a pull at his pipe. "Look here, Martin, it's not good for any young man to live so much alone as you've been doing. This lonely house, these books—it's not a healthy existence. You're inclined to be imaginative, you're a bit neurotic into the bargain, and all that combined is tempting Providence."

"Well?"

"Merely this: let us suppose for a moment that there do dwell, on the borders of this world and some other world, unclean spirits, evil elementals, forever in search, so to speak, of pliable human minds on which to impose their own will—suppose, I say, just suppose, such creatures exist, you yourself would undoubtedly have been an ideal victim for their experiments. Do you see?"

There was a pause.

"I see", Martin said, slowly, "that at least you understand my story and don't think me mad."

"I don't think you mad... Go abroad for six months, and when you come back to Burford try to interest yourself in something less solitary than study. Buy a car, but learn to repair it yourself. Keep a horse, but groom it. And don't go mooning about by yourself at pantomimes any more. Take some children with you next time."

"There won't be any next time," said Martin.

It was only when he was alone once again that Martin noticed something curious.

He was looking—for the first time for many weeks—at the pantomime prints of which he was so fond. How pretty they were, how gay, how bright were their spangles—there were Pantaloon and Harlequin, and the Demon King, and there was Columbine, and there the Cat—but no, that was the funny thing—the form of the Cat had disappeared entirely from its frame, and although the spangled background of the print remained the same, the space once occupied by the little figure was now blank and empty.

The Cat had vanished; could it, he hoped, be for ever?

THE EARLIER SERVICE

Margaret Irwin

Probably first published in *Madame Fears the Dark:
Seven Stories and a Play* (1935)

Margaret Emma Faith Irwin (1889–1967) is probably best known
as an historical novelist focusing mainly on the Elizabethan and
Stuart periods, but she also wrote a large number of short stories
mostly for publication in *The London Mercury*. This story was
printed in two collections both in 1935—the compilation volume
A Century of Horror, edited by Dennis Wheatley; and Irwin's own
book *Madame Fears the Dark: Seven Stories and a Play*. Both 'The
Earlier Service' and her other best known tale 'The Book' feature
Latin inscriptions and demonic forces, which infiltrate ordinary
modern settings and endanger the vulnerable.

Mrs. Lacey and her eldest daughter Alice hurried through the diminutive gate that led from the Rectory garden into the churchyard. Alice paused to call, "Jane, Father's gone on," under the window of her young sister's room. To her mother she added with a cluck of annoyance, "What a time she takes to dress!"

But Jane was sitting, ready dressed for church, in the window-seat of her room. Close up to her window and a little to the right, stood the square church tower with gargoyles at each corner. She could see them every morning as she lay in her bed at the left of the window, their monstrous necks stretched out as though they were trying to get into her room.

The church bell stopped. Jane could hear the shuffle of feet as the congregation rose at the entrance of her father; then came silence, and then the drone of the General Confession. She jumped up, ran downstairs and into the churchyard. Right above her now hung the gargoyles, peering down at her. Behind them the sun was setting in clouds, soft and humid as winter sunsets can only be in Somerset. She was standing in front of a tiny door studded with nails. The doorway was the oldest part of the church of Cloud Martin. It dated back to Saxon days; and the shrivelled bits of blackened, leather-like stuff, still clinging to some of the nails, were said to be the skins of heathens flayed alive.

Jane paused a moment, her hands held outwards and a little behind her. Her face was paler than it had been in her room, her eyes were half shut, and her breath came a little quickly, but then she had been running. With the same sudden movement that she had jumped from the window-seat, she now jerked her hands forward, turned the great iron ring that served as a door-handle, and stole into the church.

The door opened into the corner just behind the Rectory pew. She was late. Mrs. Lacey and Alice were standing up and chanting the monotone that had become a habitual and almost an unconscious part of their lives. Jane stole in past her mother, and knelt for an instant, her red pig-tail, bright symbol of an old-fashioned upbringing, flopping sideways on to the dark wood. "Please God, don't let me be afraid—don't, don't, *don't* let me be afraid," she whispered; then stood, and repeated the responses in clear and precise tones, her eyes fixed on the long stone figure of the Crusader against the wall in front of her.

He was in chain armour; the mesh of mail surrounded his face like the coif of a nun, and a high crown-like helmet came low down on his brows. His feet rested against a small lion, which Jane as a child had always thought was his favourite dog that had followed him to the Holy Wars. His huge mailed hand grasped the pommel of his sword, drawn an inch or two from its scabbard. Jane gazed at him as though she would draw into herself all the watchful stern repose of the sleeping giant. Behind the words of the responses, other words repeated themselves in her mind.

> The knight is dust,
> His good sword rust,
> His soul is with the saints we trust.

"But he is *here*," she told herself, "you can't really be afraid with him here."

There came the sudden silence before the hymn, and she wondered what nonsense she had been talking to herself. She knew the words of the service too well, that was what it was; how could she ever attend to them?

They settled down for the sermon, a safe twenty minutes at least, in the Rector's remote and dreamlike voice. Jane's mind raced off at a tangent, almost painfully agile, yet confined always somewhere between the walls of the church.

"You shouldn't think of other things in church," was a maxim that had been often repeated to her. In spite of it she thought of more other things in those two Sunday services than in the whole week between.

"What a lot of Other Things other people must have thought of too in this church," she said to herself; the thought shifted and changed a little; "there are lots of Other Things in this church; there are too many Other Things in this church." Oh, she *mustn't* say things like that to herself or she would begin to be afraid again—she was not afraid yet—of course, she was not afraid, there was nothing to be afraid of, and if there were, the Crusader was before her, his hand on his sword, ready to draw it at need. And what need could there be? Her mother was beside her whose profile she could see without looking at it, *she* would never be disturbed, and by nothing.

But at that moment Mrs. Lacey shivered, and glanced behind her at the little door by which Jane had entered. Jane passed her fur to her, but Mrs. Lacey shook her head. Presently she looked round again, and kept her head turned for fully a minute. Jane watched her mother until the familiar home-trimmed hat turned again to the pulpit; she wondered then if her mother would indeed never be disturbed, and by nothing.

She looked up at the crooked angel in the tiny window of mediaeval glass. His red halo was askew; his oblique face had been a friend since her childhood. A little flat-nosed face in the carving round the pillar grinned back at her and all but winked.

"How old are you?" asked Jane.

"Six hundred years old," he replied.

"Then you should know better than to wink in church, let alone always grinning."

But he only sang to a ballad tune:

> "Oh, if you'd seen as much as I,
> It's often you would wink."

"In the name of the Father and the Son and the Holy Ghost—"

Already! *Now* they would soon be outside again, out of the church for a whole safe week. But they would have to go through that door first.

She waited anxiously till her father went up to the altar to give the blessing. After she was confirmed, she, too, would have to go up to the altar. She would have to go. Now her father was going. He took so long to get there, he seemed so much smaller and darker as he turned his back on the congregation; it was really impossible sometimes to see that he had on a white surplice at all. What was he going to do up there at the altar, what was that gleaming pointed thing in his hand? *Who* was that little dark man going up to the altar? Her fingers closed tight on her prayer book as the figure turned round.

"You idiot, of course it's father! There, you can see it's father."

She stared at the benevolent nut-cracker face, distinct enough now to her for all the obscurity of the chancel. How much taller he seemed now he had turned round. And of course, his surplice was white—quite white. What *had* she been seeing?

"May the peace of God which passeth all understanding—"

She wished she could kneel under the spell of those words for ever.

"Oh yes," said the little flat-nosed face as she rose from her knees, "but you'd find it dull, you know." He was grinning atrociously.

The two Rectory girls filed out after their mother, who carefully fastened the last button on her glove before she opened the door on which hung the skins of men that had been flayed alive. As she did so, she turned round and looked behind her, but went out without stopping. Jane almost ran after her, and caught her arm. Mrs. Lacey was already taking off her gloves.

"Were you looking round for Tom Elroy, Mother?" asked Alice.

"No, dear, not specially. I thought Tom or someone had come up to our door, but the church does echo so. I think there must be a draught from that door, but it's funny, I only feel it just at the end of the Evening Service."

"You oughtn't to sit at the end of the pew then, and with your rheumatism. Janey, you always come in last. Why don't *you* sit at the end?"

"I won't!" snapped Jane.

"Whatever's the matter, Jane?" asked her mother.

"Why should I sit at the end of the pew? Why can't we move out of that pew altogether? I only wish we would."

Nobody paid any attention to this final piece of blasphemy, for they had reached the lighted hall of the Rectory by this time and were rapidly dispersing. Jane hung her coat and hat on the stand in the hall and went into the pantry to collect the cold meat and cheese. The maids were always out on Sunday evening. Alice was already making toast over the dining-room fire; she looked up as the Rector entered, and remarked severely: "You shouldn't quote Latin in your sermons, Father. Nobody in the church understands it."

"Nobody understands my sermons," said Mr. Lacey, "for nobody listens to them. So I may as well give myself the occasional pleasure of a Latin quotation, since only a dutiful daughter is likely to notice the lapse of manners. Alice, my dear, did I give out in church that next Friday is the last Confirmation class?"

"Friday!" cried Jane, in the doorway with the cheese. "Next Friday the last class? Then the Confirmation's next week."

"Of course it is, and high time, too," said Alice, "seeing that you were sixteen last summer. Only servant girls get confirmed *after* sixteen."

That settled it then. In a spirit of gloomy resignation Jane engulfed herself in an orange.

There were bright stars above the church tower when she went to bed. She kept her head turned away as she drew the curtains, so that she should not see the gargoyles stretching their necks towards her window.

Friday evening found Jane at the last Confirmation class in the vestry with her father and three farmers' daughters, who talked in a curious mixture of broad Somerset and High School education and knew the catechism a great deal better than Jane.

After they had left, she followed closely at her father's elbow into the church to remove the hymn books and other vestiges of the choir practice that had taken place just before the class. The lamp he carried made a little patch of light wherever they moved; the outlying walls of darkness shifted, but pressed hard upon it from different quarters. The Rector was looking for his Plotinus, which he was certain he had put down somewhere in the church. He fumbled all over the Rectory pew while Jane tried on vain pretexts to drag him away.

"I have looked in that corner—thoroughly," she said.

The Rector sighed.

> "What shall I say
> Since Truth is dead?"

he enquired. "So far from looking in that corner, Jane, you kept your head turned resolutely away from it."

"Did I? I suppose I was looking at the list of Rectors. What a long one it is, and all dead but you, Father."

He at once forgot Plotinus and left the Rectory pew to pore with proud pleasure over the names that began with one Johannes de Martigny and ended with his own.

"A remarkably persistent list. Only two real gaps—in the Civil Wars and in the fourteenth century. That was at the time of the Black Death, when there was no rector of this parish for many years. You see, Jane?—1349, and then there's no name till 1361—Giraldus atte Welle. Do you remember when you were a little girl, very proud of knowing how to read, how you read through all the names to me, but refused to say that one? You said, 'It is a dreadful name,' and when I pressed you, you began to cry."

"How silly! There's nothing dreadful in Giraldus atte Welle," began Jane, but as she spoke she looked round her. She caught at the Rector's arm. "Father, there isn't anyone in the church besides us, is there?"

"My dear child, of course not. What's the matter? You're not nervous, are you?"

"No, not really. But we can find the Plotinus much easier by daylight. Oh—and Father—don't let's go out by the little door. Let's pretend we're the General Congregation and go out properly by the big door."

She pulled him down the aisle, talking all the way until they were both in his study. "Father doesn't *know*," she said to herself—"he knows less than Mother. It's funny, when he would understand so much more."

But he understood that she was troubled. He asked, "Don't you want to get confirmed, Jane?" and then—"You mustn't be if you don't want it."

Jane grew frightened. There would be a great fuss if she backed out of it now after the very last class. Besides, there was the Crusader. Vague ideas of the initiation rites of knight and crusader crossed her mind in connection with the rite of Confirmation. He had spent a night's vigil in a church, perhaps in this very church. One could never fear anything else after that. If only she didn't have to go right up to the altar at the Communion Service. But she would not think of that; she told the Rector that it was quite all right really, and at this moment they reached the hall door and met Mrs. Lacey hurrying towards them with a letter from Hugh, now at Oxford, who was coming home for the vacation on Wednesday.

"He asks if he may bring an undergraduate friend for the first few days—a Mr. York who is interested in old churches and Hugh thinks he would like to see ours. He must be clever—it is such a pity Elizabeth is away—she is the only one who could talk to him; of course, he will enjoy talking with you, Father dear, but men seem to expect girls too to be clever now. And just as Janey's Confirmation is coming on—she isn't taking it seriously enough as it is."

"*Mother!* Don't you want us to play dumb crambo like the last time Hugh brought friends down?"

"Nonsense," said the Rector hastily. "Dumb crambo requires so much attention that it should promote seriousness in all things. I am very glad the young man is coming, my love, and I will try my hardest to talk as cleverly as Elizabeth."

He went upstairs with his wife, and said in a low voice: "I think Jane is worrying rather too much about her Confirmation as it is. She seems quite jumpy sometimes."

"Oh—*jumpy*—yes," said Mrs. Lacey, as though she refused to consider jumpiness the right qualification for Confirmation. The question of the curtains in the spare room however proved more immediately absorbing.

Hugh, who preferred people to talk shop, introduced his friend's hobby the first evening at dinner. "He goes grubbing over churches with a pencil and a bit of paper and finds things scratched on the walls and takes rubbings of them and you call them *graffiti*. Now, then, Father, any offers from our particular property?"

The Rector did not know of any specimens in his church. He asked what sort of things were scratched on the walls.

"Oh, anything," said York, "texts, scraps of dog Latin, aphorisms—once I found the beginning of a love song. When a monk, or anyone who was doing a job in the church, got bored, he'd begin to scratch words on the wall just as one does on a seat or log or anything today. Only we nearly always write our names and they hardly ever did."

He showed some of the rubbings he had taken. Often, he explained, you couldn't see anything but a few vague scratches, and then in the rubbing they came out much clearer. "The bottom of a pillar is a good place to look," he said, "and corners—anywhere where they're not likely to be too plainly seen."

"There are some marks on the wall near our pew," said Jane. "Low down, nearly on the ground."

He looked at her, pleased, and distinguishing her consciously for the first time from her rather sharp-voiced sister. He saw a gawky girl whose grave, beautiful eyes were marred by deep hollows under them, as though she did not sleep enough. And Jane looked back with satisfaction at a pleasantly ugly, wide, good-humoured face.

She showed him the marks next morning, both squatting on their heels beside the wall. Hugh had strolled in with them, declaring that they were certain to find nothing better than names of the present choir boys, and had retired to the organ loft for an improvisation. York spread a piece of paper over the marks and rubbed his pencil all over it and asked polite questions about the church. Was it as haunted as it should be?

Jane, concerned for the honour of their church, replied that the villagers had sometimes seen lights in the windows at midnight; but York contemptuously dismissed that. "You'd hear as much of any old church." He pulled out an electric torch and switched it on to the wall.

"It's been cut in much more deeply at the top," he remarked; "I can read it even on the wall." He spelt out slowly, "'Nemo potest duobus dominis.' That's a text from the Vulgate. It means, 'No man can serve two masters.'"

"And did the same man write the rest underneath, too?"

"No, I should think that was written much later, about the end of the fourteenth century. Hartley will tell me exactly. He's a friend of mine in the British Museum, and I send him the rubbings and he finds out all about them."

He examined the sentence on the paper by his torch, while Hugh's "improvisation" sent horrible cacophonies reeling through the church.

"Latin again, and jolly bad—monkish Latin, you know. Can't make out that word. Oh!"

"Well?"

"It's an answer to the text above, I think. I say, this is the best find I've ever had. Look here, the first fellow wrote 'No man can serve two masters,' and then, about a century after, number two squats down and writes—well, as far as I can make it out, it's like this, 'Show service therefore to the good, but cleave unto the evil.' Remarkable sentiment for a priest to leave in his church, for I'd imagine only the priest would be educated enough to write it. Now why did he say that, I wonder?"

"Because evil is more interesting than good," murmured Jane.

"Hmph. You agree with him then? What kind of evil?"

"I don't know. It's just—don't you know how words and sentences stick in your head sometimes? It's as though I were always hearing it."

"Do you think you'll hear it tomorrow?" asked York maliciously. He had been told that tomorrow was the day of her

Confirmation. She tried to jump up, but as she was cramped from squatting so long on her heels she only sat down instead, and they both burst out laughing.

"I'm sorry," said York, "I didn't mean to be offensive. But I'd like to know what's bothering you."

"What do you mean?"

"Oh, you know. But never mind. I dare say you can't say."

This at once caused an unusual flow of speech from Jane.

"Why should evil be interesting?" she gasped. "It isn't in real life—when the servants steal the spoons and the villagers quarrel with their neighbours. Mrs. Elroy came round to father in a fearful stew the other day because old Mrs. Croft had made a maukin of her."

"A what?"

"An image—you know—out of clay, and she was sticking pins in it, and Mrs. Elroy declared she knew every time a pin had gone in because she felt a stab right through her body."

"What did your father say?"

"He said it was sciatica, but she wouldn't believe it, and he had to go round to Mrs. Croft and talk about Christmas peace and goodwill, but she only leered and yammered at him in the awful way she does, and then Alice said that Christmas blessings only come to those who live at peace with their neighbours, and Mrs. Croft knew that blessings meant puddings, so she took the pins out and let the maukin be, and Mrs. Elroy hasn't felt any more stabs."

"Mrs. Croft is a proper witch then?"

York stood up, looking rather curiously at her shining eyes.

"Cloud Martin has always been a terrible bad parish for witches," said Jane proudly.

"You find *that* form of evil interesting," he said.

Jane was puzzled and abashed by his tone. She peered at the wall again and thought she could make out another mark underneath the others. York quickly took a rubbing and, examining the paper, found it to be one word only, and probably of the same date as the last sentence, which had caused so much discussion about evil.

"'Ma-ma,' ah, I have it. 'Maneo'—'I remain,' that's all."

"'*I* remain?' Who remains?"

"Why, the same 'I' who advises us to cleave to evil. Remembering, perhaps, though it hadn't been said then, that the evil that men do lives after them."

She looked at him with startled eyes. He thought she was a nice child but took things too seriously.

Hugh's attempts at jazz on the organ had faded away. As Jane and York left the church by the little door, they met him coming out through the vestry.

"Lots of luck," said York, handing him the paper. "Did you turn on the verger or anyone to look as well?"

"No—why? Aren't the family enough for you?"

"Rather. I was only wondering what that little man was doing by the door as we went out. You must have seen him, too," he said, turning to Jane, "he was quite close to us."

But as she stared at him, he wished he had not spoken.

"Must have been the organist," said Hugh, who was looking back at the church tower. "Do you like gargoyles, York? There's rather a pretty one up there of a devil eating a child—see it?"

On the Sunday morning after the Confirmation, the day of her first Communion, Jane rose early, dressed by candlelight, met her mother and sister in the hall, and followed them through the raw, uncertain darkness of the garden and churchyard. The chancel windows were lighted up; the gargoyles on the church tower could just be seen, their distorted shapes a deeper black against the dark sky.

Jane slipped past her mother at the end of the pew. Except for the lights in the chancel, and the one small lamp that hung over the middle aisle, the church was dark, and one could not see who was there. Mr. Lacey was already in the chancel, and the Service began. Jane had been to this Service before, but never when the morning was dark like this. Perhaps that was what made it so different. For it *was* different.

Her father was doing such odd things up there at the altar. Why was he pacing backwards and forwards so often, and waving his hands in that funny way? And what *was* he saying? She couldn't make out the words—she must have completely lost the place. She tried to find it in her prayer book, but the words to which she was listening gave her no clue; she could not recognise them at all, and presently she realised that not only were the words unknown to her, but so was the language in which they were spoken. Alice's rebuke came back to her: "You shouldn't quote Latin in your sermons, Father." But this wasn't a sermon, it was the Communion Service. Only in the Roman Catholic Church would they have the Communion Service in Latin, and then it would be the Mass. Was father holding Mass? He would be turned out of the Church for being Roman. It was bewildering, it was dreadful. But her mother didn't seem to notice anything.

Did she notice that there were other people up there at the altar?

There was a brief pause. People came out of the darkness behind her, and went up to the chancel. Mrs. Lacey slipped out of the pew and joined them. Jane sat back and let her sister go past her.

"You are coming, Janey?" whispered Alice as she passed.

Jane nodded, but she sat still. She had let her mother and sister leave her; she stared at the two rows of dark figures standing in the chancel behind the row of those who knelt; she could not see her mother and sister among them; she could see no one whom she knew.

She dared not look again at the figures by the altar; she kept her head bowed. The last time she had looked there had been two others standing by her father—that is, if that little dark figure had indeed been her father. If she looked now, would she see him there? Her head bent lower and sank into her hands. Instead of the one low voice murmuring the words of the Sacrament, a muffled chant of many voices came from the chancel.

She heard the scuffle of feet, but no steps came past her down into the church again. What were they doing up there? At last she had to look, and she saw that the two rows were standing facing each other across the chancel, instead of each behind the other. She tried to distinguish their faces, to recognise even one that she knew. Presently she became aware that why she could not do this was because they had no faces. The figures all wore dark cloaks with hoods, and there were blank white spaces under the hoods.

"It is possible," she said to herself, "that those are masks." She formed the words in her mind deliberately and with precision as though to distract her attention; for she felt in danger of screaming aloud with terror, and whatever happened she must not draw down on her the attention of those waiting figures.

She knew now that they were waiting for her to go up to the altar.

She might slip out by the little door and escape, if only she dared to move. She stood up and saw the Crusader lying before her, armed, on guard, his sword half drawn from its scabbard. Her breath was choking her. "Crusader, Crusader, rise and help me," she prayed very fast in her mind. But the Crusader stayed motionless. She must go out by herself. With a blind, rushing movement, she threw herself on to the little door, dragged it open, and got outside.

Mrs. Lacey and Alice thought that Jane, wishing for solitude, must have returned from the Communion table to some other pew. Only Mr. Lacey knew that she had not come up to the Communion table at all; and it troubled him still more when she did not appear at breakfast. Alice thought she had gone for a walk; Mrs. Lacey said in her vague, late Victorian way that she thought it only natural Jane should wish to be alone for a little.

"I should say it was decidedly more natural that she should wish for sausages and coffee after being up for an hour on a raw December morning," said her husband with unusual asperity.

It was York who found her half an hour later walking very fast through the fields. He took her hands, which felt frozen, and as he looked into her face he said, "Look here, you know, this won't do. What are you so frightened of?" And then broke off his questions, told her not to bother to try and speak but to come back to breakfast, and half-pulled her with him through the thick, slimy mud, back to the Rectory. Suddenly she began to tell him that the Early Service that morning had all been different—the people, their clothes, even the language, it was all quite different.

He thought over what she stammered out, and wondered if she could somehow have had the power to go back in time and see and hear the Latin Mass as it used to be in that church.

"The old Latin Mass wasn't a horrible thing, was it?"

"Jane! Your father's daughter needn't ask that."

"No. I see. Then it wasn't the Mass I saw this morning—it was—" She spoke very low so that he could hardly catch the words. "There was something horrible going on up there by the altar—and they were waiting—waiting for me."

Her hand trembled under his arm. He thrust it down into his pocket on the pretext of warming it. It seemed to him monstrous that this nice, straightforward little schoolgirl, whom he liked best of the family, should be hag-ridden like this.

That evening he wrote a long letter to his antiquarian friend, Hartley, enclosing the pencil rubbings he had taken of the words scratched on the wall by the Rectory pew.

On Monday he was leaving them, to go and look at other churches in Somerset. He looked hard at Jane as he said "goodbye." She seemed to have completely forgotten whatever it was that had so distressed her the day before, and at breakfast had been the jolliest of the party. But when she felt York's eyes upon her, the laughter died out of hers; she said, but not as though she had intended to say it, "You will come back for Wednesday."

"Why, what happens on Wednesday?"

"It is full moon then."

"That's not this Wednesday then, it must be Wednesday week. Why do you want me to come back then?"

She could give no answer to that. She turned self-conscious and began an out-of-date jazz song about "Wednesday week way down in old Bengal!"

It was plain she did not know why she had said it. But he promised himself that he would come back by then, and asked Mrs. Lacey if he might look them up again on his way home.

In the intervening ten days he was able to piece together some surprising information from Hartley which seemed to throw a light on the inscriptions he had made at Cloud Martin.

In the reports of certain trials for sorcery in the year 1474, one Giraldus atte Welle, priest of the parish of Cloud Martin in Somerset, confessed under torture to having held the Black Mass in his church at midnight on the very altar where he administered the Blessed Sacrament on Sundays. This was generally done on Wednesday or Thursday, the chief days of the Witches' Sabbath when they happened to fall on the night of the full moon. The priest would then enter the church by the little side door, and from the darkness in the body of the church those villagers who had followed his example and sworn themselves to Satan, would come up and join him, one by one, hooded and masked, that none might recognise the other. He was charged with having secretly decoyed young children in order to kill them on the altar as a sacrifice to Satan, and he was finally charged with attempting to murder a young virgin for that purpose.

All the accused made free confessions towards the end of their trial, especially in as far as they implicated other people. All however were agreed on a certain strange incident. That just as the priest was about to cut the throat of the girl on the altar, the tomb of the Crusader opened, and the knight who had lain there for two centuries arose and came upon them with drawn sword, so that they scattered and fled through the church, leaving the girl unharmed on the altar.

With these reports from Hartley in his pocket, York travelled back on the Wednesday week by slow cross-country trains that managed to miss their connections and land him at Little Borridge, the station for Cloud Martin, at a quarter-past ten. The village cab had broken down, there was no other car to be had at that hour, it was a six-mile walk up to the Rectory, there was a station hotel where it would be far more reasonable to spend the night, and finish his journey next morning. Yet York refused to consider this alternative; all through the maddening and uncertain journey, he had kept saying to himself, "I shall be late," though he did not know for what. He had promised Jane he would be back this Wednesday, and back he must be. He left his luggage at the station and walked up. It was the night of the full moon, but the sky was so covered with cloud as to be almost dark. Once or twice he missed his way in following the elaborate instructions of the station-master, and had to retrace his steps a little. It was hard on twelve o'clock when at last he saw the square tower of Cloud Martin Church, a solid blackness against the flying clouds.

He walked up to the little gate into the churchyard. There was a faint light from the chancel windows, and he thought he heard voices chanting. He paused to listen, and then he was certain of it, for he could hear the silence when they stopped. It might have been a minute or five minutes later, that he heard the most terrible shriek he had ever imagined, though faint, coming as it did from the closed church; and knew it for Jane's voice. He ran up to the little door and heard that scream again and again. As he broke through the door he heard it cry, "Crusader! Crusader!" The church was in utter darkness, there was no light in the chancel, he had to fumble in his pockets for his electric torch. The screams had stopped and the whole place was silent. He flashed his torch right and left, and saw a figure lying huddled against the altar. He knew that it was Jane; in an instant he had reached her. Her eyes were open, looking at him, but they did not know him, and she did not seem to understand him when he spoke. In a strange, rough accent of broad Somerset that he could scarcely distinguish, she said, "It was my body on the altar."

CHRISTMAS HONEYMOON

Howard Spring

First published in
The Queen's Book of the Red Cross (London, 1939)

Howard Spring (1889–1965) was born in Tiger Bay in Cardiff, the son of a gardener who died when Howard was only 12 years old. He was forced to leave school and worked initially as an errand boy, eventually managing to move into journalism. After working for local Cardiff and Yorkshire newspapers he got a job with the *Manchester Guardian* in 1915. His career as a writer of books didn't start till the early 1930s. His first great success came with his novel *O Absalom!* (1938), later retitled *My Son, my Son!* He is also remembered for his 1940 novel *Fame is the Spur*, which is set within the socialist labour movement around a fictionalised Ramsay McDonald, and was adapted into a 1947 film starring Michael Redgrave.

'Christmas Honeymoon' was published in The Queen's Book of the Red Cross (1939). Printed in the early months of the Second World War, it was sponsored by Queen Elizabeth, the wife of King George VI, and was intended to raise funds for medical aid. It included contributions from fifty authors, poets and artists, such as A. A. Milne, Daphne Du Maurier, Georgette Heyer, Cecil Beaton and Dame Laura Knight.

W e were married on December 22nd, because we had met on the 21st. It was as sudden as that. I had come down from Manchester to London. Londoners like you to say that you come up to London; but we Manchester people don't give a hoot what Londoners like. We know that we, and the likes of us, lay the eggs, and the Londoners merely scramble them. That gives us a sense of superiority.

Perhaps I have this sense unduly. Certainly I should never have imagined that I would marry a London girl. As a bachelor, I had survived thirty Manchester summers, and it seemed unlikely to me that, if I couldn't find a girl to suit me in the north, I should find one in London.

I am an architect, and that doesn't make me love London any the more. Every time I come down to the place I find it has eaten another chunk of its own beauty, so as to make more room for the fascias of multiple shops.

All this is just to show you that I didn't come to London looking for a bride; and if I had been looking for a bride, the last place I would have investigated would be a cocktail party. But it was at a cocktail party in the Magnifico that I met Ruth Hutten.

I had never been to a cocktail party in my life before. We don't go in much for that sort of thing in Manchester: scooping a lot of people together and getting rid of the whole bang shoot in one do. It seems to us ungracious. We like to have a few friends in, and give them a cut off the joint and something decent to drink, and talk in a civilised fashion while we're at it. That's what we understand by hospitality. But these cocktail parties are just a frantic St. Vitus gesture by people who don't want to be bothered.

I shouldn't have been at this party at all if it hadn't been for Claud Tunstall. It was about half-past six when I turned from the lunatic illumination of Piccadilly Circus, which is my idea of how hell is lit up, and started to walk down the Haymarket. I was wondering in an absent-minded sort of way how long the old red pillars of the Haymarket Theatre would be allowed to stand before some bright lad thought what fun it would be to tear them down, when Claud turned round from reading one of the yellow playbills, and there we were, grinning and shaking hands.

Claud had something to grin about, because the author's name on the playbill was his. It was his first play, and it looked as though it wouldn't matter to Claud, so far as money went, if it were his last. The thing had been running for over a year; companies were touring it in the provinces and Colonies; and it was due to open in New York in the coming year. No wonder Claud was grinning; but I think a spot of the grin was really meant for me. He was the same old Claud who had attended the Manchester Grammar School with me and shared my knowledge of its smell of new exercise books and old suet pudding.

Claud was on his way to this party at the Magnifico, and he said I must come with him. That's how these things are: there's no sense in them; but there would have been no sense either in trying to withstand Claud Tunstall's blue eyes and fair tumbling hair and general look of a sky over a cornfield.

That's going some, for me, and perhaps the figure is a bit mixed, but I'm not one for figures at any time. Anyway, it explains why, five minutes later, I was gritting my teeth in the presence of great boobies looking like outsizes in eighteenth-century footmen, yelling names and looking down their noses.

We stood at the door of a room, and I was aware of the gold blurs of chandeliers, and a few dozen apparent football scrums, and a hot blast of talk coming out and smacking our faces, so I deduced this was the party all right. One of the boobies yelled: "Mr. Claud Tunstall and Mr. Edward Oldham," and from what happened it might just as well have been "The Archangel Gabriel and one Worm." Because, the moment we were over the threshold, all the scrums loosened up and girls descended on Claud like a cloud of bright, skittering, squawking parrakeets, flashing their red nails at him, unveiling their pearly portals in wide grins, and bearing him off towards a bar where a chap in white was working overtime among all the sweet accessories of Sin. I never saw him again.

Well, as I say, I might have been a worm, no use at all to parrakeets, but that lets in the sparrows. I was just turning slowly on my own axis, so to speak, in the space that was miraculously cleared round me, when I saw a girl looking at me with an appreciative gleam in her brown eye. She was the brownest girl I ever saw—eyes, skin, and hair—homely as a sparrow, and just as alert.

As our eyes met, there came fluting out of one of the scrums a high-pitched female voice: "No, Basil, I'm teetotal, but I can go quite a long way on pahshun fruit."

The pronunciation of that *pahshun* was indescribable; it seemed the bogus essence of the whole damn silly occasion; and the brown girl and I, looking into one another's eyes, twinkled, savouring together the supreme idiocy. Instinctively we moved towards one another, the twinkle widening to a smile, and I found myself getting dangerously full of similes again, for when she smiled the teeth in her brown face were like the milky kernel of a brown nut.

We sat together on a couch at the deserted end of the room, and I said: "Let me get you something to drink. What would you like? Though whatever it is, it would taste nicer in civilised surroundings."

"I agree," she said simply. "Come on."

And so, ten minutes after I had entered the Magnifico, I was outside again, buttoning my overcoat warmly about me, and this girl was at my side. It was incredible. This is not the sort of thing I usually do; but it had happened so spontaneously, and to be out there in the street, with a little cold wind blowing about us, was such a relief after that gaudy Bedlam, that the girl and I turned to one another and smiled again. I could see she was feeling the same about it as I was.

Our eyes were towards the dazzle of Piccadilly Circus, when she turned and said, "Not that way," so we went the other way, and down those steps where the Duke of York's column towers up into the sky, and then we were in the park. To be walking there, with that little wind, and the sky full of stars huddling together in the cold, and the bare branches of the trees standing up against the violet pulsing of the night—this was indescribable, incredible, coming within a few minutes upon that screeching aviary.

Ruth Hutten was a typist—nothing more. Her father had been one of those old fogies who rootle for years and years in the British Museum to prove that Ben Jonson had really inserted a semi-colon where the 1739 edition or what not has a full-stop.

Things like that. Somehow he had lived on it, like a patient old rat living on scraps of forgotten and unimportant meat. Ruth had lived with him—just lived, full of admiration for the old boy's scholarship, typing his annual volume, which usually failed to earn the publisher's advance.

When he died, the typewriter was all she had; and now she typed other people's books. She had been typing a long flaming novel about Cornwall by Gregoria Gunson; and Gregoria (whom I had never heard of before, but who seemed a decent wench) had said, "I'll take you along to a party. You'll meet a lot of people there. Perhaps I can fix up some work for you."

So there Ruth Hutten was, at the Magnifico, feeling as much out of it as I did, and as glad to escape.

She told me all this as we walked through the half-darkness of the park, and I, as naturally, told her all about myself. She was hard up, but I had never known anyone so happy. And I don't mean gay, bubbling, effervescent. No; you can keep that for the Magnifico. I mean something deep, fundamental; something that takes courage when you're as near the limit as Ruth was.

To this day I don't know London as well as Londoners think everyone ought to know the place. I don't know where we had supper; but it was in a quiet place that everybody else seemed to have forgotten. There was a fire burning, and a shaded lamp on the table. The food was good and simple, and no one seemed to care how long we stayed. I wanted to stay a long time. I had a feeling that once Ruth got outside the door, shook hands, and said "Good night," I should be groping in a very dark place.

I crumbled a bit of bread on the table, and without looking at her I said: "Ruth, I like you. I've never liked anyone so much in my life. Will you marry me?"

She didn't answer till I looked up, and when our glances met she said, "Yes. If you and I can't be happy together, no two people on earth ever could."

This was five years ago. We have had time to discover that we didn't make a mistake.

We were married at a registry office the next morning. The taxi-driver, who looked like one of the seven million exiled Russian princes, and the office charwoman, who had a goitre and a hacking cough, were the witnesses. I tipped them half a sovereign each. I cling to these practical details because I find them comforting in view of the mad impracticality of what was to follow. Please remember that I am an unromantic northerner who couldn't invent a tale to save his life. If I tried to do so, I should at once begin to try and fill it with this and that—in short with Something. The remarkable thing about what happened to me and Ruth was simply that Nothing happened. If you have never come up against Nothing you have no idea how it can scare you out of your wits. When I was a child I used to be afraid of Something in the dark. I know now that the most fearful thing about the dark is that we may find Nothing in it.

It was Ruth's idea that we should spend the few days of our honeymoon walking in Cornwall. Everything was arranged in a mad hurry. Not that there was much to arrange. We bought rucksacks, stuffed a change of underclothing into them, bought serviceable shoes and waterproofs, and we were ready to start.

Walking was the idea of both of us. This was another bond: you could keep all the motor-cars in the world so far as we were concerned, and all the radio and daily newspapers, too; and we both liked walking in winter as much as in summer.

Cornwall was Ruth's idea. She had Cornwall on the brain. Her father had done some learned stuff on Malory; and her head was full of Merlin and Tintagel and the Return of Arthur. Gregoria Gunson's novel helped, too, with its smugglers and romantic inns and the everlasting beat of surf on granite coasts. So Cornwall it was—a place in which neither of us had set foot before.

We made our first contact with Cornwall at Truro. Night had long since fallen when we arrived there on our wedding day. I have not been there since, nor do I wish ever to return. Looking back on what happened, it seems appropriate that the adventure should have begun in Truro. There is in some towns something inimical, irreconcilable. I felt it there. As soon as we stepped out of the station, I wished we were back in the warm, lighted train which already was pulling out on its way to Penzance.

There was no taxi in sight. To our right the road ran slightly uphill; to our left, downhill. We knew nothing of the town, and we went to the left. Soon we were walking on granite. There was granite everywhere: grey, hard, and immemorial. The whole town seemed to be hewn out of granite. The streets were paved with it, enormous slabs like the lids of ancestral vaults. It gave me the feeling of walking in an endless graveyard, and the place was silent enough to maintain the illusion. The streets were lit with grim economy. Hardly a window had a light, and when, here and there, we passed a public-house, it was wrapped in a pall of decorum which made me wonder whether Cornishmen put on shrouds when they went in for a pint.

It did not take us long to get to the heart of the place, the few shopping streets that were a bit more festive, gay with seasonable things; and when we found an hotel, it was a good one. I signed the book, "Mr. and Mrs. Edward Oldham, Manchester," and that made me smile. After all, it was something to smile about. At this time last night, Ruth and I had just met, and now "Mr. and Mrs. Edward Oldham."

Ruth had moved across to a fire in the lounge. She had an arm along the mantelpiece, a toe meditatively tapping the fender. She looked up when I approached her and saw the smile. But her face did not catch the contagion. "Don't you hate this town?" she asked.

"I can put up with it," I said, "now that I'm in here, and now that you're in here with me."

"Yes," she answered, "this is all right. But those streets! They gave me the creeps. I felt as if every stone had been hewn out of a cliff that the Atlantic had battered for a thousand years and plastered with wrecks. Have you ever seen Tewkesbury Abbey?"

The irrelevant question took me aback. "No," I said.

"I've never seen stone so saturated with sunlight," said Ruth. "It looks as if you could wring summers out of it. The fields about it, I know, have run with blood, but it's a happy place all the same. This place isn't happy. It's under a cold enchantment."

"Not inside these four walls," I said, "because they enclose you and me and our supper and bed."

We fled from Truro the next morning. Fled is the word. As soon as breakfast was over we slung our rucksacks on to our backs and cleared out of the granite town as fast as our legs would take us. December 23rd, and utterly unseasonable weather. The sky was blue, the sun was warm, and the Christmas decorations in the shops had a farcical and inappropriate look. But we were not being bluffed by these appearances. We put that town behind us before its hoodoo could reimpose itself upon our spirits.

And soon there was nothing wrong with our spirits at all. We were travelling westward, and every step sunk us deeper into a warm enchantment. Ruth had spoken last night of a cold enchantment. Well, this was a warm enchantment. I hadn't guessed that, with Christmas only two days ahead, any part of England could be like this. We walked through woods of evergreens and saw the sky shining like incredible blue lace through the branches overhead. We found violets blooming in warm hedge bottoms, and in a cottage garden a few daffodils were ready to burst their sheaths. We could see the yellow staining the taut green. We had tea at that cottage, out of doors! I thought of Manchester, and the fog blanketing Albert Square, and the great red trams going through it, slowly, like galleons, clanging their warning bells. I laughed aloud at the incredible, the absurd things that could happen to a man in England. One day Manchester. The next London. The next marriage, Truro, and the cold shudders. The next—this! I said all this to Ruth, who was brushing crumbs off the table to feed the birds that hopped tamely round her feet. "It makes me wonder what miracle is in store for tomorrow," I said. "And, anyway, what is Cornwall? I've always thought it was beetling cliffs and raging seas, smugglers, wreckers, and excisemen."

We entered the cottage to pay the old woman, and I went close up to the wall to examine a picture hanging there. It was a fine bit of photography: spray breaking on wicked-looking rocks. "That's the Manacles," the old girl said. "That's where my husband was drowned."

The Manacles. That was a pretty fierce name, and it looked a pretty fierce place. The woman seemed to take it for granted. She made no further comment. "Good-bye, midear," she said to Ruth. "Have a good day."

We did, but I never quite recaptured the exaltation of the morning. I felt that this couldn't last, that the spirit which had first made itself felt in the hard grey streets of Truro had pounced again out of that hard grey name: the Manacles. It sounded like a gritting of gigantic teeth. We were being played with. This interlude in fairyland, where May basked in December, was something to lure us on, to bring us within striking reach of—well, of what? Isn't this England? I said to myself. Isn't Cornwall as well within the four walls of Britain as Lancashire?

We breasted a hill, and a wide estuary lay before us, shining under the evening sun. Beyond it, climbing in tier upon tier of streets, was Falmouth. I liked the look of it. "This is where we stay tonight," I said to Ruth. "We shall be comfortable here."

A ferry took us across the harbour. Out on the water it was cold. Ruth pointed past the docks, past Pendennis Castle standing on the hill. "Out there is the way to Land's End," she said.

I looked, and low down on the water there was a faint grey smudge. Even a Manchester man would know that that was fog, creeping in from the Atlantic.

All night long we heard the fog-horns moaning, and it was very cold.

I hate sleeping in an airless room, but by midnight the white coils of fog, filling every crevice, and cold as if they were the exhalation of icebergs, made me rise from bed and shut the window. Our bedroom hung literally over the sea. The wall of the room was a deep bay, and I had seen how, by leaning out of the window, one could drop a stone to the beach below. Now I could not see the beach. I could not see anything. If I had stretched my arm out into the night the fingers would have been invisible. But though I could not see, I could hear. The tide had risen, and I could hear the plash of little waves down there below me. It was so gentle a sound that it made me shudder. It was like the voice of a soft-spoken villain. The true voice of the sea and of the night was that long, incessant bellow of the fog-horns. The shutting of the window did nothing to keep that out.

I drew the curtains across the window, and, turning, saw that a fire was laid in the grate. I put a match to it. Incredible comfort! In ten minutes we felt happier. In twenty we were asleep.

There seemed nothing abnormal about Falmouth when we woke in the morning. A fairly stiff wind had sprung up. The fog was torn to pieces. It hung here and there in dirty isolated patches, but these were being quickly swept away. There was a run on the water. It was choppy and restless, and the sky was a rag-bag of fluttering black and grey. Just a normal winter day by the seaside: a marvellous day for walking, Ruth said.

At the breakfast-table we spread out the map and considered the day's journey. This was going to be something new again. There had been the grey inhospitality of Truro; the Arcadian interlude; the first contact with something vast and menacing. Now, looking at the map, we saw that, going westward, following the coast, we should come to what we had both understood Cornwall to be: a sparsely populated land, moors, a rock-bound coast. It promised to be something big and hard and lonely, and that was what we wanted.

We put sandwiches into our rucksacks, intending to eat lunch out of doors. We reckoned we should find some sort of inn for the night.

A bus took us the best part of ten miles on our westward journey. Then it struck inland, to the right. We left it at that point, climbed a stile, walked through a few winter-bare fields, and came to a path running with the line of the coast.

Now, indeed, we had found traditional Cornwall. Here, if anywhere, was the enchanted land of Merlin and of Arthur—the land that Ruth dreamed about. Never had I found elsewhere in England a sense so overpowering both of size and loneliness. To our left was the sea, down there at the foot of the mighty cliffs along whose crest we walked. The tide was low, and the reefs were uncovered. In every shape of fantastic cruelty they thrust out towards the water, great knives and swords of granite that would hack through any keel, tables of granite on which the stoutest ship would pound to pieces, jaws of granite that would seize and grind and not let go. Beyond and between these prone monsters was the innocent yellow sand, and, looking at the two—the sand and the reefs—I thought of the gentle lapping of the water under my window last night, and the crying of the fog-horns, the most desolate crying in the world.

Southward and westward the water stretched without limit; and inland, as we walked steadily forward all through the morning, was now a patch of cultivation, now the winter stretch of rusty moor with gulls and lapwings joining their lamentations as they glided and drooped across it, according to their kind. From time to time a cluster of trees broke the monotony of the inland view, and I remember rooks fussing among the bare boughs. Rooks, lapwings, and gulls: those were the only birds we saw that day.

It was at about one o'clock that we came to a spot where the cliff path made a loop inland to avoid a deep fissure into which we peered. In some cataclysm the rocks here had been torn away, tumbling and piling till they made a rough giant's stairway down which we clambered to the beach below. We ended up in a cove so narrow that I could have thrown a stone across it, and paved with sand of an unbelievable golden purity. The sun came through the clouds, falling right upon that spot. It was tiny, paradisal, with the advancing tide full of green and blue and purple lights. We sat on the sand, leaned against the bottom-most of the fallen granite blocks, and ate our lunch.

We were content. This was the loveliest thing we had found yet. Ruth recalled a phrase from the novel she had typed for Miss Gregoria Gunson. "And you will find here and there a paradise ten yards wide, a little space of warmth and colour set like a jewel in the hard iron of that coast." Far-fetched, I thought, but true enough.

It was while we were sitting there, calculating how long that bit of sun could last, that Ruth said, "We wanted a lonely place, and we've found it, my love. Has it struck you that we haven't seen a human being since we got off the bus?"

It hadn't, and it didn't seem to me a matter of concern. I stretched my arms lazily towards the sun. "Who wants to see human beings?" I demanded. "I had enough human beings at the Magnifico to last me a very long time."

"So long as we find some human beings to make us a bit of supper tonight..."

"Never fear," I said. "We'll do that. There! Going... Going... Gone."

The sun went in. We packed up, climbed to the cliff top, and started off again.

At three o'clock the light began to go out of the day. This was Christmas Eve, remember. We were among the shortest days of the year. It was now that a little uneasiness began to take hold of me. Still, I noticed, we had seen no man or woman, and, though

I kept a sharp lookout on the country inland, we saw no house, not a barn, not a shed.

We did not see the sun again that day, but we witnessed his dying magnificence. Huge spears of light fanned down out of the sky and struck in glittering points upon the water far off. Then the clouds turned into a crumble and smother of dusky red, as though a city were burning beyond the edge of the world, and when all this began to fade to grey ashes I knew that I was very uneasy indeed.

Ruth said: "I think we ought to leave this cliff path. We ought to strike inland and find a road—any road."

I thought so, too, but inland now was nothing but moor. Goodness knows, I thought, where we shall land if we embark on that.

"Let us keep on," I said, "for a little while. We may find a path branching off. Then we'll know we're getting somewhere."

We walked for another mile, and then Ruth stopped. We were on the brink of another of those deep fissures, like the one we had descended for lunch. Again the path made a swift right-hand curve. I knew what Ruth was thinking before she said it. "In half an hour or so the light will be quite gone. Suppose we had come on this in the dark?"

We had not found the path we were seeking. We did not seek it any more. Abruptly, we turned right and began to walk into the moor. So long as we could see, we kept the coast behind our backs. Soon we could not see at all. The night came on, impenetrably black and there would be no moon.

It was now six o'clock. I know that because I struck a match to look at the time, and I noticed that I had only three matches left. This is stuck in my mind because I said, "We must be careful with these. If we can't find food, we'll find a smoke a comfort."

"But, my love," said Ruth, and there was now an undoubted note of alarm in her voice, "we *must* find food. Surely, if we just keep on we'll see a light, or hear a voice, or come to a road—"

She stopped abruptly, seized my arm, held on to prevent my going forward. I could not see her face, but I sensed her alarm. "What is it?" I asked.

"I stepped in water."

I knelt and tested the ground in front of me with my hands. It was a deep oozy wetness; not the clear wetness of running water. "Bog," I said; and we knew we could go forward no longer. With cliff on the one hand and the possibility of stumbling into a morass on the other, there seemed nothing for it but to stay where we were till heaven sent us aid or the dawn came up.

I put my arm round Ruth and felt that she was trembling. I want to put this adventure down exactly as it happened. It would be nice to write that her nerves were steady as rock. Clearly they weren't, and I was not feeling very good either. I said as gaily as I could, "This is where we sit down, smoke a cigarette, and think it out."

We went back a little so as to be away from the bog, and then we plumped down among the heather. We put the cigarettes to our lips and I struck a match. It did not go out when I threw it to the ground. In that world of darkness the little light burning on the earth drew our eyes, and simultaneously we both stood up with an exclamation of surprised delight. The light had shown us an inscribed stone, almost buried in the heather. There were two matches left. Fortunately, we were tidy people. We had put our sandwich papers into the rucksacks. I screwed these now into little torches. Ruth lit one and held it to the stone while I knelt to read. It seemed a stone of fabulous age. The letters were mossy and at first illegible. I took out a penknife and scraped at them. "2 Miles—" we made out, but the name of this place two miles off we do not know to this day. I scraped away, but the letters were too defaced for reading, and just as the last of the little torches flared to extinction the knife slipped from my hand into the heather. There was nothing to do but leave it there.

We stood up. Two miles. But two miles to where, and two miles in what direction? Our situation seemed no happier, when suddenly I saw the stones.

I had seen stones like them on the Yorkshire moors, round about the old Brontë parsonage. But were they the same sort of stones, and did they mean the same thing? I was excited now. "Stay here," I said to Ruth, and I stepped towards the first stone. As I had hoped, a third came into view in line with the second, and, as I advanced, a fourth in line with the third. They were the same: upright monoliths set to mark a path, whitewashed half way up so that they would glimmer through the dark as they were doing now, tarred on their upper half to show the way when snow was on the ground. I shouted in my joy: "Come on! Supper! Fires! Comfort! Salvation!" but Ruth came gingerly. She had not forgotten the bog.

But the stones did not let us down. They led us to the village. It must have been about nine o'clock when we got there.

Half-way through that pitch-black two-mile journey we were aware that once more we were approaching the sea. From afar we could hear its uneasy murmur growing louder, and presently threaded with a heart-darkening sound: the voice of a bell-buoy tolling its insistent warning out there on the unseen water.

As the murmur of the sea and the melancholy clangour of the bell came clearer we went more warily, for we could not see more than the stone next ahead; and presently there was no stone where the next stone should be. We peered into the darkness, our hearts aching for the light which would tell us that we were again among houses and men. There was no light anywhere.

"We have one match," I said. "Let us light a cigarette apiece and chance seeing something that will help us."

We saw the wire hawser: no more than the veriest scrap of it, fixed by a great staple into the head of a post and slanting down into darkness. I first, Ruth behind me, we got our hands upon it, gripping for dear life, and went inching down towards the sound of water.

So we came at last to the village. Like many a Cornish village, it was built at the head of a cove. The sea was in front; there was a horse-shoe of cliffs; and snuggling at the end was a half-moon of houses behind a seawall of granite.

All this did not become clear to us at once. For the moment, we had no other thought than of thankfulness to be treading on hard cobbles that had been laid by human hands, no other desire than to bang on the first door and ask whether there was in the place an inn or someone who would give us lodging for the night.

Most of the cottages were whitewashed; their glimmer gave us the rough definition of the place; and I think already we must have felt some uneasy presage at the deathly mask of them, white as skulls with no light in their eyes.

For there was no living person, no living thing, in the village. That was what we discovered. Not so much as a dog went by us in the darkness. Not so much as a cock crowed. The tolling from the water came in like a passing bell, and the sea whispered incessantly, and grew to a deep-throated threatening roar as the tide rose and billows beat on the sand and at last on the seawall; but there was no one to notice these things except ourselves; and our minds were almost past caring, so deeply were we longing for one thing only—the rising of the sun.

There was nothing wrong with the village. It contained all the apparatus of living. Bit by bit we discovered that. There was no answer to our knocking at the first door we came to. There was nothing remarkable in that, and we went on to the next. Here, again, there was no welcome sound of feet, no springing up of a light to cheer us who had wandered for so long in the darkness.

At the third house I knocked almost angrily. Yes; anger was the feeling I had then: anger at all these stupid people who shut down a whole village at nine o'clock, went to their warm beds, and left us standing there, knocking in the cold and darkness. I thudded the knocker with lusty rat-tat-tats; and suddenly, in the midst of that noisy assault, I stopped, afraid. The anger was gone. Plain fear took its place. At the next house I *could* not knock, because I knew there was no one to hear me.

I was glad to hear Ruth's voice. She said, surprisingly, "It's no good knocking. Try a door."

I turned the handle and the door opened. Ruth and I stepped over the threshold, standing very close together. I shouted, "Is there anyone at home?" My voice sounded brutally loud and defiant. Nothing answered it.

We were standing in the usual narrow passageway of a cottage. Ruth put out her hand and knocked something to the floor from a little table. "Matches," she said; and I groped on the floor and found them. The light showed us a hurricane lantern standing on the table. I lit it, and we began to examine the house, room by room.

This was a strange thing to do, but at the time it did not seem strange. We were shaken and off our balance. We wanted to reassure ourselves. If we had found flintlocks, bows and arrows, bronze hammers, we might have been reassured. We could have told ourselves that we had wandered, bewitched, out of our century. But we found nothing of the sort. We found a spotless cottage full of contemporary things. There was a wireless set. There was last week's *Falmouth Packet*. There were geraniums in a pot in the window; there were sea-boots and oilskins in the passage. The bed upstairs was made, and there was a cradle beside it. There was no one in the bed, no child in the cradle.

Ruth was white. "I want to see the pantry," she said, inconsequentially I thought.

We found the pantry, and she took the cloth off a breadpan and put her hand upon a loaf. "It's warm," she said. "It was baked today." She began to tremble.

We left the house and took the lantern with us. Slowly, with the bell tolling endlessly, we walked through the curved length of the village. There was one shop. I held up the light to its uncurtained window. Toys and sweets, odds and ends of grocery, all the stock-in-trade of a small general store, were there behind the glass. We hurried on.

We were hurrying now, quite consciously hurrying; though where we were hurrying to we did not know. Once or twice I found myself looking back over my shoulder. If I had seen man, woman, or child I think I should have screamed. So powerfully had the death of the village taken hold of my imagination that the appearance of a living being, recently so strongly desired, would have affected me like the return of one from the dead.

At the centre of the crescent of houses there was an inn, the Lobster Pot, with climbing geraniums ramping over its front in the way they do in Cornwall; then came more cottages; and at the farther tip of the crescent there was a house standing by itself. It was bigger than any of the others; it stood in a little garden. In the comforting daylight I should have admired it as the sort of place some writer or painter might choose for a refuge.

Now I could make it out only bit by bit, flashing the lantern here and there; and, shining the light upon the porch, I saw that the door was open. Ruth and I went in. Again I shouted, "Is anyone here?" Again I was answered by nothing.

I put the lantern down on an oak chest in the small square hall, and that brought my attention to the telephone. There it was, standing on the chest, an up-to-date microphone in ivory white. Ruth saw it at the same moment, and her eyes asked me, "Do you dare?"

I did. I took up the microphone and held it to my ear. I could feel at once that it was dead. I joggled the rest. I shouted, "Hallo! Hallo!" but I knew that no one would answer. No one answered.

We had stared through the windows of every cottage in the village. We had looked at the shop and the inn. We had banged at three doors and entered two houses. But we had not admitted our extraordinary situation in words. Now I said to Ruth, "What do you make of it?"

She said simply, "It's worse than ghosts. Ghosts are something. This is nothing. Everything is absolutely normal. That's what seems so horrible."

And, indeed, a village devastated by fire, flood, or earthquake would not have disturbed us as we were disturbed by that village which was devastated by nothing at all.

Ruth shut the door of the hall. The crashing of the sea on granite, the tolling of the bell, now seemed far off. We stood and looked at one another uneasily in the dim light of the hurricane lamp. "I shall stay here," said Ruth, "either till the morning or till something happens."

She moved down the hall to a door which opened into a room at the back. I followed her. She tapped on the door, but neither of us expected an answer, and there was none. We went in.

Nothing that night surprised us like what we saw then. Holding the lantern high above my head, I swung its light round the room. It was a charming place, panelled in dark oak. A few fine pictures were on the walls. There were plenty of books, some pieces of good porcelain. The curtains of dark-green velvet fringed with gold were drawn across the window. A fire was burning on the hearth. That was what made us start back almost in dismay—the fire.

If it had been a peat fire—one of those fires that, once lit, smoulder for days—we should not have been surprised. But it was not. Anyone who knew anything about fires could see that this fire had been lit within the last hour. Some of the coals were still black; none had been consumed. And the light from this fire fell upon the white smooth texture of an excellent linen cloth upon the table. On the table was supper, set for one. A chair was placed before the knife and fork and plates. There was a round of cold beef waiting to be cut, a loaf of bread, a jar of pickles, a fine cheese, a glass, and a jug containing beer.

Ruth laughed shrilly. I could hear that her nerves were strained by this last straw. "At least we shan't starve," she cried. "I'm nearly dying of hunger. I suppose the worst that could happen would be the return of the bears, demanding 'Who's been eating my beef? Who's been drinking my beer?' Sit down. Carve!"

I was as hungry as she was. As I looked at the food the saliva flowed in my mouth, but I could as soon have touched it as robbed a poor-box. And Ruth knew it. She turned from the table, threw herself into an easy chair by the fire, and lay back, exhausted. Her eyes closed. I stood behind the chair and stroked her forehead till she slept. That was the best that could happen to her.

That, in a way, was the end of our adventure. Nothing more happened to us. Nothing *more*? But, as you see, nothing at all had happened to us. And it was this nothingness that made my vigil over Ruth sleeping in the chair the most nerve-destroying experience of all my life. A clock ticking away quietly on the chimney-piece told me that it was half-past nine. A tear-off calendar lying on a writing-table told me that it was December 24th. Quite correct. All in order.

The hurricane-lamp faded and went out. I lit a lamp, shaded with green silk, that stood on the table amid the waiting supper. The room became cosier, even more human and likeable. I prowled about quietly, piecing together the personality of the man or woman who lived in it. A man. It was a masculine sort of supper, and I found a tobacco jar and a few pipes. The books were excellently bound editions of the classics, with one or two modern historical works. The pictures, I saw now, were Medici reprints of French Impressionists, all save the one over the fireplace, which was an original by Paul Nash.

I tried, with these trivial investigations, to divert my mind from the extraordinary situation we were in. It wouldn't work. I sat down and listened intently, but there was nothing to hear save the bell and the water—water that stretched, I reminded myself, from here to America. This was one of the ends of the world.

At one point I got up and locked the door, though what was there to keep out? All that was to be feared was inside me.

The fire burned low, and there was nothing for its replenishment. It was nearly gone, and the room was turning cold, when Ruth stirred and woke. At that moment the clock, which had a lovely silver note, struck twelve. "A merry Christmas, my darling," I said.

Ruth looked at me wildly, taking some time to place herself. Then she laughed and said, "I've been dreaming about it. It's got a perfectly natural explanation. It was like this... No... It's gone. I can't remember it. But it was something quite reasonable."

I sat with my arm about her. "My love," I said, "I can think of a hundred quite reasonable explanations. For example, every man in the village for years has visited his Uncle Henry at Bodmin on Christmas Eve, taking wife, child, dog, cat, and canary with him. The chap in this house is the only one who hasn't got an Uncle Henry at Bodmin, so he laid the supper, lit the fire, and was just settling down for the evening when the landlord of the Lobster Pot thought he'd be lonely, looked in, and said: 'What about coming to see *my* Uncle Henry at Bodmin?' And off they all went. That's perfectly reasonable. It explains everything. Do you believe it?"

Ruth shook her head. "You must sleep," she said. "Lay your head on my shoulder."

We left the house at seven o'clock on Christmas morning. It was slack tide. The sea was very quiet, and in the grey light, standing in the garden at the tip of the crescent, we could see the full extent of the village with one sweep of the eye, as we had not been able to do last night.

It was a lovely little place, huddled under the rocks at the head of its cove. Every cottage was well cared for, newly washed in cream or white, and on one or two of them a few stray roses were blooming, which is not unusual in Cornwall at Christmas.

At any other time, Ruth and I would have said, "Let's stay here." But now we hurried, rucksacks on backs, disturbed by the noise of our own shoes, and climbed the path down which we had so cautiously made our way the night before.

There were the stones of black and white. We followed them till we came to the spot where we found the stone with the obliterated name. "And, behold, there was no stone there, but your lost pocket-knife was lying in the heather," said a sceptical friend to whom I once related this story.

That, I suppose, would be a good way to round off an invented tale if I were a professional story-teller. But, in simple fact, the stone *was* there, and so was my knife. Ruth took it from me, and when we came to the place where we had left the cliff path and turned into the moor, she hurled it far out and we heard the faint tinkle of its fall on the rocks below.

"And now," she said with resolution, "we go back the way we came, and we eat our Christmas dinner in Falmouth. Then you can inquire for the first train to Manchester. Didn't you say there are fogs there?"

"There are an' all," I said broadly.

"Good," said Ruth. "After last night, I feel a fog is something substantial, something you can get hold of."

THE CHEERY SOUL

Elizabeth Bowen

First published in *The Listener*, 24 December 1942

Elizabeth Dorothea Cole Bowen (1899–1973) was born in Dublin but lived for most of her life in England. Her most famous novels include *The Death of the Heart* (1938) and *The Heat of the Day* (1949), both of which explore the theme of loneliness—the former between the wars, and the latter, against the backdrop of the London Blitz. She did not use supernatural tropes in her novels, but was an enthusiastic writer of short ghost stories, seeing them as a perfect way of manifesting the problems and uncertainties of the modern world.

Although this story was first published in *The Listener* in 1942, we have chosen to use the slightly altered version which appeared in the April 1952 issue of *The Magazine of Fantasy and Science Fiction*. There it is described as *'one of the most difficult of all supernatural feats: a truly funny ghost story. Not since the denizens of Richard Middleton's "The Ghost Ship" have we encountered so purely comic a phantasm as the outraged and outrageous cook whom Miss Bowen calls "The Cheery Soul".'*

On arriving, I first met the aunt of whom they had told me, the aunt who had not yet got over being turned out of Italy. She sat resentfully by the fire, or rather the fireplace, and did not look up when I came in. The acrid smell that curled through the drawing-room could be traced to a grate full of sizzling fir cones that must have been brought in damp. From the mantelpiece one lamp, with its shade tilted, shed light on the parting of the aunt's hair. It could not be said that the room was cheerful: the high, curtained bow windows made draughty caves; the armchairs and sofas, pushed back against the wall, wore the air of being renounced forever. Only a row of discreet greeting-cards along a bureau betrayed the presence of Christmas.

I coughed and said: "I feel I should introduce myself," and followed this up by giving the aunt my name, which she received with apathy. When she did stir, it was to look at the parcel that I coquettishly twirled from its loop of string. "They're not giving presents, this year," she said in alarm. "If I were you, I should put that back in my room."

"It's just—my rations."

"In that case," she remarked, "I really don't know what you had better do." Turning away from me she picked up a small bent poker, and with this began to interfere with the fir cones, of which several, steaming, bounced from the grate. "A good wood stove," she said, "would make all the difference. At Sienna, though they say it is cold in winter, we never had troubles of this kind."

"How would it be," I said, "if I sat down?" I pulled a chair a little on to the hearthrug, if only for the idea of the thing. "I gather our hosts are out. I wonder where they have gone to?"

"Really, I couldn't tell you."

"My behaviour," I said, "has been shockingly free-and-easy. Having pulled the bell three times, waited, had a go at the knocker..."

"...I heard," she said, slightly bowing her head.

"I gave *that* up, tried the door, found it unlocked, so just marched in."

"Have you come about something?" she said with renewed alarm.

"Well, actually, I fear that I've come to stay. They have been so very kind as to..."

"...Oh, I remember—someone *was* coming." She looked at me rather closely. "Have you been here before?"

"Never. So this is delightful," I said firmly. "I am billeted where I work" (I named the industrial town, twelve miles off, that was these days in a ferment of war production), "my landlady craves my room for these next two days for her daughter, who is on leave, and, on top of this, to be frank, I'm a bit old-fashioned: Christmas alone in a strange town didn't appeal to me. So you can see how I sprang at..."

"Yes, I can see," she said. With the tongs, she replaced the cones that had fallen out of the fire. "At Orvieto," she said, "the stoves were so satisfactory that one felt no ill effects from the tiled floors."

As I could think of nothing to add to this, I joined her in listening attentively to the hall clock. My entry into the drawing-room having been tentative, I had not made so bold as to close the door behind me, so a further coldness now seeped through from the hall. Except for the clock—whose loud tick was reluctant—there was not another sound to be heard: the very silence seemed to produce echoes. The Rangerton-Karneys' absence from their own house was becoming, virtually, ostentatious. "I understand," I said, "that they are tremendously busy. Practically never not on the go."

"They expect to have a finger in every pie."

Their aunt's ingratitude shocked me. She must be (as they had hinted) in a difficult state. They had always spoken with the most marked forbearance of her enforced return to them out of Italy. In England, they said, she had no other roof but theirs, and they were constantly wounded (their friends told me) by her saying she would have preferred internment in Italy.

In common with all my fellow-workers at —, I had a high regard for the Rangerton-Karneys, an admiration tempered, perhaps, with awe. Their energy in the promotion of every war effort was only matched by the austerity of their personal lives. They appeared to have given up almost everything. That they never sat down could be seen from their drawing-room chairs. As "local people" of the most solid kind they were on terms with the bigwigs of every department, the key minds of our small but now rather important town. Completely discreet, they were palpably "in the know."

Their house in the Midlands, in which I now so incredibly found myself, was largish, built of the local stone, *circa* 1860 I should say from its style. It was not very far from a railway junction, and at a still less distance from a canal. I had evaded the strictures on Christmas travel by making the twelve-mile journey by bicycle—indeed, the suggestion that I should do this played a prominent part in their invitation. So I bicycled over. My little things for the two nights were contained in one of those useful American-cloth suitcases, strapped to my back-wheel carrier, while my parcel of rations could be slung, I found, from my handlebar. The bumping of this parcel on my right knee as I pedalled was a major embarrassment. To cap this, the misty damp of the afternoon had caused me to set off in a mackintosh. At the best of times I am not an expert cyclist. The grateful absence of hills (all this country is very flat) was cancelled out by the greasiness of the roads, and army traffic often made me dismount—it is always well to be on the safe side. Now and then, cows or horses loomed up abruptly to peer at me over the reeking hedgerows. The few anonymous villages I passed through all appeared, in the falling dusk, to be very much the same: their inhabitants wore an air of war-time discretion, so I did not dare risk snubs by asking how far I had come. My pocket map, however, proved less unhelpful when I found that I had been reading it upside down. When, about half way, I turned on my lamp, I watched mist curdle under its wobbling ray. My spectacles dimmed steadily; my hands numbed inside my knitted gloves (the only Christmas present I had received so far) and the mist condensed on my muffler in fine drops.

I own that I had sustained myself through this journey on thoughts of the cheery welcome ahead. The Rangerton-Karneys' invitation, delivered by word of mouth only three days ago, had been totally unexpected, as well as gratifying. I had had no reason to think they had taken notice of me. We had met rarely, when I reported to the committees on which they sat. That the brother and two sisters (so much alike that people took them for triplets) had attracted *my* wistful notice, I need not say. But not only was my position a quite obscure one; I am not generally sought out; I make few new friends. None of my colleagues had been to the Rangerton-Karneys' house: there was an idea that they had given up guests. As the news of their invitation to me spread (and I cannot say I did much to stop it spreading) I rose rapidly in everyone's estimation.

In fact, their thought had been remarkably kind. Can you wonder that I felt myself favoured? I was soon, now, to see their erstwhile committee faces wreathed with seasonable and genial smiles. I never was one to doubt that people unbend at home. Perhaps a little feverish from my cycling, I pictured blazing hearths through holly-garlanded doors.

Owing to this indulgence in foolish fancy, my real arrival rather deflated me.

"I suppose they went out after tea?" I said to the aunt.

"After lunch, I think," she replied. "There was no tea." She picked up her book, which was about Mantegna, and went on reading, pitched rather tensely forward to catch the light of the dim-bulbed lamp. I hesitated, then rose up, saying that perhaps I had better deliver my rations to the cook. "If you can," she said, turning over a page.

The whirr of the clock preparing to strike seven made me jump. The hall had funny acoustics—so much so that I strode across the wide breaches from rug to rug rather than hear my step on the stone flags. Draught and dark coming down a shaft announced the presence of stairs. I saw what little I saw by the flame of a night-light, palpitating under a blue glass inverted shade. The hall and the staircase windows were not blacked out yet. (Back in the drawing-room, I could only imagine, the aunt must have so far bestirred herself as to draw the curtains.)

The kitchen was my objective—as I had said to the aunt. I pushed at a promising baize door: it immediately opened upon a vibration of heat and rich, heartening smells. At these, the complexion of everything changed once more. If my spirits, just lately, had not been very high, this was no doubt due to the fact that I had lunched on a sandwich, then had not dared leave my bicycle to look for a cup of tea. I was in no mood to reproach the Rangerton-Karneys for this Christmas break in their well-known austere routine.

But, in view of this, the kitchen was a surprise. Warm, and spiced with excellent smells, it was in the dark completely but for the crimson glow from between the bars of the range. A good deal puzzled, I switched the light on—the black-out, here, had been punctiliously done.

The glare made me jump. The cook must have found, for her own use, a quadruple-power electric bulb. This now fairly blazed down on the vast scrubbed white wood table, scored and scarred by decades of the violent chopping of meat. I looked about—to be staggered by what I did not see. Neither on range, table, nor outsize dresser were there signs of the preparation of any meal. Not a plate, not a spoon, not a canister showed any signs of action. The heat-vibrating top of the range was bare; all the pots and pans were up above, clean and cold, in their places along the rack. I went so far as to open the oven door—a roasting smell came out, but there was nothing inside. A tap drip-drop-dripped on an upturned bowl in the sink—but nobody had been peeling potatoes there.

I put my rations down on the table and was, dumbfounded, preparing to turn away, when a white paper on the white wood caught my eye. This paper, in an inexpert line of block-printing, bore the somewhat unnecessary statement: I AM NOT HERE. To this was added, in brackets: "Look in the fish kettle." Though this be no affair of mine, could I fail to follow it up? Was this some new demonstration of haybox cookery; was I to find our dinner snugly concealed? I identified the fish kettle, a large tin object (about the size, I should say, of an infant's bath) that stood on a stool half way between the sink and range. It wore a tight-fitting lid, which came off with a sort of plop: the sound in itself had an ominous hollowness. Inside, I found, again, only a piece of paper. This said: "Mr. & the 2 Misses Rangerton-Karney can boil their heads. This holds 3."

I felt that the least I could do for my hosts the Rangerton-Karneys was to suppress this unkind joke, so badly out of accord with the Christmas spirit. I *could* have dropped the paper straight into the kitchen fire, but on second thought I went back to consult the aunt. I found her so very deep in Mantegna as to be oblivious of the passage of time. She clearly did not like being interrupted. I said: "Can you tell me if your nephew and nieces had any kind of contretemps with their cook today?"

She replied: "I make a point of not asking questions."

"Oh, so do I," I replied, "in the normal way. But I fear..."

"You fear what?"

"She's gone," I said. "Leaving this..."

The aunt looked at the paper, then said: "How curious." She added: "Of course, she has gone: that happened a year ago. She must have left several messages, I suppose. I remember that Etta found one in the mincing machine, saying to tell them to

197

mince their gizzards. Etta seemed very much put out. That was *last* Christmas Eve, I remember—dear me, what a coincidence... So you found this, did you?" she said, re-reading the paper with less repugnance than I should have wished to see. "I expect, if you went on poking about the kitchen..."

Annoyed, I said tartly: "A reprehensible cook!"

"No worse than other English cooks," she replied. "They all declare they have never heard of a *pasta*, and that oil in cookery makes one repeat. But I always found her cheerful and kind. And of course I miss her—Etta's been cooking since." (This was the elder Miss Rangerton-Karney.)

"But look," I said, "I was led to *this* dreadful message, by another one, on the table. *That* can't have been there a year."

"I suppose not," the aunt said, showing indifference. She picked up her book and inclined again to the lamp.

I said: "You don't think some other servant..."

She looked at me like a fish.

"They *have* no other servants. Oh no: not since the cook..." Her voice trailed away. "Well, it's all very odd, I'm sure."

"It's worse than odd, my dear lady: there won't be any dinner."

She shocked me by emitting a kind of giggle. She said: "Unless they *do* boil their heads."

The idea that the Rangerton-Karneys might be out on a cook-hunt rationalised this perplexing evening for me. I am always more comfortable when I can tell myself that people are, after all, behaving accountably. The Rangerton-Karneys always acted in trio. The idea that one of them should stay at home to receive me while the other two went ploughing round the dark country would, at this crisis, never present itself. The Rangerton-Karneys' three sets of thoughts and feelings always appeared to join at the one root: one might say that they had a composite character. One thing, I could reflect, about misadventures is that they make for talk and often end in a laugh. I tried in vain to picture the Rangerton-Karneys laughing—for that was a thing I had never seen.

But if Etta is now resigned to doing the cooking...? I thought better not to puzzle the thing out.

Screening my electric torch with my fingers past the uncurtained windows, I went upstairs to look for what might be my room. In my other hand I carried my little case—to tell the truth, I was anxious to change my socks. Embarking on a long passage, with doors ajar, I discreetly projected my torch into a number of rooms. All were cold; some were palpably slept in, others dismantled. I located the resting-places of Etta, Max and Paulina by the odour of tar soap, shoe-leather and boiled woollen underclothes that announced their presences in so many committee rooms. At an unintimate distance along the passage, the glint of my torch on Florentine bric-à-brac suggested the headquarters of the aunt. I did at last succeed, by elimination, in finding the spare room prepared for me. They had put me just across the way from their aunt. My torch and my touch revealed a made-up bed, draped in a glacial white starched quilt, two fringed towels straddling the water-jug, and virgin white mats to receive my brushes and comb. I successively bumped my knee (the knee still sore from the parcel) on two upright chairs. Yes, this must be the room for me. Oddly enough, it was much less cold than the others—but I did not think of that at the time. Having done what was necessary to the window, I lit up, to consider my new domain.

Somebody had been lying on my bed. When I rest during the day, I always remove the quilt, but whoever it was had neglected to do this. A deep trough, with a map of creases, appeared. The creases, however, did not extend far. Whoever it was had lain here in a contented stupor.

I worried—Etta might blame me. To distract my thoughts, I opened my little case and went to put my things on the dressing-table. The mirror was tilted upwards under the light, and something was written on it in soap: DEARIE, DON'T MIND ME. I at once went to the washstand, where the soap could be verified—it was a used cake, one corner blunted by writing. On my way back, I kicked over a black bottle, which, so placed on the floor as to be in easy reach from the bed, now gaily and noisily bowled away. It was empty—I had to admit that its contents, breathed out again, gave that decided character to my room.

The aunt was to be heard, pattering up the stairs. Was this belated hostess-ship on her part? She came into view of my door, carrying the night-light from the hall table. Giving me a modest, affronted look she said: "I thought I'd tidy my hair."

"The cook has been lying on my bed."

"That would have been very possible, I'm afraid. She was often a little—if you know what I mean. But, she left last Christmas."

"She's written something."

"I don't see what one can do," the aunt said, turning into her room. For my part, I dipped a towel into the jug and reluctantly tried to rub out the cook's message, but this only left a blur all over the glass. I applied to this the drier end of the towel. Oddly enough (perhaps) I felt fortified: this occult good feeling was, somehow, warming. The cook was supplying that touch of nature I had missed since crossing the Rangerton-Karneys' threshold. Thus, when I stepped back for another look at the mirror, I was barely surprised to find that a sprig of mistletoe had been twisted around the cord of the hanging electric light.

My disreputable psychic pleasure was to be interrupted. Downstairs, in the caves of the house, the front door bell jangled, then jangled again. This was followed by an interlude with the knocker: an imperious rat-a-tat-tat. I called to the aunt: "Ought one of us to go down? It might be a telegram."

"I don't think so—why?"

We heard the glass door of the porch (the door through which I had made my so different entry) being rattled open; we heard the hall traversed by footsteps with the weight of authority. In response to a mighty "*Anyone there?*" I defied the aunt's judgment and went hurrying down. Coming on a policeman outlined in the drawing-room door, my first thought was that this must be about the black-out. I edged in, silent, just behind the policeman: he looked about him suspiciously, then saw me. "And who might you be?" he said. The bringing out of his notebook gave me stage fright during my first and other replies. I explained that the Rangerton-Karneys had asked me to come and stay.

"Oh, they did?" he said. "Well, that is a laugh. Seen much of them?"

"Not so far."

"Well, you won't." I asked why: he ignored my question, asked for all my particulars, quizzed my identity card. "I shall check up on all this," he said heavily. "So they asked you for Christmas, did they? And just *when*, may I ask, was this invitation issued?"

"Well, er—three days ago."

This made me quite popular. He said: "Much as I thought. Attempt to cover their tracks and divert suspicion. I daresay you blew off all round about them having asked you here?"

"I may have mentioned it to one or two friends."

He looked pleased again and said: "Just what they reckoned on. Not a soul was to guess they had planned to bolt. As for you—*you're* a cool hand, I must say. Just walked in, found the place empty and dossed down. Never once strike you there was anything fishy?"

"A good deal struck me," I replied austerely. "I took it, however, that my host and his sisters had been unexpectedly called out—perhaps to look for a cook."

"Ah, cook," he said. "Now what brought that to your mind?"

"Her whereabouts seemed uncertain, if you know what I mean."

Whereupon, he whipped over several leaves of his notebook. "The last cook employed here," he said, "was in residence here four days, departing last Christmas Eve, December 24th, 194—. We have evidence that she stated locally that she was unable to tolerate certain goings-on. She specified interference in her department, undue advantage taken of the rationing system, mental cruelty to an elderly female refugee..."

I interposed: "That would certainly be the aunt."

"...and failure to observe Christmas in the appropriate manner. On this last point she expressed herself violently. She further adduced (though with less violence of feeling) that her three employers were 'dirty spies, with their noses in everything.' Subsequently, she withdrew this last remark; her words were, 'I do not wish to make trouble, as I know how to make trouble in a way of my own.' However, certain remarks she had let drop have been since followed up, and proved useful in our inquiries. Unhappily, we cannot check up on them, as the deceased met her end shortly after leaving this house."

"The *deceased*?" I cried, with a sinking heart.

"Proceeding through the hall door and down the approach or avenue, in an almost total state of intoxication, she was heard singing 'God rest you merry, gentlemen, let nothing you dismay.' She also shouted: 'Me for an English Christmas!' Accosting several pedestrians, she informed them that in her opinion times were not what they were. She spoke with emotion (being intoxicated) of turkey, mince pies, ham, plum pudding, etc. She was last seen hurrying in the direction of the canal, saying she must get brandy to make her sauce. She was last heard in the vicinity of the canal. The body was recovered from the canal on Boxing Day, December 26th, 194—"

"But what," I said, "has happened to the Rangerton-Karneys?"

"Now, now!" said the policeman, shaking his finger sternly. "You *may* hear as much as is good for you, one day—or you may not. Did you ever hear of the Safety of the Realm? I don't mind telling you one thing—you're lucky. You might have landed yourself in a nasty mess."

"But, good heavens—the *Rangerton-Karneys*! They know everyone."

"Ah!" he said, "but it's that kind you have to watch." Heavy with this reflection, his eyes travelled over the hearth-rug. He stooped with a creak and picked up the aunt's book. "Foreign name," he said, "propaganda: sticks out a mile. Now, don't you cut off anywhere, while I am now proceeding to search the house."

"Cut off?" I nearly said. "What do you take me for?" Alone, I sat down in the aunt's chair and dropped a few more fir cones into the extinct fire.

BETWEEN SUNSET
AND MOONRISE

R. H. Malden

First verified publication in *Nine Ghosts* (London, 1943)

Richard Henry Malden (1879–1951) was a prominent Church of England clergyman who served as the editor of *Crockford's Clerical Dictionary* from 1920–1944, and as the Dean of Wells from 1933–1950. Like the great ghost story writer M. R. James, he was educated at Eton and King's College Cambridge, and the two men shared a long friendship. 'Between Sunset and Moonrise' was published in Malden's 1943 story collection *Nine Ghosts*, which he dedicated to the memory of James who had died in 1936. However, Malden explains in his preface to the volume that this story, along with 'The Sundial' and 'The Blank Leaves', had already appeared in a Christmas parish magazine produced by the Leeds Parish Church. We have not been able to trace a copy of this so the original date of the tale is unknown—although it must have been sometime between 1909 and 1942, the period when Malden states all the stories were written.

D uring the early part of last year it fell to me to act as executor for an old friend. We had not seen much of each other of late, as he had been living in the west of England, and my own time had been fully occupied elsewhere. The time of our intimacy had been when he was vicar of a large parish not very far from Cambridge. I will call it Yaxholme, though that is not its name.

The place had seemed to suit him thoroughly. He had been on the best of terms with his parishioners, and with the few gentry of the neighbourhood. The church demanded a custodian of anti-quarian knowledge and artistic perception, and in these respects too my friend was particularly well qualified for his position. But a sudden nervous breakdown had compelled him to resign. The cause of it had always been a mystery to his friends, for he was barely middle-aged when it took place, and had been a man of robust health. His parish was neither particularly laborious nor harassing; and, as far as was known, he had no special private anxieties of any kind. But the collapse came with startling sud-denness, and was so severe that, for a time, his reason seemed to be in danger. Two years of rest and travel enabled him to lead a normal life again, but he was never the man he had been. He never revisited his old parish, or any of his friends in the county; and seemed to be ill at ease if conversation turned upon the part of England in which it lay. It was perhaps not unnatural that he should dislike the place which had cost him so much. But his friends could not but regard as childish the length to which he carried his aversion.

He had had a distinguished career at the University, and had kept up his intellectual interests in later life. But, except for an occasional *succès d'estime* in a learned periodical, he had published nothing. I was not without hope of finding something completed among his papers which would secure for him a permanent place in the world of learning. But in this I was disappointed. His literary remains were copious, and a striking testimony to the vigour and range of his intellect. But they were very fragmentary. There was nothing which could be made fit for publication, except one document which I should have preferred to suppress. But he had left particular instructions in his will that it was to be published when he had been dead for a year. Accordingly I subjoin it exactly as it left his hand. It was dated two years after he had left Yaxholme, and nearly five before his death. For reasons which will be apparent to the reader I make no comment of any kind upon it.

The solicitude which my friends have displayed during my illness has placed me under obligations which I cannot hope to repay. But I feel that I owe it to them to explain the real cause of my breakdown. I have never spoken of it to anyone, for, had I done so, it would have been impossible to avoid questions which I should not wish to be able to answer. Though I have only just reached middle-age I am sure that I have not many more years to live. And I am therefore confident that most of my friends will survive me, and be able to hear my explanation after my death.

Nothing but a lively sense of what I owe to them could have enabled me to undergo the pain of recalling the experience which I am now about to set down.

Yaxholme lies, as they will remember, upon the extreme edge of the Fen district. In shape it is a long oval, with a main line of railway cutting one end. The church and vicarage were close to the station, and round them lay a village containing nearly five-sixths of the entire population of the parish. On the other side of the line the Fen proper began, and stretched for many miles. Though it is now fertile corn land, much of it had been permanently under water within living memory, and would soon revert to its original condition if it were not for the pumping stations. In spite of these it is not unusual to see several hundred acres flooded in winter.

My own parish ran for nearly six miles, and I had therefore several scattered farms and cottages so far from the village that a visit to one of them took up the whole of a long afternoon. Most of them were not on any road, and could only be reached by means of droves. For the benefit of those who are not acquainted with the Fen I may explain that a drove is a very imperfect sketch of the idea of a road. It is bounded by hedges or dykes, so that the traveller cannot actually lose his way, but it offers no further assistance to his progress. The middle is simply a grass track, and as cattle have to be driven along it the mud is sometimes literally knee-deep in winter. In summer the light peaty soil rises in clouds of sable dust. In fact I seldom went down one without recalling Hesiod's unpatriotic description of his native village in Bœotia. "Bad in winter; intolerable in summer; good at no time."

At the far end of one of these lay a straggling group of half a dozen cottages, of which the most remote was inhabited by an old woman whom I will call Mrs. Vries. In some ways she was the most interesting of all my parishioners, and she was certainly the most perplexing. She was not a native, but had come to live there some twenty years before, and it was hard to see what had tempted a stranger to so unattractive a spot. It was the last house in the parish: her nearest neighbour was a quarter of a mile away, and she was fully three miles from a hard road or a shop. The house itself was not at all a good one. It had been unoccupied, I was told, for some years before she came to it, and she had found it in a semi-ruinous condition. Yet she had not been driven to seek a very cheap dwelling by poverty, as she had a good supply of furniture of very good quality, and, apparently, as much money as she required. She never gave the slightest hint as to where she had come from, or what her previous history had been. As far as was known she never wrote or received any letters. She must have been between fifty and sixty when she came. Her appearance was striking, as she was tall and thin, with an aquiline nose, and a pair of very brilliant dark eyes, and a quantity of hair—snow-white by the time I knew her. At one time she must have been handsome; but she had grown rather forbidding, and I used to think that, a couple of centuries before, she might have had some difficulty in proving that she was not a witch. Though her neighbours, not unnaturally, fought rather shy of her, her conversation showed that she was a clever woman who had at some time received a good deal of education, and had lived in cultivated surroundings. I used to think that she must have been an upper servant—most probably lady's maid—in a good house, and, despite the ring on her finger, suspected that the "Mrs." was brevet rank.

One New Year's Eve I thought it my duty to visit her. I had not seen her for some months, and a few days of frost had made the drove more passable than it had been for several weeks. But, in spite of her interesting personality, I always found that it required a considerable moral effort to call at her cottage. She was always civil, and expressed herself pleased to see me. But I could never get rid of the idea that she regarded civility to me in the light of an insurance, which might be claimed elsewhere. I always told myself that such thoughts were unfounded and unworthy, but I could never repress them altogether, and whenever I left her cottage it was with a strong feeling that I had no desire to see her again. I used, however, to say to myself that that was really due to personal pique (because I could never discover that she had any religion, nor could I instil any into her), and that the fault was therefore more mine than hers.

On this particular afternoon the prospect of seeing her seemed more than usually distasteful, and my disinclination increased curiously as I made my way along the drove. So strong did it become that if any reasonable excuse for turning back had presented itself I am afraid I should have seized it. However, none did: so I held on, comforting myself with the thought that I should begin the New Year with a comfortable sense of having discharged the most unpleasant of my regular duties in a conscientious fashion.

When I reached the cottage I was a little surprised at having to knock three times, and by hearing the sound of bolts cautiously drawn back. Presently the door opened and Mrs. Vries peered out. As soon as she saw who it was she made me very welcome as usual. But it was impossible not to feel that she had been more or less expecting some other visitor, whom she was not anxious to see. However, she volunteered no statement, and I thought it better to pretend to have noticed nothing unusual. On a table in the middle of the room lay a large book in which she had obviously been reading. I was surprised to see that it was a Bible, and that it lay open at the Book of Tobit. Seeing that I had noticed it Mrs. Vries told me—with a little hesitation, I thought—that she had been reading the story of Sarah and the fiend Asmodeus. Then—the ice once broken—she plied me almost fiercely with questions. "To what cause did I attribute Sarah's obsession, in the first instance?" "Did the efficacy of Tobias' remedy depend upon the fact that it had been prescribed by an angel?" and much more to the same effect. Naturally my answers were rather vague, and her good manners could not conceal her disappointment. She sat silent for a minute or two, while I looked at her—not, I must confess, without some alarm, for her manner had been very strange—and then said abruptly, "Well, will you have a cup of tea with me?" I assented gladly, for it was nearly half-past four, and it would take me nearly an hour and a half to get home. She took some time over the preparations and during the meal talked with even more fluency than usual. I could not help thinking that she was trying to make it last as long as possible.

Finally, at about half-past five, I got up and said that I must go, as I had a good many odds and ends awaiting me at home. I held out my hand, and as she took it said, "You must let me wish you a very happy New Year." She stared at me for a moment, and then broke into a harsh laugh, and said, "If wishes were horses beggars might ride. Still, I thank you for your good will. Goodbye." About thirty yards from her house there was an elbow in the drove. When I reached it I looked back and saw that she was still standing in her doorway, with her figure sharply silhouetted against the red glow of the kitchen fire. For one instant the play of shadow made it look as if there were another, taller, figure behind her, but the illusion passed directly. I waved my hand to her and turned the corner.

It was a fine, still, starlight night. I reflected that the moon would be up before I reached home, and my walk would not be unpleasant. I had naturally been rather puzzled by Mrs. Vries' behaviour, and decided that I must see her again before long, to ascertain whether, as seemed possible, her mind were giving way.

When I had passed the other cottages of the group I noticed that the stars were disappearing, and a thick white mist was rolling up. This did not trouble me. The drove now ran straight until it joined the high-road, and there was no turn into it on either side. I had therefore no chance of losing my way, and anyone who lives in the Fens is accustomed to fogs. It soon grew very thick, and I was conscious of the slightly creepy feeling which a thick fog very commonly inspires. I had been thinking of a variety of things, in somewhat desultory fashion, when suddenly—almost as if it had been whispered into my ear—a passage from the Book of Wisdom came into my mind and refused to be dislodged. My nerves were good then, and I had often walked up a lonely drove in a fog before; but still just at that moment I should have preferred to have recalled almost anything else. For this was the extract with which my memory was pleased to present me. "For neither did the dark recesses that held them guard them from fears, but sounds rushing down rang around them; and phantoms appeared, cheerless with unsmiling faces. And no force of fire prevailed to give them light, neither were the brightest flames of the stars strong enough to illumine that gloomy night. And in terror they deemed the things which they saw to be worse than that sight on which they could not gaze. And they lay helpless, made the sport of magic art." (*Wisdom* xvii. 4–6).

Suddenly I heard a loud snort, as of a beast, apparently at my elbow. Naturally I jumped and stood still for a moment to avoid blundering into a stray cow, but there was nothing there. The next moment I heard what sounded exactly like a low chuckle. This was more disconcerting: but common sense soon came to my aid. I told myself that the cow must have been on the other side of the hedge and not really so close as it had seemed to be. What I had taken for a chuckle must have been the squelching of her feet in a soft place. But I must confess that I did not find this explanation as convincing as I could have wished.

I plodded on, but soon began to feel unaccountably tired. I say "unaccountably" because I was a good walker and often covered much more ground than I had done that day.

I slackened my pace, but, as I was not out of breath, that did not relieve me. I felt as if I were wading through water up to my middle, or through very deep soft snow, and at last was fairly compelled to stop. By this time I was thoroughly uneasy, wondering what could be the matter with me. But as I had still nearly two miles to go there was nothing for it but to push on as best I might.

When I started again I saw that the fog seemed to be beginning to clear, though I could not feel a breath of air. But instead of thinning in the ordinary way it merely rolled back a little on either hand, producing an effect which I had never seen before. Along the sides of the drove lay two solid banks of white, with a narrow passage clear between them. This passage seemed to stretch for an interminable distance, and at the far end I "perceived" a number of figures. I say advisedly "perceived," rather than "saw," for I do not know whether I saw them in the ordinary sense of the word or not. That is to say—I did not know then, and have never been able to determine since, whether it was still dark. I only know that my power of vision seemed to be independent of light or darkness. I perceived the figures, as one sees the creatures of a dream, or the mental pictures which sometimes come when one is neither quite asleep nor awake.

They were advancing rapidly in orderly fashion, almost like a body of troops. The scene recalled very vividly a picture of the Israelites marching across the Red Sea between two perpendicular walls of water, in a set of Bible pictures which I had had as a child. I suppose that I had not thought of that picture for more than thirty years, but now it leapt into my mind, and I found myself saying aloud, "Yes: of course it must have been exactly like that. How glad I am to have seen it."

I suppose it was the interest of making the comparison that kept me from feeling the surprise which would otherwise have been occasioned by meeting a large number of people marching down a lonely drove after dark on a raw December evening.

At first I should have said there were thirty or forty in the party, but when they had drawn a little nearer they seemed to be not more than ten or a dozen strong. A moment later I saw to my surprise that they were reduced to five or six. The advancing figures seemed to be melting into one another, something after the fashion of dissolving views. Their speed and stature increased as their numbers diminished, suggesting that the survivors had, in some horrible fashion, absorbed the personality of their companions. Now there appeared to be only three, then one solitary figure of gigantic stature rushing down the drove towards me at a fearful pace, without a sound. As he came the mist closed behind him, so that his dark figure was thrown up against a solid background of white: much as mountain climbers are said sometimes to see their own shadows upon a bank of cloud. On and on he came, until at last he towered above me and I saw his face. It has come to me once or twice since in troubled dreams, and may come again. But I am thankful that I have never had any clear picture of it in my waking moments. If I had I should be afraid for my reason. I know that the impression which it produced upon me was that of intense malignity long baffled, and now at last within reach of its desire. I believe I screamed aloud. Then after a pause, which seemed to last for hours, he broke over me like a wave. There was a rushing and a streaming all round me, and I struck out with my hands as if I were swimming. The sensation was not unlike that of rising from a deep dive: there was the same feeling of pressure and suffocation, but in this case coupled with the most intense physical loathing. The only comparison which I can suggest is that I felt as a man might feel if he were buried under a heap of worms or toads.

Suddenly I seemed to be clear, and fell forward on my face. I am not sure whether I fainted or not, but I must have lain there for some minutes. When I picked myself up I felt a light breeze upon my forehead and the mist was clearing away as quickly as it had come. I saw the rim of the moon above the horizon, and my mysterious fatigue had disappeared. I hurried forward as quickly as I could without venturing to look behind me. I only wanted to get out of that abominable drove on to the high-road, where there were lights and other human beings. For I knew that what I had seen was a creature of darkness and waste places, and that among my fellows I should be safe. When I reached home my housekeeper looked at me oddly. Of course my clothes were muddy and disarranged, but I suspect that there was something else unusual in my appearance. I merely said that I had had a fall coming up a drove in the dark, and was not feeling particularly well. I avoided the looking-glass when I went to my room to change.

Coming downstairs I heard through the open kitchen door some scraps of conversation—or rather of a monologue delivered by my housekeeper—to the effect that no one ought to be about the droves after dark as much as I was, and that it was a providence that things were no worse. Her own mother's uncle had—it appeared—been down just such another drove on just such another night, forty-two years ago come next Christmas Eve. "They brought 'im 'ome on a barrow with both 'is eyes drawed down, and every drop of blood in 'is body turned. But 'e never would speak to what 'e see, and wild cats couldn't ha' scratched it out of him."

An inaudible remark from one of the maids was met with a long sniff, and the statement: "Girls seem to think they know everything nowadays." I spent the next day in bed, as besides the shock which I had received I had caught a bad cold. When I got up on the second I was not surprised to hear that Mrs. Vries had been found dead on the previous afternoon. I had hardly finished breakfast when I was told that the policeman, whose name was Winter, would be glad to see me.

It appeared that on New Year's morning a half-witted boy of seventeen, who lived at one of the other cottages down the drove, had come to him and said that Mrs. Vries was dead, and that he must come and enter her house. He declined to explain how he had come by the information: so at first Mr. Winter contented himself with pointing out that it was the first of January not of April. But the boy was so insistent that finally he went. When repeated knockings at Mrs. Vries' cottage produced no result he had felt justified in forcing the back-door. She was sitting in a large wooden armchair quite dead. She was leaning forward a little and her hands were clasping the arms so tightly that it proved to be a matter of some difficulty to unloose her fingers. In front of her was another chair, so close that if anyone had been sitting in it his knees must have touched those of the dead woman. The seat cushions were flattened down as if it had been occupied recently by a solid personage. The tea-things had not been cleared away, but the kitchen was perfectly clean and tidy. There was no suspicion of foul play, as all the doors and windows were securely fastened on the inside. Winter added that her face made him feel "quite sickish like," and that the house smelt very bad for all that it was so clean.

A post-mortem examination of the body showed that her heart was in a very bad state, and enabled the coroner's jury to return a verdict of "Death from Natural Causes." But the doctor told me privately that she must have had a shock of some kind. "In fact," he said, "if anyone ever died of fright, she did. But goodness knows what can have frightened her in her own kitchen unless it was her own conscience. But that is more in your line than mine."

He added that he had found the examination of the body peculiarly trying: though he could not, or would not, say why.

As I was the last person who had seen her alive, I attended the inquest, but gave only formal evidence of an unimportant character. I did not mention that the second armchair had stood in a corner of the room during my visit, and that I had not occupied it.

The boy was of course called and asked how he knew she was dead. But nothing satisfactory could be got from him. He said that there was right houses and there was wrong houses—not to say persons—and that "they" had been after her for a long time. When asked whom he meant by "they" he declined to explain, merely adding as a general statement that he could see further into a milestone than what some people could, for all they thought themselves so clever. His own family deposed that he had been absolutely silent, contrary to his usual custom, from tea-time on New Year's Eve to breakfast-time next day. Then he had suddenly announced that Mrs. Vries was dead; and ran out of the house before they could say anything to him. Accordingly he was dismissed, with a warning to the effect that persons who were disrespectful to Constituted Authorities always came to a bad end.

It naturally fell to me to conduct the funeral, as I could have given no reason for refusing her Christian burial. The coffin was not particularly weighty, but as it was being lowered into the grave the ropes supporting it parted, and it fell several feet with a thud. The shock dislodged a quantity of soil from the sides of the cavity, so that the coffin was completely covered before I had had time to say "Earth to earth: Ashes to ashes: Dust to dust."

Afterwards the sexton spoke to me apologetically about the occurrence. "I'm fair put about, Sir, about them ropes," he said. "Nothing o' that sort ever 'appened afore in my time. They was pretty nigh new too, and I thought they'd a done us for years. But just look 'ere, Sir." Here he showed two extraordinarily ravelled ends. "I never see a rope part like that afore. Almost looks as if it 'ad been scratted through by a big cat or somethink."

That night I was taken ill. When I was better my doctor said that rest and change of scene were imperative. I knew that I could never go down a drove alone by night again, so tendered my resignation to my Bishop. I hope that I have still a few years of usefulness before me: but I know that I can never be as if I had not seen what I have seen. Whether I met with my adventure through any fault of my own I cannot tell. But of one thing I am sure. There are powers of darkness which walk abroad in waste places: and that man is happy who has never had to face them.

If anyone who reads this should ever have a similar experience and should feel tempted to try to investigate it further, I commend to him the counsel of Jesus-ben-Sira.

"My son, seek not things that are too hard for thee: and search not out things that are above thy strength."

THE MIRROR IN ROOM 22

James Hadley Chase

First published in *The Royal Air Force Journal*, vol. 2, no. 12,
1 December 1944

James Hadley Chase was the main *nom de plume* used by René
Lodge Brabazon Raymond (24 December 1906—6 February
1985). He was one of the twentieth century's most successful and
prolific thriller writers, producing 90 books over his lifetime.
The son of a veterinary surgeon in the colonial Indian Army,
Raymond served in the Royal Air Force in the Second World
War, attaining the rank of Squadron Leader. Together with the
cartoonist David Langdon he edited the Royal Air Force Journal,
which contained stories, essays and articles written by service-
men as a morale-boosting activity. After the war, some of the
best stories were published in the collection *Slipstream* (1946).
Among them was 'The Mirror in Room 22'. In both publications
the story appeared under the author's real name, Squadron
Leader R. Raymond.

The wartime setting and Air Force banter of the tale gives a
different feel to the motif of the haunted mirror, which had previously appeared in E. F. Benson's 1915 story 'The Chippendale
Mirror' (adapted into part of the classic horror anthology film
Dead of Night in 1945).

There were not more than a half a dozen officers in the mess that Christmas Eve. The big comfortably furnished room, in spite of its gay decorations and blazing log fire, looked forlorn and a trifle bleak now that the usual noisy crowd was absent.

The six officers who, for one reason or another, were spending Christmas Day on the station, had finished dinner and arranged themselves in a semicircle before the fire. For once the radio was silent and the officers seemed content to watch the leaping flames in the brick grate and listen to the wind as it whistled round the massive old house which served as their mess.

Hopkins, red-faced with a big blond moustache, half wing and two gongs, remarked suddenly that he would be glad when the Squadron moved on.

The Adjutant, a trifle sleepy, reminded him that they had only just arrived.

"I don't like this station," Hopkins complained, stretching out his long legs and sliding farther down into his chair. "Of all the lonely, god-forsaken holes, this is it. Besides, this house depresses me."

"It depresses me, too," the equipment officer agreed from his corner. "Hark at that dog howling. He's been howling like that for the last two nights."

"I know." Hopkins unbuttoned his jacket and made himself more comfortable. "The brute kept me awake half the night."

"Why didn't you get up and kick it?" asked the Adjutant, who was of a practical turn of mind.

"I did get up, as a matter of fact, but though the howling seemed right under my window there was no sign of any dog."

The equipment officer grinned. "You're not trying to make us believe the mess is haunted, are you?"

"Don't be an ass," Hopkins returned shortly. "All the same, you must admit it is pretty creepy."

"I suppose all lonely old country houses are creepy," Meadowfield, the catering officer, remarked. "If you're afraid that a spook will jump out on you when you go to bed I don't mind convoying you along the corridor for a slight consideration."

There was a general laugh, in which Hopkins joined, and then came a pause in the conversation. The wind rose to a sudden crescendo, sending a flurry of twigs and small stones against the windows, for a moment drowning the ghoulish howling of the dog.

The Squadron C.O. came in with a wing commander who was a stranger to the men around the fire.

"Don't get up, chaps," the C.O. said. "This is Wing Commander Adams, the late C.O. of this station. He's spending Christmas with us."

There was a general movement to make room for the newcomers, and the six officers regarded the wing commander curiously. He was a big, fleshy, cheerful looking man with powerful shoulders and a bull neck.

"What a dreary place to spend Christmas in, sir," Hopkins said as soon as everyone had settled down again.

"I've known worse," the wing commander replied, filling his pipe, "but I must say I would have chosen a better spot, only we moved out so quickly—there was some work left undone here and I took the opportunity of slipping back to tie up the loose ends." He glanced suddenly towards the window. "The old dog's at it again, from the sound of that howling."

"Know who it belongs to, sir?" Meadowfield asked. "It's been howling like that for the past two nights."

"It always does at Christmas time, so I'm told," the wing commander replied. "Odd thing... the people in the village think it's a spook. No one has ever seen it and it's never heard except three days before Christmas."

"Hopkins here was trying to make us believe the mess is haunted," the equipment officer said with a sly grin. "You're not trying to make us think so too, are you, sir?"

"Well, no," the wing commander said slowly, "but something odd does happen here at Christmas time. When I first heard the story I thought it was an old wives' tale, but—well, these old houses—you hear strange things—" He lifted his shoulders and stared into the fire.

"You can't leave it like that," the C.O. said. "What story? Come on, Adams, you've aroused my curiosity."

"There's a popular tale in the village that the owner of this house committed suicide in his bedroom on Christmas Eve. It was about six years ago. He was in business in a big way and his partner swindled him. The business went smash and the news reached him on Christmas Eve. Not a very nice Christmas present, was it? Well, he cut his throat and they found him lying before the mirror in his bedroom. His dog disappeared that day and no one has seen sight of it since." He glanced towards the windows again. "They do say in the village that it howls every Christmas Eve outside the house, mourning for its master."

Meadowfield lit a cigarette. "Extraordinary the nonsense some villagers talk. By the way, what was the number of the room in which the old boy died?"

The wing commander looked round at the expectant faces. "Number Twenty-two," he said.

Hopkins made a little grimace. "That's my room," he said. "It's a jolly good room, too."

The wing commander nodded. "I know it is," he said. "As a matter of fact I used to have that room when I was on the station."

Hopkins grinned. "Then that's all right," he said. "You didn't notice anything peculiar about it, did you?"

"Nothing much," the wing commander returned, and once more lit his pipe.

"There was something?"

"Well, yes, but I guess it was due to one Scotch too many. It is easy to imagine things in the candlelight, especially after one has been talking about ghosts."

Hopkins leaned forward. "Did you see anything?"

"Perhaps I had better go on with my story," the wing commander said, "as it was told me last Christmas Eve. We had invited the village squire to dinner and he asked quite suddenly who was occupying Room Twenty-two—just as I asked you—and when I told him he gave me such a peculiar look that I took him aside and asked him if anything was the matter."

The Adjutant suddenly kicked the fire into a blaze. "It's getting chilly in here," he said, leaning forward to warm his hands. "Haven't you noticed it?"

"Go on, sir," Hopkins said; scowling at the adjutant. "What did he tell you?"

"It seems that the last two occupants of Room Twenty-two were found lying before the mirror with a razor in their hands and their throats cut. Both of them had occupied the room on successive Christmas Eves and since then the room had been kept locked. It was only when my squadron moved in that the room was opened again." He gave a chuckle.

"I thought it was absolute rot and told the squire so. As the evening went on I forgot all about it. The next morning I was on early duty and got up about six o'clock. It was dark and the room was lit only by flickering candles. The dog was howling as it is howling now but even then I did not think of those odd deaths that had taken place in the room. I began to shave before the mirror, watching as one does the reflection of my face. Then quite suddenly I had an extraordinary illusion. It could have been nothing but that, of course, but I found I was no longer looking at myself in the mirror, but at someone completely different. He was a man about my own build and his face was sad. He was apparently going through the motions of shaving himself with a glittering old fashioned razor, his motions coinciding with mine, and then suddenly he paused and deliberately drew the razor across his throat, smiling fixedly at me as he did so. I must admit the apparition gave me a nasty shock and I stepped away from the mirror, dropping my razor as I did so. When I looked again I only saw myself, looking, I must admit, a little green about the gills. It was, to say the least, a most disagreeable experience, but of course it was nothing but an illusion."

Hopkins stared at him. "It's a wonder you didn't cut yourself," he said seriously.

The wing commander nodded. "I use a safety razor," he said. "Otherwise I might have met with a serious accident especially if I used an old fashioned cut throat."

"Like I do," Hopkins said thoughtfully. "H'm—well, I think we all ought to have a drink after that."

Someone else started a ghost story, and after a little while Hopkins slipped from the ante room for a few minutes. When he returned he seemed somewhat relieved, and joined in the conversation in his usual noisy fashion.

Later the group of officers broke up, and the wing commander and the C.O. were the last to retire.

"You're fixed up all right?" the C.O. asked, as he was leaving to go to his own little cottage across the way.

The wing commander smiled. "I think so," he said, and beckoned to the airman who was waiting with his luggage. "Has Flight Lieutenant Hopkins moved his things from Room Twenty-two yet?"

The airmen nodded. "Yes, sir," he said. "It's all ready for you."

"Good, then take up my bag, will you?" The wing commander turned to the C.O. "I always believe in taking a little trouble to secure the best room, don't you? I wouldn't feel happy to stay here and not be in my old room. After all, Hopkins can have it back when I've gone. Good night. I hope my little story won't disturb your dreams. It certainly won't disturb mine." And still smiling, the wing commander followed the airman up the broad staircase.

AT THE CHALET LARTREC

Winston Graham

First published in *John Bull*, 31 May 1947

Winston Mawdsley Graham (1908–2003) was the adopted name of Winston Grime. He is best known today as the author of the immensely popular Poldark novels, which have twice been adapted for television. Grime was born in Manchester, the son of a prosperous commercial traveller. At the age of seventeen he moved with his family to the coastal town of Perranporth in Cornwall, where he would go on to live for 34 years. His childhood ambition to become a writer came to pass when his first novel, murder mystery *The House with the Stained Glass Windows*, was published in 1934—although he only earned £29 from the book. During the Second World War he served in the Coastguard, and then in 1945 the first Poldark novel, *Ross Poldark: a novel of Cornwall* was published. He went on to write eleven more books in the series, as well as a large number of thrillers and suspense novels—the latter including *Marnie* (1961), made into a film by Alfred Hitchcock in 1964.

This story, 'At the Chalet Lartrec', was published in the magazine *John Bull* in May 1947, at around the same time that the author formally changed his name by deed poll to Winston Mawdsley Graham (incorporating his mother's maiden name as a middle name). The editor of *John Bull* chose to present the story as a thriller rather than a ghost story, with the strapline 'The

Englishman had no sympathy to spare for informers. But he little realised that his advice might implicate him in a murder'. The tale speaks to the chaos and trauma of life in mainland Europe in the period directly after the war.

I was looking out for a village. Almost any sort of a village would have done if there was somewhere to find shelter. Things had been difficult this last hour.

The clouds were lowering all round and it was lonely up there, more than a mile high, with nothing human or alive anywhere, the great peaks jutting up into the clouds, the first fall of the winter long overdue and nothing but a complicated and unreliable piece of manmade machinery to get me down among the safe things again.

It isn't an easy road at the best of times. You go down and down but never seem to get much lower, round dozens of acute hairpin bends and through echoing tunnels with faint relics of daylight at the far end; and every time your tyres slither on the loose surface of the bends you look down thousands of feet into dark, pine-wooded valleys wreathed in cloud.

It's like some supreme artist's vision of Judgment; and, of course, if you slither too far the vision becomes an immediate fact.

In a mile or two it was snowing hard, and the car had no chains. It was nearly five o'clock and very soon I knew it would be quite dark. The snow was dry, powdery stuff, very fine and soft, and for a bit the strong wind blew it off the centre of the road, piling it in drifts in the sheltered corners.

I'd hoped to make Tirano and find an hotel there. It was no distance on the map, but today it just wasn't going to work out.

My screen wipers made heavy going of it and I had to stop and get out to clear them. Somewhere nearer at hand, just for a moment, I caught the musical note of a cow bell. But there was no other traveller, no other human being in sight. They might have all gone long ago to some more civilised land.

As darkness fell I had to stop again and again, because the wipers made streaks on the screen and it was easy to miss the turns of the road. I could see the paragraph in the papers: "The victim of a sudden storm in the Bernina Alps was Major Frederick Vane, aged thirty-three, a British officer attached to U.N.R.R.A., who unwisely attempted to cross from Switzerland into Italy by the Bernina Pass, which is normally closed to vehicular traffic at this time of the year. His car..."

And then I turned one more contorted bend and the head-lights showed up a few farm huts and the narrow cobbled street of a village.

It was a welcome sight. My arrival attracted some attention even on that bleak night. Faces were pressed to windows, and two or three people came out. No, they said, there was nowhere here to stay; nothing here, and doubts about Bagnolo, the next village, fifteen kilometres on. Beyond that was the frontier and then Tirano, but...

Then, quite suddenly, as a sort of afterthought, someone mentioned the Chalet Lartrec, and at once everyone agreed it might be worth trying at the Chalet Lartrec, which was off this road and only about a kilometre distant. The season being over, they said, Monsieur Lartrec would have closed down his house, but it was probable he would make an exception in a case like this.

I thanked them and drove on, thinking how often it was people forgot the important thing until nearly too late.

At a stone marked ten I turned as instructed down a narrow track barely wide enough for the car. It was now pitch dark, but I had a feeling that somewhere near the land fell away into further cloudy depths. I was glad when a gate showed up and beyond that a light. I left the car in the shelter of some tall poplar trees and picked my way across a field towards the light, carrying my smallest suitcase.

The chalet was a three-storeyed place, painted in some light colour, cream or green, and all the shutters were up except in the window that showed the light.

I knocked on the door and waited.

There was no reply. I knocked again, picturing the unknown Lartrec crouching ill-temperedly by his fire. But just then there was the rattle of bolts, and I retreated a step.

Light came out and I saw a woman.

"Er—Monsieur Lartrec?" I said.

She was staring at me. I think she was surprised at seeing a stranger.

"You wish to see my husband?" she said in a soft voice.

I explained. While I was speaking the wind was pushing at the door in her hand, and it blew flurries of snow into the hall. She was young, with a lot of dark hair and wide-set mild black eyes.

When I'd finished she said: "I regret, m'sieu, we can't put you up. We have no bed, no food. We are closed for the winter."

I pointed to the snow. "The first fall. The roads are treacherous. I can't go on until daybreak."

"We are closed, m'sieu."

"But in the circumstances..."

She hesitated. "I will see my husband."

She shut the door tight, leaving me on the step. I stamped my feet and thought unkind thoughts for about three minutes that seemed like ten. I reflected that Italian was not her language any more than it was mine. Then the door came open and this time a tall man stood there. He peered out at me in the dark.

Wearily I explained it all again, and again came the same refusal. I was not to be moved from the doorstep. We lapsed into French, and after a while, with a gesture of resignation, the man gave way.

"We will do what we can, m'sieu. I see that it is bad for you."

None of it had been very gracious, and I felt a bit uncomfortable. But once having capitulated, M. Lartrec and his wife did their best to put a good face on it. They gave me a pleasant bedroom and put a fire in it.

When I'd had a meal—it was spaghetti, stewed meat, and cheese, I remember, with a rather sour chianti—I began to feel a whole lot better towards them and to see their point of view.

Lartrec was about thirty-five, rather distinguished in an angular way, with great, bony shoulders which he would nervously shrug at times as if to rid them of some oppressive weight. Madam Lartrec was a little younger, with the good looks of her type and finely-shaped hands which had been spoiled with rough work. She might have been ill, for the fresh complexion that often goes with such looks was absent.

Their only servant seemed to be a half-wit boy with hair that fell in his eyes, who followed his mistress—in person or with his gaze—wherever she went. Of Lartrec he seemed afraid.

The house was big and empty and cold, and I sat by myself in the large bare hall with my feet on the only square of carpet and tried to read a three-day-old Swiss newspaper. But most of the time I listened to the howl of the wind and wondered if the roads would be quite blocked in the morning.

The fingers of the clock in the corner climbed up to nine, and when it had struck I rose to go to bed. There was no point in sitting miserably here when there was a fire burning upstairs. I wandered round, staring at the pictures, a view of Lake Maggiore, three small etchings of snow scenes and a photograph of a fat man with beady eyes, then I went through the dining-room to the kitchen door and tapped.

There was no answer for a moment, then the door was suddenly flung open and Lartrec looked at me.

"Yes?" he said.

Behind him I saw the tear-stained face of his wife.

"I thought I'd tell you," I said. "I'm going to bed."

"Certainly, m'sieu. Everything is to your liking?"

"Yes, thanks."

"Can you find your room again? I'll show you."

I said this wasn't necessary, but he took no notice and I followed him upstairs. In my bedroom we forced a few minutes' conversation, and then I said good night.

Lartrec stood in the door. He looked as if he didn't want to stay but couldn't pluck up the initiative to go. I could see that he was wavering between two impulses.

He suddenly said: "D'you think it strange, m'sieu, that my wife should be in tears?"

"I'm married myself," I said. He stiffened a little. Perhaps I'd touched his pride on a weak spot.

"It is not at all what you think. It is not domestic."

I said I was pleased to know it.

"You are in part responsible for this tonight."

I stared at him. "Sorry. I assure you I'll not stay here a minute longer than I can help."

"No, no. It's not just your coming, it is your coming tonight. That gave her a shock. It is the anniversary of something which happened twelve months ago." He looked at me doubtfully, seemed to be weighing me up. "You are from England?"

"Yes."

"I thought so. Helene, my wife, was in England for a few years when a baby. After the first war..."

"Really?"

There was a pause. We didn't seem to be getting far. "Cigarette?" I said.

He said: "In England you suffered from the wars, but not in the same way. In France it was a bad way..." He stopped.

"You are French?"

"Yes," he said, half reluctantly.

"Not Swiss French?"

"No. From the Loire."

I sat on the edge of the bed. "I was in Nantes two months ago."

Glancing at me suddenly he gave that nervous twitch to his shoulders. "It is my native town. It suffered much."

"Oh? I noticed very little damage."

"It is not the sort that shows. That is what I mean, m'sieu, as the difference between England and France. One is the damage to buildings, the other the damage to people."

"You mean—collaboration..."

"It is what corrodes a people: the civil strife, the suspicion, the *informing*. When I see France today I am amazed that she has come through so well."

"You were here during the war?" I ventured.

He came slowly into the room. "No. I was in the Loire for three years. Then after that I was in Germany."

"In Germany?"

"In a concentration camp."

"Oh," I said.

I lit his cigarette and studied his lean, dark face. I had seen these men before. They are of all nationalities. But once you have seen the signs in one man you recognise them in others. "You were in the underground movement?" I said.

"When war broke out, I was on a newspaper, in Paris," he said. "I served during that first winter, and in the following May was evacuated from Dunkirk by your navy and re-landed at Brest. When the final collapse came I made my way back to Nantes, where my family still lived, and took work. I met there old school friends, who were already in the resistance, and I naturally went the same way.

"Among them was my good friend Maurice, whose sister Helene had married Charles Ruol, a lawyer of the town. As very young children Helene and I had been sweethearts. While I was in Paris she had married Ruol, a man much older than herself. Coming back as I did then, I soon realised that I had lost my chance of happiness."

*

Lartrec frowned at his cigarette, moved to tap the ash into a tray on the table beside the bed. "But happiness—domestic happiness—was not much to be thought of in those days. I saw something of Helene, and once or twice we used Ruol and his knowledge of law. But he was not one of us, for we felt he hadn't the nerve to hold his tongue if things went wrong."

He stopped there and moved slowly over to the window to peer out. Even yet there was something furtive in his actions; the caution of the conspirator had been stamped on him for ever.

"It has stopped snowing," he said. "You will be able to continue your journey in the morning, m'sieu."

"And things went wrong?" I prompted.

"Things went very wrong. It was just before that that I discovered Helene loved me in return. The details don't matter: it was just an expression on her face when her brother told her about the bridge that was to be blown and my part in it. No more, but it was enough for me. You understand.

"Well, the bridge was blown, with great efficiency. It is interesting, watching the collapse of a bridge. The centre pillar seems to crumble like a sandstone cliff falling, and the two arches fold towards each other like a knife. There is a certain pleasure in destruction. We in France found it so—to our later cost.

"But that was one of the early ones, and, since it was a very useful bridge, the Germans were annoyed. We did not mind that—until, two mornings later, we were all arrested."

Lartrec came back from the window. I was leaning back against the bed rail watching him and smoking.

"It was the Germans who told me that Ruol had informed on us. It amused them, knowing I should never go back. Maurice and two others they shot the next morning. For reasons of their own they spared my life, and I and the remaining six were sent into Germany, where we stayed till the end of the war..."

"I'm sorry," I said. "I know just a little of what that means."

"When it was over," he said, "the others were all dead, but not I. I walked three or four hundred miles; it took me nearly two months to reach Nantes. I had one thought; but when I got there Ruol had gone—and with him Helene. He had made his escape. Helene, of course, knew nothing of his betrayals, though she began to suspect something when he chose to leave his native town.

"I searched but found nothing. It became my whole life. You see, there were two motives urging me on: revenge and love. I don't know which was the stronger. I had two pictures before me always."

"And... you found them?"

His shadow gave a jerk on the wall as he hitched his shoulders. "It was twelve months ago, m'sieu. You understand. He had money in Switzerland and had settled here. He had changed his name; that does not matter. In the afternoon I came to this chalet just as it was going dark. I was not sure even then, not at all sure.

"I came up to it, but did not knock on the door as you knocked on the door. Instead, I crept round to the kitchen and looked in at the window. They were *there*, unchanged it seemed, Helene putting food on his plate, and Ruol bending greedily to eat it. He was as fat as a pig, m'sieu, and had small eyes, old eyes, m'sieu, with short, pale lids."

Suddenly I was reminded of the photograph of the fat man in the hall. Lartrec had paused. Up to now he had spoken with detachment, but he could no longer keep the feeling out of his voice.

I said: "Don't you think you've told me enough?"

He said: "I went round to the front then and knocked. The boy came, the idiot boy. I pushed past him and went into the kitchen, shutting the boy out. They looked at me as if frozen suddenly where they sat. It was going dusk but they hadn't lit the lamp.

"I said to Ruol: 'There are ten of us here, Ruol, all of that first batch. Maurice, and Bernard and Rene, who were shot, and Boulanger who died of starvation, and Moreau who was killed by the hounds...' I went on to the end, and all the time he sat there with the stain of food on the corner of his mouth.

"When I'd finished I looked at Helene. And then I heard him move. He'd jumped—so quick for a fat man—to a drawer, and I went after him. As he turned with a revolver I hit him across the head with the iron poker."

Lartrec dropped his smouldering cigarette in the ash tray.

"He was dead within five minutes. I felt no sorrow or sense of guilt. It was what I had come for. But we had to face the outcome. It seemed the only way would be to escape while there was still time. In France I might be safe, and Helene could come with me.

"But it was Helene who suggested another way. No one knew of my presence in the neighbourhood. If I were to carry the body to the bottom of the cellar steps and leave it in the right position it might appear that he had fallen and caught his head on the iron stairs.

"The idiot boy was devoted to Helene and would say anything she told him. Suppose I went away again as I had come. There was no one in the house strong enough to inflict such a blow. And he was a heavy man and the fall down the steps would be great.

240

"There was danger, of course; but the other way there was the other danger, of extradition proceedings and of Helene being involved as an accessory. The way she suggested, if it worked, I would not be a hunted man. In a few months I could come to this district and meet Helene and marry her with no fear of suspicion. Those were the alternatives, m'sieu. What would you have done?"

My own cigarette was finished, too, and I shifted uncomfortably on the bed.

"My opinion now won't help much, will it. I think you were lucky to get away with it. And you won't get away with it much longer if you start telling the story to perfect strangers."

"You are the first and will be the last. It was something... it came out. I can rely on your discretion?"

"Yes," I said. Travelling over the turbulent, sickly Europe of today, one becomes inured to violence. A collaborator more or less... "Is your idiot boy a Catholic?"

"Yes."

"Then I think I should have been afraid of your wife's scheme for three reasons. I should have been afraid of the boy telling what he knew in confession. I should have been afraid of the police finding something inconsistent with her story of a fall. And I should have preferred the risk of trying to escape to France, where, I imagine, there are plenty to give shelter to such crimes as yours. But I wish you hadn't told me this."

"And the murder?" said Lartrec. "As an Englishman would you have done different?"

"No," I said. "Probably not."

"Thank you," he said.

There was silence. Outside, the wind was thundering through the valley.

"I, too, am a Catholic," he said. "The instinct of confession is strong in me. But in the *right* way this can never come out. I think it is my excuse for troubling you. That and the anniversary. Your coming tonight... We could not get over that."

I thought of the men I had seen in the hospital in Austria. "I shouldn't let your conscience get too active," I said. "Ruol deserved what he got. But I think you have made a mistake in continuing to live here. In this house you'll never be quite free."

Downstairs in the hall the clock was striking ten. It seemed to bring him back to his duties as host. He smiled a little, courteously.

"What time would monsieur wish to be knocked in the morning?"

I was a long time dropping off to sleep. My leg was aching, and whichever way I moved it wouldn't stop. And I thought of Lartrec's story. Presently I got up and bolted the door.

I woke at seven and the wind had dropped. I was almost afraid to look out, but to my joy no snow had fallen. The roads would be safe enough.

I thought of Lartrec's story and wondered if he would refer to it again. He would probably be bitterly repenting the confidences of the night. Inured to violence or not, I should be glad to be on my way. It is not pleasant to be guest to a murderer whose safety now rests on your silence.

I'd not ordered breakfast till nine, but I washed and shaved in luke-warm water and stuffed my things into my bag. It was now getting on for eight, and I thought I'd go out to inspect the car. I could hear someone chopping wood, but that was the only movement below so far.

It's always vaguely depressing to be the only person in an hotel, and the place looked shabby in the morning light. The first thing I saw in the hall were my other two bags. It was thoughtful of Lartrec to have brought them in.

The shutters were closed in the dining-room, and the hall was untidy and desolate. I opened the front door and stepped out. The sun was bright now but slightly hazy, and I made for the tall poplar trees. When I got to them I stopped. The car was no longer there.

I looked round, rejecting unpleasant thoughts. The snow was so dry that it had blown away the track marks and I thought perhaps Lartrec had moved the car into one of the sheds for protection. Still, he should have told me.

I went back.

"Lartrec!" I called in the hall.

"Lartrec!" came the echo upstairs.

"Lartrec!" I called in the dining-room.

They were probably all at the back. Someone was chopping wood again.

I went into the kitchen. The remains of my supper were on the table. It was not chopping but knocking. It came from the small larder. I pulled back the bolt.

The half-wit boy stared at me stupidly. His hair was a damp mat on his forehead. He burst into tears and began to gabble.

I took him and shook him.

"Where is your mistress, boy?"

He stared at me in fright, owlishly.

"Gone, signor," he whispered at last.

"Gone? Gone where?"

"I do not know, signor."

"And Monsieur Lartrec? Has he gone, too?"

"No, signor, he is still here."

"Then take me to him."

"No, signor. I am afraid."

"Don't be a fool. I'll not let him hurt you."

The tears running down to his chin, the boy faltered across the kitchen to another door, which I opened. There were steps leading down and a smell of old wine. He tried to run then, but I stopped him and lit a lamp and pushed him down the steps before me.

It was a long flight and half way down the boy clung to the side and wouldn't move at all. I peered past him and saw something lying at the bottom. I went down then and pulled at a tweed-clad shoulder. A stranger, yet it was a familiar face: a fat man with staring eyes and blood dried on his forehead.

I stepped back and nearly upset the lamp. The boy hadn't moved.

"This—this is not Monsieur Lartrec," I said.

"Yes, signor; that is Monsieur Lartrec."

There was a silence in the cellar.

"But," I said, "this... all this... happened twelve months ago."

"No, signor," said the boy. "Last evening."

Then the strength came back to his limbs and, with the echoes shaking among the wine vats, he went swarming up the steps and through the empty house out into the winter sunlight beyond.

ACCOUNT RENDERED

W. F. Harvey

First published in *The Arm of Mrs. Egan and Other Stories* (1951)

William Fryer Harvey (1885–1937) was born in Leeds, West Yorkshire into a well-to-do Quaker family, and had a very happy childhood. Harvey qualified as a doctor and when the First World War broke out he joined the Friends' Ambulance Unit, going first to Flanders, before transferring to the Royal Navy and serving as surgeon-lieutenant. On 28 June 1918 two British torpedo boat destroyers collided. Harvey was sent in to see what could be done for the injured sailors. He freed one man from the wreckage by amputating his arm, whilst breathing in poisonous fumes from the nearby boiler room. Harvey was awarded the Albert Medal for Gallantry but his lungs were permanently damaged and he suffered ill health for the rest of his life. He wrote many short stories during repeated periods of recuperation.

Harvey died in 1937 aged only 52, having never recovered from the lung damage he sustained in the war. In 1946 his story 'The Beast with Five Fingers' was made into a successful film starring Peter Lorre. Its popularity led to a surge of interest in the writer's work, and in 1951 a collection of previously unseen tales was published under the title *The Arm of Mrs. Egan and Other Stories*. 'Account Rendered', featuring a doctor and a question of medical ethics, was among them.

"**M**edical ethics," said my uncle, "is a very curious subject. If my plate were four times its present size, or if the lettering were in scarlet instead of black, my conduct might be judged unethical. I remember once a distinguished surgeon getting hot and bothered over what he called the ethical principle involved if qualified chiropodists were permitted to treat bunions. Any condition, he maintained, involving any structure below the level of the true skin was outside their province. It was a deep, not a superficial question, and a question of principle."

He took down the tobacco jar from the mantelpiece and, though it was eight o'clock in the evening, filled his first pipe of the day.

"Here's a case in point," he went on. "A man came to me this morning with a request, a very queer request. He seemed rather surprised that I did not immediately accede to it in view of the fee he offered. He wanted me to give him an anaesthetic the day after tomorrow at twelve o'clock at night."

"They chose a most inconvenient hour for the operation," I said.

"But there wasn't to be an operation. That was the curious thing. All he wanted was to be fully anaesthetised between 11:45 and 12:15. As soon as I had recovered from my natural astonishment I put as tactfully as I could some of the difficulties which my caller had overlooked. I reminded him that I know nothing whatever about him. For all I knew he might be contemplating suicide. At 11:30 he might swallow a dangerous drug and then when he expired half an hour later I should have been responsible for a death under anaesthetic.

"Mr. Tolson (I'm not guilty of unethical conduct in telling you his name because you, too, may be concerned in the matter) rather naturally took offence at this idea. He explained to me that he could produce unimpeachable references to his character, that his health was excellent, and that he was perfectly prepared to submit to a rigorous medical examination. The reason for his request, which he now admitted, might appear strange, was that he was engaged upon a piece of research, partly mathematical, partly psychological, into what might be called the relation of space-time and the unconscious.

"He went off the deep end and I soon gave up all attempts to follow him. The gist of the matter was that he wished to verify certain scientific conclusions he had come to by recording his impressions before and after being anaesthetised. That put a rather different light on things. I am not prepared to give an anaesthetic to any Tom, Dick, or Harry who thinks that all he has got to do is stop me and buy one. On the other hand, there is no reason why I should not co-operate in a piece of research. Tolson evidently saw that I was hesitating and produced from his pocket a telegram. He told me that he had previously arranged with the honorary anaesthetist to the County Hospital at Wilchester to do the job on the day and hour mentioned, but only that morning a wire had come to say that he was ill. He showed it to me. I have met Dr. Hancock once or twice. He is a shrewd man and I told myself that if he was satisfied with Tolson's bona fides there was no reason why I should not be. The matter finally ended like this. I told Tolson that I would give him a definite answer tomorrow. If I then decided to do his job of work, I should give him a thorough overhaul and I should bring my niece, a trained nurse, along with me. I explained to him that the after-effects of an anaesthetic are sometimes unpleasant, but I really wanted to have you there to safeguard my interests as much as his. He hummed and hawed a bit but finally agreed, and there the matter rests. That is our little problem in medical ethics. What are we going to do about it?"

I think my uncle had already made up his mind, but he is an old bachelor who likes to have the support of his womenfolk.

"I should certainly anaesthetise Mr. Tolson," I said.

All this happened many years ago. I was young and inexperienced. It is hardly to be wondered at that I gave the wrong answer. I see now that my uncle would have been probably better advised to have nothing to do with Mr. Tolson, but his sense of curiosity was very strongly developed—that was partly what made him so good a doctor—and he liked his own way—that was partly what had kept him a bachelor.

At a quarter past eleven on 17th December, my uncle's car stopped outside the door of Lebanon Lodge, a square, old-fashioned residence that stood out white behind the solitary cedar that had given to the house its name. We were not kept long waiting. Hardly had the bell ceased ringing when the door was opened by Mr. Tolson himself. He was a man of nearer fifty than forty, short and wiry in build, dark hair tinged with grey, and dark, restless-looking eyes. He was wearing a dressing gown.

"I'm glad to see you, doctor," he said. "I was afraid you might be late. I have everything ready, so we can go straight upstairs. I told my old housekeeper to go off to bed an hour ago, so we shall be quite undisturbed."

The room on the first floor into which he led us had almost as much the appearance of a study as of a bedroom. It was lined with books. At the opposite end from the bed a fire was burning brightly. Heavy crimson curtains were drawn across the bow windows that looked out on to the cedar, while a *portière* of the same colour screened the door.

My uncle wasted no time. He had overhauled his patient on the previous day and had instructed him as to what preparations he should make. By the time the hands of the clock on the mantelpiece pointed to a quarter to twelve Mr. Tolson was completely unconscious.

"There's this at least to be said," remarked my uncle, "the man knows how to take an anaesthetic."

Outside the night was still. The only sound in the room was the deep, regular breathing of the man in the bed and the ticking of the clock. It struck twelve. And then, about five minutes past the hour a curious thing happened. Without any warning the door opened and an old man looked into the room. I could only see his head and shoulders. He wore a little black skull-cap, and as he stood there, his lean scraggy neck peering forward, his toothless mouth half open, he gave me the impression of a timid but inquisitive tortoise slowly intruding itself into a hostile world.

"Ah, you are busy, Charles," he said. "You can't see me now. But there is no hurry, no need for hurry at all. Another time will do." Then he closed the door as quietly as he had opened it and disappeared.

"Who the devil was that?" said my uncle. "There, hold his legs; he's not so deeply under as I thought he was. Steady now, my hearties. That's better," as the deep, regular breathing began again. "Who was that, Margaret? I wasn't watching. The housekeeper?"

"It may have been the housekeeper's husband," I said. "He seemed quite at home. We'll ask Mr. Tolson when he comes round."

At a quarter past twelve my uncle stopped the anaesthetic and began to put his things together. And then in the hall below we heard the telephone ring. No one seemed to answer the bell; the housekeeper, or whoever it was who had looked into the room a quarter of an hour before, must either have been very deaf or have gone to bed.

"I'll go," said my uncle. "It's probably a emergency call for me. My luck's out tonight."

He was back again in a few minutes.

"Yes," he said, "that young ass Jerry Polegate has collided with a lamp-post again and will probably need a couple of stitches. He's round at the surgery. The only comfort is that the motor-bicycle is a complete wreck. What are we to do with you, my dear? Do you mind being left alone here for an hour or so? Of course Tolson is all right, but I should be easier in my mind if there was someone with him. I'll call for you as soon as I have finished branding that young road-hog."

Naturally, I agreed. Tolson was sleeping quietly, the fire was burning brightly. I drew up a chair and settled down to read. The book I took down from the shelf was a beautifully bound copy of *John Buncle*. The fly-leaf was inscribed "Ex-libris Jarvis Effington." The name had a slightly familiar ring and I tried in vain to place it, until I remembered that I had once gathered primroses at a place called Effington in Kent. The book itself, however, was as unfamiliar as it was delightful and I read on, regardless of the time.

As the clock struck one Mr. Tolson stirred uneasily and began to mutter to himself. A little later he opened his eyes.

"Where am I?" he asked. "Where has he gone to?"

"Dr. Parkinson has been called out to a case," I replied. "He will be back very soon."

"It's all over then," he said, "it's all safely over," and he closed his eyes with a weary sigh of satisfaction, only to open them a few minutes later.

"Tell me," he said, "did anything happen when I was under?"

"You took the anaesthetic splendidly. The only thing that surprised us was when an old man came up the stairs a little after twelve and looked into the room without knocking. I think he, too, was surprised to see us and said something about seeing you another time."

Mr. Tolson glanced at me in a curious way. I saw fear, dismay, and a suggestion of something else, of wily satisfaction that gave one the impression that he was well pleased to have escaped from a tiresome visitor.

"That would be my old uncle," he said at last. "He ought to have been in bed hours ago."

"That's where *my* uncle ought to have been," I thought to myself, but I had not very long to wait before I heard his steps again on the stairs.

"Sorry to run off and leave you like that, Mr. Tolson," he said as he came into the room. "You see, there is no end to a doctor's day. You will be going off to sleep now, I expect. Is there anything I can do for you before we go?"

Apparently there was nothing. Tolson thanked him for his services and handed him an envelope from the table by his bedside.

"I won't keep you waiting," he said, with a rather attractive smile, "not even for your fee. I think you will find it is right. Again many thanks, and to you, too, nurse."

As we got into the car we could see that the lights were still burning in Mr. Tolson's room in Lebanon Lodge.

"A rum sort of cove," my uncle remarked. "He is probably going to write up his notes on what I hope will have proved a satisfactory experiment."

Some three years later I was nursing a doctor in the midlands. Clergymen and doctors are, in my experience, far the most unsatisfactory patients to deal with, but Dr. Gilkes was an exception. He was an excellent talker—his fractured thigh was no impediment—and he had knocked about all over the world. Something or other had made me tell him about the strange case of the man who wanted to be anaesthetised. He listened with, I thought, unusual interest and then he burst out laughing.

"That's a funny thing," he said. "I've met Mr. Tolson. At least, I think I have, though Drewit was the name he went by. How long ago would it be? Five years, perhaps. At any rate, I hadn't started in general practice. I was ship's surgeon in the *Valumeria*, a venerable survivor of pre-war days that used to make the trip to Australia by way of the Cape. Four days out from Hobart something went wrong with the propeller, and though things were patched up—the weather, thank goodness, was fine—it meant our proceeding in whatever was the nautical equivalent of bottom gear and we were three days behind our schedule. We all put as cheerful a face on things as we could with the exception of this

Drewit fellow, who seemed to think that the fates had personally insulted him. He had, it appeared, a most important engagement in Hobart. We did our best to console him, partly because a man with a most important engagement in sleepy Tas (that's Tasmania, you know) is a rare bird, but I never knew its actual nature until the day before we were due in port. No, it wasn't time-space and its relation to the psychology of the unconscious. The dope he dealt out to me had to do with telepathy. Drewit, it seemed, was writing a treatise on telepathy which was to include the results of some entirely new experiments. He and a friend in England had arranged to be put under an anaesthetic at the same hour. A third friend—what curious friends some people do seem to have!—was then to broadcast on the appropriate brain wave-length and the other two, on coming round, would record their impressions. You see the idea? Telepathy and the unconscious mind. Unmitigated nonsense!

"Well, Drewit had fixed everything up with a doctor he knew in Hobart, when this unforeseen delay occurred. He was most anxious that I should do the job. Anxious, indeed, is hardly the word to describe his dithering importunity. I didn't know what to do, but when he produced a letter from his friend in England to convince me of his bona fides and mentioned a twenty-guinea fee without turning a hair, I hesitated no longer. I was human and I was stony broke.

"The time Drewit had chosen for his experiment, between 11:45 and 12:15 at night, suited me well, since it was unlikely that we should be disturbed. Some of the bright young sparks among the passengers had fixed up a fancy-dress ball. I slipped away soon after eleven and got my things ready. I had rather expected that Drewit would have been nervous. Not a bit of it. When I examined his heart he took it as a matter of ordinary routine, and when I started to anaesthetise him he made not the slightest effort to resist, but went on breathing away as if he enjoyed it. It was the easiest twenty guineas that I had ever earned or was likely to earn. I could feel myself in Harley Street. The only thing that happened was that when I was half way through, the door of the cabin opened and someone popped in his head. Then, seeing what was going on he apologised, said something about looking in again later, and withdrew. I thought at the time it was Dow, the third engineer, dressed up as one of our ancestors. I taxed him with it next day, but he said the only time he had worn fancy dress was at his sister's wedding, when he had a gardenia in his buttonhole. He had, moreover, an alibi. At the time I mentioned it, it appeared that he was endeavouring to point out the glories of the Southern Cross—they need a lot of searching—to a girl from Dulwich.

"Of course I never heard of Drewit again. You are the first person I've met who ever came across him, because obviously it must be the same man masquerading under another name. I suppose you don't remember the date?"

"It was the seventeenth of December," I said, "the day before my uncle's birthday."

Dr. Gilkes asked me to hand him his diary.

"I'll make a note of that," he said. "It would be about the middle of December that we got to Hobart. I can't be sure of the actual day, but I'll look it up as soon as I'm on my pins again. I should dearly like to know what has happened to Drewit, if he still indulges in this annual stunt and why he does it. It makes a good story, but we want the closing chapter. There's one thing that's certain. The man's medical attendants are pretty certain to remember him; it is the sort of case, too, about which they might easily talk. If I hear anything that will throw light on our mysterious patient, I will let you know, and I expect you to do the same to me."

Dr. Gilkes, I am glad to say, made an excellent recovery from his accident. I did not expect to hear from him again, and the letter I received two years later came as a surprise.

"I haven't forgotten my promise," he wrote, "to let you know if anything more turned up about our friend Tolson-Drewit. Three weeks ago I was staying with a doctor, an old University College man, who told me a story almost precisely similar to the one we could tell. It happened on the same date in December, and the patient was evidently the same, though on this occasion he passed under the name of Royce. He persuaded my friend into giving him an anaesthetic by propounding an ingenious theory about the nature of memory. Soon after twelve there was the usual interruption, but Handysides had kept his patient only very lightly under, and when the door opened and the old fellow poked his head in, it was all he could do to hold Drewit down. When he came round he was extremely indignant and declared that he had been conscious half the time, and poor old Handysides had to be content with only ten guineas. As he is a Scotsman he naturally remembers the incident very well. That's the story in brief; the same in all the principal features as ours. If I ever hear more, I'll let you know."

Then there was silence for four years, but I was to hear once more from Dr. Gilkes.

"I have just come across this extract," he wrote, "from a three months' old copy of a local paper. I wonder if it is the sort of explanation that satisfies you. If you care to do so, you will be able to look up the case in greater detail by consulting the newspaper files. To me it seems that Drewit was for once speaking the truth when he told my friend on the last occasion on which we heard of him that he was investigating the nature of memory. Reading between the lines I can guess who and what it was he wanted to forget."

And this was the cutting:

SUDDEN DEATH OF A WADDISLOW VISITOR
Mystery of a famous poisoning case recalled

On Monday last an inquest was held at the Crown Inn, Waddislow, upon the body of Mr. Charles Spenser Newcombe, who had for some weeks been a resident in the district. Mr. Newcombe, who was a victim of insomnia, was found dead in his bedroom. Medical evidence showed that the deceased died from an overdose of laudanum. A curious feature of the case was brought forward in Dr. Edward's evidence. He said that he had been attending the deceased gentleman for the last ten days, and had arranged at his express desire to administer a general anaesthetic on the night of his death, but that owing to his being called away in connection with a motor accident, he had been unable to fulfil his engagement.

The deceased gentleman, who was travelling under the name of Fuller, came prominently before the public in the early nineties in what was known as the Sulphonal Case. He acted as librarian and confidential secretary to the eccentric Sir Jarvis Effington, who died under curious circumstances in Naples from an overdose of that drug, leaving his entire property to Mr. Newcombe. The will was contested by the family, and many of the leading counsel of the day appeared in the case. The jury's decision in favour of the defendant caused general surprise in view of the comments of the presiding judge.

Portraits of Sir Jarvis Effington and Mr. Newcombe will be found on another page.

Dr. Gilkes had cut out the two portraits. Tolson's face I recognised at once. The other, though I had seen it for only a moment on a night more years ago than I cared to remember, I recognised too. There were the dark eyes, the long scraggy neck, the thin lips, mocking and cruel. I can well believe that to one man at least it would be a face to forget.

THE WILD WOOD

Mildred Clingerman

First published in *The Magazine of Fantasy and Science Fiction*, January 1957

Mildred Clingerman, nee McElroy (1918–1997), was born in Oklahoma, moving to Arizona when she was a child. She attended the University of Arizona, and married in 1937. She was not a full-time author but contributed a number of stories to *The Magazine of Fantasy and Science Fiction*, starting in 1952 with 'Minister without Portfolio'. The magazine's editor, Anthony Boucher, rated her work highly, republishing the Christmas horror story 'The Wild Wood' (which had first appeared in January 1957) in the seventh volume of *The Best from Fantasy and Science Fiction* (1958), and even dedicating the collection to Clingerman as the 'most serendipitous of discoveries'.

Clingerman was a great fan of Kenneth Grahame, and collected editions of his works. The name of this story, 'The Wild Wood' recalls the title of chapter three of *The Wind in the Willows* (1908), in which Mole ventures into the wood despite warnings, and begins to see malevolent faces and hear sinister footsteps among the darkening trees.

'The Wild Wood', like several others of Clingerman's stories (notably 'A Red Heart and Blue Roses') depicts the terror and dread experienced by a powerless married woman at the mercy of a predatory man. The domestic horror of a seemingly wholesome 1950s scene can be likened to the work of Clingerman's contemporary, Shirley Jackson.

I t seemed to Margaret Abbott that her children, as they grew older, clung more and more jealously to the family Christmas traditions. Her casual suggestion that, just this once, they try something new in the way of a Christmas tree met with such teenage scorn and genuine alarm that Margaret hastily abandoned the idea. She found it wryly amusing that the body of ritual she herself had built painstakingly through the years should now have achieved sacrosanctity. Once again, then, she would have to endure the secret malaise of shopping for the tree at Cravolini's Christmas Tree Headquarters. She tried to comfort herself with the thought that one wretchedly disquieting hour every year was not too much to pay for her children's happiness. After all, the episode always came far enough in advance of Christmas so that it never *quite* spoiled the great day for her.

Buying the tree at Cravolini's began the year Bonnie was four. Bruce had been only a toddler, fat and wriggling, and so difficult for Margaret to carry that Don had finally loaded Margaret with the packages and perched his son on his shoulder. Margaret remembered that night clearly. All day the Abbotts had promised Bonnie that when evening came, when all the shop lights blazed inside the fairy-tale windows, the four of them would stroll the crowded streets, stopping or moving on at Bonnie's command. At some point along the way, the parents privately assured each other, Bonnie would grow tired and fretful but unwilling to relinquish the dazzling street and her moment of power. That would be the time to allow her to choose the all-important tree, which must then, of course, be carried to their car in triumph with Bonnie as valiant, proud helper. Once she had been lured to the car it would be simple to hurry her homeward and to bed. The fragrant green mystery of the tree, sharing their long ride home, would insure her sleepiness and contentment.

As it turned out (why hadn't they foreseen it?), the child showed no sign of fatigue that evening other than her captious rejection of every Christmas tree pointed out to her. Margaret, whose feet and back ached with Bruce's weight, swallowed her impatience and shook out yet another small tree and twirled its dark bushiness before Bonnie's cool, measuring gaze.

"No," Bonnie said. "It's too little. Daddy, let's go that way." She pointed down one of the darker streets, leading to the area of pawnshops and narrow little cubbyholes that displayed cheap jewellery. These, in turn, verged on the ugly blocks that held credit clothiers, shoe repair shops, and empty, boarded-up buildings where refuse gathered ankle-deep in the entrance ways.

"I won't," Margaret said. "This is silly. What's the matter with this tree, Bonnie? It isn't so small. We certainly aren't going to wander off down there. I assure you, they don't *have* Christmas trees on that street, do they, Don?"

Don Abbott shook his head, but he was smiling down at his daughter, allowing her to drag him to the street crossing.

Like a damn, lumbering St. Bernard dog, Margaret thought, *towed along by a simpering cheeild*. She stared after her husband and child as if they were strangers. They were waiting for her at the corner, Don, with the uneasy, sheepish look of a man who knows his wife is angry but unlikely to make a scene. Bonnie was still tugging at his hand, flashing sweet, smug little smiles at her mother. Margaret dropped the unfurled tree with a furious, open-fingered gesture, shifted Bruce so that he rode on one hip, and joined them.

The traffic light changed and they all crossed together. Don slowed and turned a propitiating face to his wife. "You all right, hon? Here, you carry the packages and I'll take Bruce. If you want to, you could go sit in the car. Bonnie and I, we'll just check down this street a little way to make sure... She says they've got some big trees someplace down here." He looked doubtfully down at his daughter then. "Are you sure, Bonnie? How do you know?"

"I saw them. Come on, Daddy."

"Probably she *did* see some," Don said. "Maybe last week when we drove through town. You know, kids see things we don't notice. Lord, with traffic the way it is, who's got time to see anything? And besides, Margaret, you said she could pick the tree. You said it was time to start building traditions, so the kids would have... uh... security and all that. Seems to me the tree won't mean much to her if we make her take the one we choose. Anyway, that's the way I figure it."

Margaret moved close to him and took his arm, squeezing it to show both her forgiveness and apology. Don smiled down at her and Margaret's whole body warmed. For a long moment she allowed her eyes to challenge his with the increased moisture and blood-heat that he called "smoky," and which denoted for both of them her frank desire. He stared back at her with alerted male tension, and then consciously relaxed.

"Well, not right here and now," he said. "See me later."

Margaret, reassured, skipped a few steps. This delighted the children. The four of them were laughing, then, when they found themselves in front of the derelict store that housed Cravolini's Christmas Tree Headquarters.

Perhaps it was their gaiety, that first year, that made Cravolini's such a pleasant memory for Don and the children. For the first few minutes Margaret, too, had found the dim, barny place charming. It held a bewildering forest of upright trees, aisles and aisles of them, and the odour of fir and spruce and pine was a tingling pleasure to the senses. The floor was covered with damp sawdust, the stained old walls hung with holly wreaths and Della Robbia creations that showed real artistry. Bonnie had gone whooping off in the direction of the taller trees, disappearing from sight so quickly that Don had hurried after her, leaving Margaret standing just inside the door.

She found herself suddenly struggling with that queer and elusive conviction that "this has happened before." Not since her own childhood had she felt so strongly that she was capable of predicting in detail the events that would follow this moment. Already her flesh prickled with foreknowledge of the touch that would come... *now*.

She whirled to stare into the inky eyes of the man who stood beside her, his hand poised lightly on her bare forearm. Yes, he was part of the dream she'd returned to—the long, tormenting dream in which she cried out for wholeness, for decency, and love, only to have the trees close in on her, shutting away the light. "The trees, the trees..." Margaret murmured. The dream began to fade. She looked down across the packages she held at the dark hand that smoothed the golden hairs on her forearm. *I got those last summer when I swam so much.*

She straightened suddenly as the dream ended, trying to shake off the languor that held her while a strange, ugly man stroked her arm. She managed to jerk away from him, spilling the packages at her feet. He knelt with her to pick them up, his head so close to hers that she smelled his dirty, oily hair. The odour of it conjured up for her (*again?*) the small, cramped room and the bed with the thin mattress that never kept out the cold. Onions were browning in olive oil there over the gas plate. The man standing at the window with his back turned... *He needed her; nobody else needed her in just that way. Besides, Mama had said to watch over Alberto. How could she leave him alone? But Mama was dead... And how could Mama know all the bad things Alberto had taught her?*

"Margaret." Don's voice called her rather sharply out of the dream that had again enveloped her. Margaret's sigh was like a half-sob. She laughed up at her husband, and he helped her to her feet, and gathered up the packages. The strange man was introducing himself to Don. He was Mr. Cravolini, the proprietor. He had seen that the lady was very pale, ready to faint, perhaps. He'd stepped up to assist her, unfortunately frightening her, since his step had not been heard—due, doubtless, to the great depth of the sawdust on the floor. Don, she saw, was listening to the overtones of the apology. If Mr. Cravolini's voice displayed the smallest hint of insolence and pride in the lies he was telling, then Don would grab him by the shirt front and shake him till he stopped lying and begged for mercy. Don did not believe in fighting. Often while he and Margaret lay warmly and happily in bed together Don spoke regretfully of his "wild-kid" days, glad that with maturity he need not prove on every street corner that he was not afraid to fight, glad to admit to Margaret that often he'd been scared, and always he'd been sick afterwards. Don approved of social lies, the kind that permitted people to live and work together without too much friction. So Mr. Cravolini had made a mistake. Finding Margaret alone, he'd made a pass. He knew better now. OK. Forget it. Thus Margaret read her husband's face and buried very deeply the sharp, small stab of disappointment. *A fight would have ended it, for good.* She frowned a little with the effort to understand her own chaotic thoughts, her vision of a door that had almost closed on a narrow, stifling room, but was now wedged open... waiting.

Don led her down one of the long aisles of trees to where Bonnie and Bruce were huddled beside their choice. Margaret scarcely glanced at the tree. Don was annoyed with her—half-convinced, as he always was, that Margaret had invited the pass. Not by any overt signal on her part, but simply because she forgot to look busy and preoccupied.

"Don't go dawdling along in that wide-eyed dreamy way," he'd said so often. "I don't know what it is, but you've got that look—as if you'd say yes to a square meal or to a panhandler or to somebody's bed."

Bonnie was preening herself on the tree she'd chosen, chanting a maddening little refrain that Bruce would comprehend at any moment: "And Bru-cie did-unt he-ulp..." Already Bruce recognised that the singsong words meant something scornful and destructive to his dignity. His face puckered, and he drew the three long breaths that preceded his best screaming.

Margaret hoisted him up into her arms, while Don and Bonnie hastily beat a retreat with the excuse that they must pay Mr. Cravolini for the tree. Bruce screamed his fury at a world that kept trying to confine him, limit him, or otherwise squeeze his outsize ego down to puny, civilised proportions. Margaret paced up and down the aisles with him, wondering why Don and Bonnie were taking so long.

Far back at the rear of the store building, where the lights were dimmest, Margaret caught sight of a display of handmade candles. Still joggling Bruce up and down as if she were churning butter, she paused to look them over. Four pale blue candles of varying lengths rose gracefully from a flat base moulded to resemble a sheaf of laurel leaves. Very nice, and probably very expensive. Margaret turned away to find Mr. Cravolini standing immediately in front of her.

"Do you like those candles?" he asked softly.

"Where is my husband?" Margaret kept her eyes on Bruce's fine, blonde hair. *Don't let the door open any more...*

"Your husband has gone to bring his car. He and your daughter. The tree is too large to carry so far. Why are you afraid?"

"I'm not afraid..." She glanced fleetingly into the man's eyes, troubled again that her knowledge of his identity wavered just beyond reality. "Have we met before?" she asked.

"I almost saw you once," Cravolini said. "I was standing at a window. You were reflected in it, but when I turned around you were gone. There was nobody in the room but my sister... the stupid cow..." Cravolini spat into the sawdust. "That day I made a candle for you. Wait." He reached swiftly behind the stacked packing boxes that held the candles on display. He had placed it in her hand before she got a clear look at it. Sickeningly pink, loathsomely slick and hand-filling. It would have been cleaner, more honest, she thought, if it had been a frank reproduction of what it was intended to suggest. She dropped it and ran awkwardly with the baby towards the lights at the entrance way. Don was just parking the car. She wrenched the door open and half fell into the front seat. Bonnie had rushed off with Don to bring out the tree. Margaret buried her face in Bruce's warm, sweet-smelling neck and nuzzled him till he laughed aloud. She never quite remembered afterwards the ride home that night. She must have been very quiet—in one of her "lost" moods, as Don called them. The next morning she was surprised to see that Bonnie had picked one of Cravolini's largest, finest trees, and to discover the tissue-wrapped pale blue candles he had given Bonnie as a special Christmas gift.

Every year after that Margaret promised herself that this year she'd stay at home on the tree-buying night. But something always forced her to go—some errand, a last bit of shopping, or Don's stern injunctions not to be silly, that he could not handle Bonnie, Bruce, *and* the biggest tree in town. Once there, she never managed to escape Cravolini's unctuous welcome. If she sat in the car, then he came out to speak to her. Much better go inside and stick close by Don and the children. But that never quite worked, either. Somehow the three of them eluded her; she might hear their delighted shouts two aisles over, but when she hastened in their direction, she found only Cravolini waiting. She never eluded him. Sometimes on New Year's Day, when she heard so much about resolutions on radio and television, she thought that surely this year she'd tell Don at least some of the things Cravolini said to her—did to her—enough, anyway, to assure the Abbotts never going back there again. But she never did. It would be difficult to explain to Don why she'd waited so long to speak out about it. Why hadn't she told him that first night?

She could only shake her head in puzzlement and distaste for motivations that were tangled in a long, bad dream. And how could a woman of almost-forty explain and deeply explore a woman in her twenties? Even if they were the same woman, it was impossible.

When Cravolini's "opening announcement" card arrived each year, Margaret was jolted out of the peacefulness that inevitably built in her between Christmases. It was as if a torn and raw portion of her brain healed in the interim. *But the door was still invitingly wedged open, and every Christmas something tried to force her inside.* Margaret's spirit fought the assailant that seemed to accompany Mr. Cravolini (hovering there beyond the lights, flitting behind the trees), but the fighting left her weak and tired and without any words to help her communicate her distress. *If only Don would see,* she thought. *If there were no need for words. It ought to be like that…* At such times she accused herself of indulging in Bruce's outgrown baby fury, crying out against things as they are.

Every time she saw Cravolini the dream gained in reality and continuity. He was very friendly with the Abbotts now. They were among his "oldest customers," privileged to receive his heartiest greetings along with the beautiful candles and wreaths he gave the children. Margaret had hoped this year that she could convince Bonnie and Bruce to have a different kind of tree—something modern and a little startling, perhaps, like tumbleweeds sprayed pink and mounted on a tree-shaped form. Anything. But they laughed at her bad taste, and were as horrified as if she were trying to by-pass Christmas itself.

I wonder if I'll see *her* this year, Margaret thought. Alberto's sister. She knew so much about her now—that she was dumb, but that she had acute, morbidly sensitive hearing—that once she'd heard Cravolini murmuring his lust to Margaret, because that was the time the animal-grunting, laughing sounds had come from the back of the store, there where extra trees lay stacked against the wall. Her name was Angela, and she was very gross, very fat, very ugly. Unmarriageable, Alberto said. Part of what Margaret knew of Angela came from Alberto's whispered confidences (unwanted, oh unasked for!), and the rest grew out of the dream that lived and walked with Margaret there in the crumbling building, beginning the moment she entered the door, ending only with Don's voice, calling her back to sanity and to another life.

There were self-revelatory moments in her life with Don when Margaret was able to admit to herself that the dream had power to call her back. She would like to know the ending. It was like a too-short book that left one hungry and dissatisfied. So this year she gave way to the children, to tradition, and went once again to Cravolini's.

Margaret was aware that she looked her best in the dull red velveteen suit. The double golden hoops at her ears tinkled a little when she walked and made her feel like an arrogant gypsy. She and Don had stopped at their favourite small bar for several drinks while the children finished their shopping.

Maybe it's the drinks, Margaret thought, and maybe it's the feeling that tonight, at last, I'll settle Mr. Cravolini, that makes me walk so jut-bosomed and proud. Don, already on his way with her to Cravolini's, had dropped into a department store with the mumbled excuse that always preceded his gift-buying for Margaret. He had urged her to go on alone, reminding her that the children might be there waiting. For once, Margaret went fearlessly, almost eagerly.

The children were not waiting, but the woman was. *Angela.* Margaret knew her instantly, just as she'd known Alberto. Angela stared up and down at Margaret and did not bother to hide her amusement, or her knowledge of Margaret's many hot, protesting encounters with her brother. Margaret started to speak, but the woman only jerked her head meaningfully towards the back of the store. Margaret did not move. The dream was beginning. *Alberto is waiting, there beyond the stacked-high Christmas trees. See the soft, springy nest he has built for you with pine boughs.* Margaret stirred uneasily and began to move down the aisle, Angela beside her.

I must go to him. He needs me. Mama said to look after Alberto. That I would win for myself a crown in Heaven... Did she know how unnatural a brother Alberto is? Did she know how he learned the seven powers from the old, forbidden books? And taught them to me? He shall have what he desires, and so shall I. Here, Alberto, comes the proud, silly spirit you've won... and listen, Don and the children are coming in the door.

Margaret found the soft, springy bed behind the stacked trees. Alberto was there, waiting. She heard Don call for her and struggled to answer, struggled desperately to rise to go to him. But she was so fat, so heavy, so ugly... She heard the other woman's light, warm voice answering, heard her happy, foolish joking with the children, her mock-protestations, as always, at the enormous tree they picked. Margaret fought wildly and caught a last glimpse of the Abbotts, the four of them, and saw the dull, red suit the woman wore, heard the final, flirtatious tinkling of the golden earrings, and then they were gone.

A whole year I must wait, Margaret thought, *and maybe next year they won't come. She will see to that.*

"My sister, my love..." Alberto crooned at her ear.

THE WAITS

L. P. Hartley

First published in *Two for the River* (1961)

Leslie Poles Hartley (1895–1972) started his literary career as a book reviewer, before having a first short story collection published in 1924 and later moving on to novel writing. His most famous book is probably *The Go-Between* (1953), generally regarded as a modern classic. He was a close friend of Cynthia Asquith, and she supported him by including his work in several of her edited collections; he wrote the introduction to her *Third Ghost Book* in 1955, and contributed the story 'Someone in the Lift' to the same volume.

'The Waits', featuring some carol singers who are not what they seem, includes one of the recurring themes of Hartley's works—a scenario in which comfortable ordinariness becomes a source of horror.

Christmas Eve had been for all the Marriners, except Mr. Marriner, a most exhausting day. The head of the house usually got off lightly at the festive season, lightly that is as far as personal effort went. Financially, no; Mr. Marriner knew that financially quite a heavy drain was being made on his resources. And later in the evening when he got out his cheque-book to give his customary presents to his family, his relations and the staff, the drain would be heavier. But he could afford it, he could afford it better this Christmas than at any other Christmas in the history of his steadily increasing fortune. And he didn't have to think, he didn't have to choose; he only had to consult a list and add one or two names, and cross off one or two. There was quite a big item to cross off, quite a big item, though it didn't figure on the list or on the counterfoil of his cheque-book. If he saw fit he would add the sum so saved to his children's cheques. Jeremy and Anne would then think him even more generous than he was, and if his wife made any comment, which she wouldn't, being a tactful woman, he would laugh and call it a Capital Distribution—"capital in every sense, my dear!"

But this could wait till after dinner.

So of the quartet who sat down to the meal, he was the only one who hadn't spent a laborious day. His wife and Anne had both worked hard decorating the house and making arrangements for the party on Boxing Day. They hadn't spent the time in getting presents, they hadn't had to. Anne, who was two years older than Jeremy, inherited her mother's gift for present-giving and had made her selections weeks ago; she had a sixth sense for knowing what people wanted. But Jeremy had left it all to the last moment. His method was the reverse of Anne's and much less successful; he thought of the present first and the recipient afterwards. Who would this little box do for? Who would this other little box do for? Who should be the fortunate possessor of this third little box? In present-giving his mind followed a one-way track; and this year it was little boxes. They were expensive and undiscriminating presents and he was secretly ashamed of them. Now it was too late to do anything more: but when he thought of the three or four friends who would remain un-boxed his conscience smote him.

Silent and self-reproachful, he was the first to hear the singing outside the window.

"Listen, there's some carol-singers!" His voice, which was breaking, plunged and croaked.

The others all stopped talking and smiles spread over their faces.

"Quite good, aren't they?"

"The first we've had this year," said Mrs. Marriner.

"Well, not the first, my dear; they started coming days ago, but I sent them away and said that waits must wait till Christmas Eve."

"How many of them are there?"

"Two, I think," said Jeremy.

"A man and a woman?"

Jeremy got up and drew the curtain. Pierced only by a single distant street-lamp, the darkness in the garden pressed against the window-pane.

"I can't quite see," he said, coming back. "But I think it's a man and a boy."

"A man and a boy?" said Mr. Marriner. "That's rather unusual."

"Perhaps they're choristers, Daddy. They do sing awfully well."

At that moment the front-door bell rang. To preserve the character of the house, which was an old one, they had retained the original brass bell-pull. When it was pulled the whole house seemed to shudder audibly, with a strangely searching sound, as if its heart-strings had been plucked, while the bell itself gave out a high yell that split into a paroxysm of jangling. The Marriners were used to this phenomenon, and smiled when it made strangers jump: tonight it made them jump themselves. They listened for the sound of footsteps crossing the stone flags of the hall, but there was none.

"Mrs. Parfitt doesn't come till washing-up time," said Mrs. Marriner. "Who'll go and give them something?"

"I will," Anne said, jumping up. "What shall I give them, Daddy?"

"Oh, give them a bob," said Mr. Marriner, producing the coin from his pocket. However complicated the sum required he always had it.

Anne set off with the light step and glowing face of an eager benefactor; she came back after a minute or two at a much slower pace and looking puzzled and rather frightened. She didn't sit down but stood over her place with her hands on the chair-back.

"He said it wasn't enough," she said.

"Wasn't enough?" her father repeated. "Did he really say that?"

Anne nodded.

"Well, I like his cheek." Even to his family Mr. Marriner's moods were unforeseeable; by some chance the man's impudence had touched a sympathetic chord in him. "Go back and say that if they sing another carol they shall have another bob."

But Anne didn't move.

"If you don't mind, Daddy, I'd rather not."

They all three raised questioning faces to hers.

"You'd rather not? Why?"

"I didn't like his manner."

"Whose, the man's?"

"Yes. The boy—you were right, Jeremy, it is a boy, quite a small boy—didn't say anything."

"What was wrong with the man's manner?" Mr. Marriner, still genial, asked.

"Oh, I don't know!" Anne began to breathe quickly and her fingers tightened on the chair-back. "And it wasn't only his manner."

"Henry, I shouldn't—" began Mrs. Marriner warningly, when suddenly Jeremy jumped up. He saw the chance to redeem himself in his own eyes from his ineffectiveness over the Christmas shopping—from the general ineffectiveness that he was conscious of whenever he compared himself with Anne.

"Here's the shilling," Anne said, holding it out. "He wouldn't take it."

"This will make it two," their father said, suiting the action to the word. "But only if they sing again, mind you."

While Jeremy was away, they all fell silent, Anne still trying to compose her features, Mr. Marriner tapping on the table, his wife studying her rings. At last she said:

"They're all so class-conscious nowadays."

"It wasn't that," said Anne.

"What was it?"

Before she had time to answer—if she would have answered—the door opened and Jeremy came in, flushed and excited but also triumphant, with the triumph he had won over himself. He didn't go to his place but stood away from the table looking at his father.

"He wouldn't take it," he said. "He said it wasn't enough. He said you would know why."

"I should know why?" Mr. Marriner's frown was an effort to remember something. "What sort of man is he, Jeremy?"

"Tall and thin, with a pulled-in face."

"And the boy?"

"He looked about seven. He was crying."

"Is it anyone you know, Henry?" asked his wife.

"I was trying to think. Yes, no, well, yes, I might have known him." Mr. Marriner's agitation was now visible to them all, and even more felt than seen. "What did you say, Jeremy?"

Jeremy's breast swelled.

"I told him to go away."

"And has he gone?"

As though in answer the bell pealed again.

"I'll go this time," said Mrs. Marriner. "Perhaps I can do something for the child."

And she was gone before her husband's outstretched arm could stop her.

Again the trio sat in silence, the children less concerned with themselves than with the gleam that kept coming and going in their father's eyes like a dipping headlight.

Mrs. Marriner came back much more self-possessed than either of her children had.

"I don't think he means any harm," she said, "he's a little cracked, that's all. We'd better humour him. He said he wanted to see you, Henry, but I told him you were out. He said that what we offered wasn't enough and that he wanted what you gave him last year, whatever that means. So I suggest we give him something that isn't money. Perhaps you could spare him one of your boxes, Jeremy. A Christmas box is quite a good idea."

"He won't take it," said Anne, before Jeremy could speak.

"Why not?"

"Because he can't," said Anne.

"Can't? What do you mean?" Anne shook her head. Her mother didn't press her.

"Well, you are a funny girl," she said. "Anyhow, we can but try. Oh, and he said they'd sing us one more carol."

They set themselves to listen, and in a moment the strains of "God rest you merry, gentlemen" began.

Jeremy got up from the table.

"I don't believe they're singing the words right," he said. He went to the window and opened it, letting in a puff of icy air.

"Oh, do shut it!"

"Just a moment. I want to make sure."

They all listened, and this is what they heard:

"God blast the master of this house,
Likewise the mistress too,

280

> And all the little children
> That round the table go."

Jeremy shut the window. "Did you hear?" he croaked.

"I thought I did," said Mrs. Marriner. "But it might have been 'bless', the words sound so much alike. Henry, dear, don't look so serious."

The door-bell rang for the third time. Before the jangling died down, Mr. Marriner rose shakily.

"No, no, Henry," said his wife. "Don't go, it'll only encourage them. Besides, I said you were out." He looked at her doubtfully, and the bell rang again, louder than before. "They'll soon get tired of it," she said, "if no one comes. Henry, I beg you not to go." And when he still stared at her with groping eyes, she added:

"You can't remember how much you gave him last year?" Her husband made an impatient gesture with his hand.

"But if you go take one of Jeremy's boxes."

"It isn't a box they want," he said, "it's a bullet."

He went to the sideboard and brought out a pistol. It was an old-fashioned saloon pistol, a relic from the days when Henry's father, in common with others of his generation, had practised pistol-shooting, and it had lain at the back of a drawer in the sideboard longer than any of them could remember.

"No, Henry, no! You mustn't get excited! And think of the child!"

She was on her feet now; they all were.

"Stay where you are!" he snarled.

"Anne! Jeremy! Tell him not to! Try to stop him." But his children could not in a moment shake off the obedience of a lifetime, and helplessly they watched him go.

"But it isn't any good, it isn't any good!" Anne kept repeating.

"What isn't any good, darling?"

"The pistol. You see, I've seen through him!"

"How do you mean, seen through him? Do you mean he's an imposter?"

"No, no. I've really seen through him," Anne's voice sank to a whisper. "I saw the street-lamp shining through a hole in his head."

"Darling, darling!"

"Yes, and the boy, too—"

"Will you be quiet, Anne?" cried Jeremy from behind the window curtain. "Will you be quiet? They're saying something. Now Daddy's pointing the gun at him—he's got him covered! His finger's on the trigger, he's going to shoot! No, he isn't. The man's come nearer—he's come right up to Daddy! Now he's showing him something, something on his forehead—oh, if I had a torch—and Daddy's dropped it, he's dropped the gun!"

As he spoke they heard the clatter; it was like the sound that gives confirmation to a wireless commentator's words. Jeremy's voice broke out again:

"He's going off with them—he's going off with them! They're leading him away!"

Before she or any of them could reach the door, Mrs. Marriner had fainted.

The police didn't take long to come. On the grass near the garden gate they found the body. There were signs of a struggle—a slither, like a skid-mark, on the gravel, heel-marks dug deep into the turf. Later it was learnt that Mr. Marriner had died of coronary thrombosis. Of his assailants not a trace was found. But the motive couldn't have been robbery, for all the money he had had in his pockets, and all the notes out of his wallet (a large sum), were scattered around him, as if he had made a last attempt to buy his captors off, but couldn't give them enough.

DEADMAN'S CORNER

George Denby

First published in *The Illustrated London News*, Christmas 1963

We have not been able to find out anything at all about George Denby, the author of this story. 'Deadman's Corner' appeared in the Christmas number of the *Illustrated London News* for 1963, but Denby doesn't appear to have contributed any other stories or articles to the publication in other years. It may have been a *nom de plume*, used by a journalist for what was seen as a light-weight entertainment unlike their more serious job reporting on real events.

The Illustrated London News was published between 1842 and 2003, having been founded by the newsagent Herbert Ingram when he noticed that customers were more likely to buy news-papers when they included illustrations. It was the first illustrated weekly news magazine in the world. The *ILN* didn't often publish fiction except in its Christmas special issues. 'Deadman's Corner' is a short, old-fashioned ghost story that harkens back to some of the earliest examples of the genre.

Where the road swung round the corner of the hill on its course, a length of it had been picked up by the roadmenders. And now the area where they had been working was screened by a temporary fencing, suspended from which warning lamps shone with red lights. The watchman had a great fire blazing in his brazier and the brazier itself almost in the mouth of his canvas shelter, for the night was very bitter and off and on fine powdery snow came eddying down.

As he spread his hands to the blaze the watchman saw that he was not alone. A stranger, a tall, gaunt man with a deeply lined face and a straggling grey moustache, had come up like a ghost from behind him and now stood shivering in the outmost circle of the firelight.

"'Ullo, mate, I didn't 'ear yer," said the watchman. "Where you come from?"

"I jest come down from 'ill," said the stranger. "May I warm meself by your fire?" He was shivering violently. Patches of snow rested here and there on his old worn overcoat and on the front of his soft old bowler hat.

"Step right in, chum... From 'ill, eh? I thought as there was nobbut cemet'ry on 'ill."

"Ah. Cemet'ry and footpath to Crowley. You'm a stranger in these parts, seemin'."

287

"Ah. I come gangin'. Pretty cold over 'ill, wan't it?"

With stiff, awkward movements the stranger advanced and crouched over the watchman's fire, spreading his dirty, bony old hands over the blaze. He raised a pair of dull, fish-like eyes to the night watchman.

"Cold, ah. Pretty cold it were... So they're mendin' old road at last."

"Ah."

"'Bout time too. Bad name this corner's allus 'ad."

"Accidents?"

"Ah, and more'n accidents." With the palms of his hands he essayed to brush the snow off the front of his old worn overcoat.

"W'y, wot more'n accidents?"

"W'y, it's 'ereabout, by the roadside like, many a year agone, as they took and 'anged Dancing Jack. Ah, and buried 'un too nigh about."

"Dancin' Jack? Never 'eard tell on 'im. 'Oo was 'e?"

"'Ighwayman, that's wot 'e was. 'E robbed mail 'ereabouts, and they took 'im and 'anged, drawed and quartered 'im, ah, and buried 'un too nigh round about. And folk won't come nigh this place 'o nights accordin'."

"Well, I ain't seed 'im, mate, and I lay I never shall. I tell you wot. I bin a night watchman nigh on forty year and I can tell yer that I've watched in some mighty queer places. And I ain't never seed no ghost yet."

"No. Folk will talk. It's all talk, most like. And they skeers each other with the talk. They say as Dancin' Jack useter wait in the shadders like, on 'is 'orse and all, with 'is pistol in 'is 'and, ready to jump on any as come by."

"You ain't never seed 'im, I'll lay."

"No, I ain't never seed 'im. And some say as 'e ain't to be seen no more. They say 'e 'ad to 'aunt until 'e'd found summun to take over from 'im like. And they say as Farmer Stubbins took over from 'im. And they do say as 'e killed Farmer Stubbins accordin'."

"And 'ow did 'e do that?" asked the night watchman.

"W'y, nobody dursn't come nigh the place o' nights, 'cos they knew as old ghost wants 'is rest and 'e's arter killin' summun to take over from 'im like. But Farmer Stubbins, it's years gone by, 'e laughed at them stories—a devil-may-care feller 'e was by all accounts and they do say over fond of the bottle—and, bein' 'e was out to 'orse fair and drinkin' like, they say to 'im, if 'e don't 'urry back, 'e'll not be by Deadman's Corner till arter dark. But 'e jest laughs, not believin' there was anything in it like. So 'e 'arnesses 'is gig and drives 'ome and passes 'ere nigh on midnight. And there is old ghost waitin' fer 'im in the shadders, sittin' on 'is 'orse with 'is pistol in 'is 'and. And Farmer Stubbins' cob 'e shys and bolts and upsets gig and Farmer Stubbins 'e is thrown out and killed, and cob don't stop till 'e's come to village and gig all smashed and broke be'ind 'im."

"That's a likely story, mate, that is. If Farmer's dead, 'oo tells folks as it were old ghost as done it? Did cob tell 'em?"

"Ah, you use yer 'ead, you do. They don't think of things like that, folk as tells ghost stories don't, do they?"

"So," said the night watchman, "it ain't Dancin' Jack on 'is 'orse I gotter watch for, but Farmer Stubbins in 'is gig?"

"W'y, no," said the stranger, pressing closer to the brazier and almost laying his cold old hands on the blazing coals. "They do say as Farmer Stubbins 'ad to find summun to take over from 'im like, and they do say as it were 'im as killed old Silas Claypole."

"Well, wot 'appened to old Silas Claypole?" asked the night watchman with comic resignation.

"W'y, they do say as old Silas were greedy arter money, come 'ow it might come. A miser they say 'e was. And up at village folk bet 'im 'e wouldn't walk to Deadman's Corner at midnight. It was a 'ard thing to do, 'im 'avin' a load on his conscience like, and, if they was arter makin' game of 'im, as some folks say, it might be the death of 'im, for they do say as 'e 'ad good cause to be skeered of some as was dead. But if there were money to be 'ad, old Silas, they say, would face old devil 'imself. So 'e asks 'ow much they lay 'im, and betwigst 'em they make up a tidy sum, and so old Silas walks to Deadman's Corner on a night with snow in it, as it might be tonight... Cold, ain't it mate?"

"Well, and wot 'appened to old Silas?"

"W'y, 'e's found next mornin' like 'e's bin trampled to death by a 'orse. And they do say as it was Farmer Stubbins drove 'is gig over 'im."

"Another likely story that is. For w'y, if old Silas is dead, 'ow folks know wot 'appened to 'im?"

"Ah, you use yer 'ead, like I said." The stranger pulled himself even closer to the fire and bent over it, so that the steam rose from him in little wisps.

"And did *you* ever see 'im?... And leave me a bit o' me own fire to sit over, won't you, chum?"

"Sorry, mate. I'm fair froze. No, I never seed 'im. Time 'e were killed I were away like. But folk up to village say as 'e mun 'aunt till 'e finds summun to take over from 'im like."

"So it ain't Dancin' Jack I gotter watch for, and it ain't Farmer Stubbins in 'is gig. It's old Silas Claypole."

"That's right, mate."

"Lookin' for summun to take over from 'im, as it might be me."

"That's right, mate."

"Well, if 'e comes, 'e's welcome to warm 'isself by old fire… if you leave 'im room and don't go 'oggin' it. You want a fire to yersel, don't you, chum?"

"Sorry, mate."

"Well, if night watchmen started believin' yarns like that o' yourn, where should we all be?"

"That's right, mate. I don't 'old with ghosts meself."

"I mean, 'ave you ever seed Dancin' Jack?"

"No, I ain't never seed 'im."

"Or old Silas Claypole?"

"No, I can't say as I 'ave."

"Well, there you are then."

"Yes, 'ere I am." The stranger was pressing forward to the fire again like a moth fascinated by a flame.

"Yes, there you are."

"That's wot I say. 'Ere I am." By now he was almost on top of the brazier.

"Cold, ain't yer, chum?" said the night watchman ironically.

"Cold?" said the stranger fiercely. "So would you be cold, if you'd bin lyin' in cemet'ry these twenty year, like I 'ave." The stranger flung himself forward on the brazier, clasping it in both his arms and burying his face among the blazing coals, which wavered and darkened as if it were a block of ice which had been suddenly put upon them. "Cold? I should think I *am* cold."

With a startled cry the night watchman leaped to his feet and started running down the road.

DON'T TELL CISSIE

Celia Fremlin

First published in *By Horror Haunted* (1974)

Celia Margaret Fremlin (1914–2009) was born in Kingsbury, then in the county of Middlesex but now a district of northwest London. Her father was a doctor and the family were middle class. Celia studied Classics at Somerville College, Oxford, and her brother John Heaver Fremlin, became a nuclear physicist and anti-war campaigner. During her studies, Celia worked in domestic service, saying that she wanted 'to observe the peculiarities of the class structure of our society'. She wrote about the experience in her first book, the non-fiction *The Seven Chars of Chelsea* (1940). During the Second World War she furthered her knowledge of the everyday lives of ordinary people by working with Mass-Observation, an organisation which recorded the views and activities of the British public.

Fremlin started submitting short stories to magazines in the 1950s, and in 1956 'The Locked Room' was the first to appear in print (in *The London Mystery Magazine*). She had a long association with the publication *Ellery Queen's Mystery Magazine*, writing many stories for them between 1967 and 1999. Her first novel, *The Hours before Dawn*, came out in 1958, and she produced fifteen further novels and three story collections.

'Don't Tell Cissie' is taken from Fremlin's collection of domestic horror and mystery stories, *By Horror Haunted*, which was published in 1974.

"**F**riday, then. The six-ten from Liverpool Street," said Rosemary, gathering up her gloves and bag. "And don't tell Cissie!" she added, "You *will* be careful about that, won't you, Lois?"

I nodded. People are always talking like this about Cissie, she's that kind of person. She was like that at school, and now, when we're all coming up towards retirement, she's like it still.

You know the kind of person I mean? Friendly, good-hearted, and desperately anxious to be in on everything, and yet with this mysterious knack of ruining things—of bringing every project grinding to a halt, simply by being there.

Because it wasn't ever her fault. Not really. "Let me come! Oh, *please* let me come too!" she'd beg, when three or four of us from the Lower Fourth had schemed up an illicit trip to the shops on Saturday afternoon. And, because she was our friend (well, sort of—anyway, it was *our* set that she hovered on the fringe of all the time, not anyone else's)—because of this, we usually let her come; and always it ended in disaster. *She'd* be the one to slip on the edge of the kerb outside Woolworth's, and cut her knee so that the blood ran, and a little crowd collected, and a kind lady rang up the school to have us fetched home. *She'd* be the one to get lost... to miss the bus... to arrive back at school bedraggled and tear-stained and late for evening preparation, hopelessly giving the game away for all of us.

You'd think, wouldn't you, that after a few such episodes she'd have given up, or at least have learned caution. But no. Her persistence (perhaps one would have called it courage if only it hadn't been so annoying)—well, her persistence, then, was indomitable. Neither school punishments nor the reproaches of her companions ever kept her under for long. "Oh, *please* let me come!" she'd be pleading again, barely a week after the last débâcle. "Oh, plee-ee-ease! Oh, don't be so *mean*!"

And so there, once again, she'd inexorably be, back in action once more. Throwing-up in the middle of the dormitory feast. Crying with blisters as we trudged back from a ramble out of bounds. Soaked, and shivering, and starting pneumonia from having fallen through the ice of the pond we'd been forbidden to skate on.

So you can understand, can't you, why Rosemary and I didn't want Cissie with us when we went to investigate the ghost at Rosemary's new weekend cottage. Small as our chances might be of pinning down the ghost in any case, Cissie could have been counted on to reduce them to zero. Dropping a tray of tea-things just as the rapping began... Calling out, "What? *I* can't hear anything!" as we held our breaths trying to locate the ghostly sobbing... Falling over a tombstone as we tiptoed through the moonlit churchyard... No, Cissie must at all costs be kept out of our little adventure; and by now, after nearly half a century, we knew that the only way of keeping Cissie out of anything was to make sure that she knew nothing about it, right from the beginning.

*

But let me get back to Rosemary's new cottage. I say "new", because Rosemary has only recently bought it—not because the cottage itself is new. Far from it. It is early eighteenth-century, and damp, and dark, and built of the local stone, and Rosemary loves it (*did* love it, rather—but let me not get ahead of myself). Anyway, as I was saying, Rosemary loved the place, loved it on sight, and bought it almost on impulse with the best part of her life's savings. *Their* life's savings, I suppose I should say, because she and Norman are still married to each other, and it must have been his money just as much as hers. But Norman never seems to have much to do with these sort of decisions—indeed, he doesn't seem to have much to do with Rosemary's life at all, these days—certainly, he never comes down to the cottage. I think that was part of the idea, really—that they should be able to get away from each other at weekends. During the week, of course, it's all right, as they are both working full-time, and they both bring plenty of work home in the evenings. Rosemary sits in one room correcting history essays, while Norman sits in another working out Export Quotas, or something; and the mutual non-communication must be almost companionable, in an arid sort of a way. But the crunch will come, of course, when they both retire in a year or so's time. I think Rosemary was thinking of this when she bought the cottage; it would become a real port in a storm then—a bolt-hole from what she refers to as "the last and worst lap of married life".

At one time, we used to be sorry for Cissie, the only one of our set who never married. But now, when the slow revolving of the decades has left me a widow and Rosemary stranded among the flotsam of a dead marriage—now, lately I have begun wondering whether Cissie hasn't done just as well for herself as any of us, in the long run. Certainly, she has had plenty of fun on the fringes of other people's lives, over the years. She wangles invitations to silver-wedding parties; worms her way into other people's family holidays—and even if it ends up with the whole lot of them in quarantine at the airport because of Cissie coming out in spots—well, at least she's usually had a good run for her money first.

And, to be fair to her, it's not just the pleasures and luxuries of our lives that she tries to share; it's the problems and crises, too. I remember she managed to be present at the birth of my younger son, and if only she hadn't dropped the boiling kettle on her foot just as I went into the second stage of labour, her presence would have been a real help. As it was, the doctor and midwife were both busy treating her for shock in the kitchen, and binding up her scalded leg, while upstairs my son arrived unattended, and mercifully without fuss. Perhaps even the unborn are sensitive to atmosphere? Perhaps he sensed, even then, that, with Cissie around, it's just *no use* anyone else making a fuss about anything?

But let me get back to Rosemary's haunted cottage (or not haunted, as the case may be—let me not prejudge the issue before I have given you all the facts). Of course, to begin with, we were half playing a game, Rosemary and I. The tension tends to go out of life as you come up towards your sixties. Whatever problems once tore at you, and kept you fighting, and alive, and gasping for breath—they are solved now, or else have died, quietly, while you weren't noticing. Anyway, what with one thing and another, life can become a bit dull and flavourless when you get to our age; and, to be honest, a ghost was just what Rosemary and I were needing. A spice of danger; a spark of the unknown to reactivate these waterlogged minds of ours, weighed down as they are by such a lifetime's accumulation of the known.

I am telling you this because I want to be absolutely honest. In evaluating the events I am to describe, you must remember, and allow for, the fact that Rosemary and I *wanted* there to be a ghost. Well, no, perhaps that's putting it too strongly; we wanted there to *might* be a ghost—if you see what I so ungrammatically mean. We wanted our weekend to bring us at least a small tingling of the blood; a tiny prickling of the scalp. We wanted our journey to reach a little way into the delicious outskirts of fear, even if it *did* have to start from Liverpool Street.

We felt marvellously superior, Rosemary and I, as we stood jam-packed in the corridor, rocking through the rainy December night. We glanced with secret pity at all those blank, commuter faces, trundling towards the security of their homes. *We* were different. *We* were travelling into the Unknown.

Our first problems, of course, were nothing to do with ghosts. They were to do with milk, and bread, and damp firewood, and why Mrs. Thorpe from the village hadn't come in to air the beds as she'd promised. She hadn't filled the lamps, either, or brought in the paraffin... how did she think Rosemary was going to get it from the shed in all this rain and dark? And where were all those tins she'd stocked up with in the summer? They couldn't *all* have been eaten...?

I'm afraid I left it all to Rosemary. I know visitors are supposed to trot around at the heels of their hostesses, yapping helpfully, like terriers; but I just won't. After all, I know how little help it is to *me*, when I am a hostess, so why should I suppose that everyone else is different? Besides, by this time I was half-frozen, what with the black, sodden fields and marshlands without, and the damp stone within; and so I decided to concentrate my meagre store of obligingness on getting a fire going.

What a job it was, though! It was as if some demon was working against me, spitting and sighing down the cavernous chimney, whistling wickedly along the icy, stone-flagged floor, blowing out each feeble flicker of flame as fast as I coaxed it from the damp balls of newspaper piled under the damper wood.

Fortunately there were plenty of matches, and gradually, as each of my abortive efforts left the materials a tiny bit drier than before, hope of success came nearer. Or maybe it was that the mischievous demon grew tired of his dance of obstruction—the awful sameness of frustrating me time and time again—anyway, for whatever reason, I at last got a few splinters of wood feebly smouldering. Bending close, and cupping my hands around the precious whorls to protect them from the sudden damp gusts and sputters of rain down the chimney, I watched, enchanted, while first one tiny speck of gold and then another glimmered on the charred wood. Another... and yet another... until suddenly, like the very dawn of creation, a flame licked upwards.

It was the first time in years and years that I had had anything to do with an open fire. I have lived in centrally heated flats for almost all of my adult life, and I had forgotten this apocalyptic moment when fire comes into being under your hands. Like God on the morning of creation, I sat there, all-powerful, tending the spark I had created. A sliver more of wood here... a knob of coal there... soon my little fire was bright, and growing, and needing me no more.

But still I tended it—or pretended to—leaning over it, spreading my icy hands to the beginnings of warmth. Vaguely, in the background, I was aware of Rosemary blundering around the place, clutching in her left hand the only oil-lamp that worked, peering disconsolately into drawers and cupboards, and muttering under her breath at each new evidence of disorder and depletion.

Honestly, it was no use trying to help. We'd have to manage, somehow, for tonight, and then tomorrow, with the coming of the blessed daylight, we'd be able to get everything to rights. Fill the lamps. Fetch food from the village. Get the place properly warm…

Warm! I shivered, and huddled closer into the wide chimney-alcove. Although the fire was burning up nicely now, it had as yet made little impact on the icy chill of the room. It was cold as only these ancient, little-used cottages *can* be cold. The cold of centuries seems to be stored up in their old stones, and the idea that you can warm it away with a single brisk weekend of paraffin heaters and hastily lit fires has always seemed to me laughable.

Not to Rosemary, though. She is an impatient sort of person, and it always seems to her that heaters *must* produce heat. That's what the word *means*! So she was first angered, then puzzled, and finally half-scared by the fact that she just *couldn't* get the cottage warm. Even in late August, when the air outside was still soft, and the warmth of summer lingered over the fields and marshes—even then, the cottage was like an ice-box inside. I remember remarking on it during my first visit—"Marvellously cool!" was how I put it at the time, for we had just returned, hot and exhausted, from a long tramp through the hazy, windless countryside; and that was the first time (I think) that Rosemary mentioned to me that the place was supposed to be haunted.

"One of those tragic, wailing ladies that the Past specialises in," she explained, rather facetiously. "She's supposed to have drowned herself away on the marsh somewhere—for love, I suppose; it always was, wasn't it? My God, though, what a thing to drown oneself for!—if only she'd *known*...!"

This set us off giggling, of course; and by the time we'd finished our wry reminiscences, and our speculations about the less-than-ecstatic love-lives of our various friends—by this time, of course, the end of the ghost story had rather got lost. Something about the woman's ghost moaning around the cottage on stormy nights (or was it moonlight ones?), and about the permanent, icy chill that had settled upon the cottage, and particularly upon the upstairs back bedroom, into which they'd carried her body, all dripping wet from the marsh.

"As good a tale as any, for when your tenants start demanding proper heating," I remember remarking cheerfully (for Rosemary, at that time, had vague and grandiose plans for making a fortune by letting the place for part of the year) and we had both laughed, and that, it had seemed, was the end of it.

But when late summer became autumn, and autumn deepened into winter, and the north-east wind, straight from Siberia, howled in over the marshes, then Rosemary began to get both annoyed and perturbed.

"I just *can't* get the place warm," she grumbled. "I can't understand it! And as for that back room—the one that looks out over the marsh—it's uncanny how cold it is! Two oil-heaters, burning day and night, and it's *still*...!"

I couldn't pretend to be surprised: as I say, I *expect* my friends' weekend cottages to be like this. But I tried to be sympathetic; and when, late in November, Rosemary confessed, half-laughing, that she really *did* think the place was haunted, it was I who suggested that we should go down together and see if we could lay the ghost.

She welcomed the suggestion with both pleasure and relief.

"If it was just the cold, I wouldn't be bothering," she explained. "But there seems to be something eerie about the place—there really does, Lois! It's like being in the presence of the dead." (Rosemary never has been in the presence of the dead, or she'd know it's not like that at all, but I let it pass.) "I'm getting to hate being there on my own. Sometimes—I know it sounds crazy, but sometimes I really *do* seem to hear voices!" She laughed, uncomfortably. "I must be in a bad way, mustn't I? *Hearing voices...! Me...!*"

To this day, I don't know how much she was really scared, and how much she was just trying to work a bit of drama into her lonely—and probably unexpectedly boring—trips down to her dream cottage. I don't suppose she even knows herself. All I can say for certain is that her mood of slightly factitious trepidation touched exactly on some deep need of my own, and at once we knew that we would go. And that it would be fun. And that Cissie must at all costs be kept out of it. Once *her* deep needs get involved, you've had it.

A little cry from somewhere in the shadows, beyond the circle of firelight, jerked me from my reverie, and for a moment I felt my heart pounding. Then, a moment later, I was laughing, for the cry came again:

"Spaghetti! Spaghetti bolognese! Four whole tins of it, all stacked up under the sink! Now, *who* could have...?"

And who could care, anyway? Food, real food, was now within our grasp! Unless... Oh dear...!

"I bet you've lost the tin-opener!" I hazarded, with a sinking heart—for at the words "spaghetti bolognese" I had realised just how hungry I was—and it was with corresponding relief that, in the flickering firelight, I saw a smug smile overspreading her face.

"See?" She held up the vital implement; it flickered through the shadows like a shining minnow as she gesticulated her triumph. "*See?* Though of course, if *Cissie* had been here...!"

We both began to giggle; and later, as we sat over the fire scooping spaghetti bolognese from pottery bowls, and drinking the red wine which Rosemary had managed to unearth—as we sat there, revelling in creature comforts, we amused ourselves by speculating on the disasters which would have befallen us by now had Cissie been one of the party. How she would have dropped the last of the matches into a puddle, looking for a lost glove... would have left the front door swinging open in the wind, blowing out our only oil-lamp. And the tin-opener, of course, would have been a write-off from the word go; if she hadn't lost it in some dark corner, it would certainly have collapsed into two useless pieces under her big, willing hands... By now, we would have been without light, heat or food...

This depressing picture seemed, somehow, to be the funniest thing imaginable as we sat there, with our stomachs comfortably full and with our third helping of red wine gleaming jewel-like in the firelight.

"To absent friends!" we giggled, raising our glasses. "And let's hope they *remain* absent," I added, wickedly, thinking of Cissie; and while we were both still laughing over this cynical toast, I saw Rosemary suddenly go rigid, her glass an inch from her lips, and I watched the laughter freeze on her face.

"Listen!" she hissed. "Listen, Lois! Do you *hear*?"

For long seconds, we sat absolutely still, and the noises of the night impinged, for the first time, on my consciousness.

The wind, rising now, was groaning and sighing around the cottage, moaning in the chimney and among the old beams. The rain spattered in little gusts against the windows, which creaked and rattled on their old hinges. Beyond them, in the dark, overgrown garden, you could hear the stir and rustle of bare twigs and sodden leaves... and beyond that again there was the faint, endless sighing of the marsh, mile upon mile of it, half-hidden under the dry, winter reeds.

"No..." I began, in a whisper; but Rosemary made a sharp little movement, commanding silence. "*Listen!*" she whispered once more; and this time—or was it my imagination?—I did begin to hear something.

"Ee... ee... ee...!" came the sound, faint and weird upon the wind. "Ee... ee... ee...!"—and for a moment it sounded so human, and so imploring, that I, too, caught my breath. It must be a trick of the wind, of course; it *must*—and as we sat there, tensed almost beyond bearing by the intentness of our listening, another sound impinged upon our preternaturally sharpened senses—a sound just as faint, and just as far away, but this time very far from ghostly.

"Pr-rr-rr! Ch-ch-ch...!"—the sound grew nearer... unmistakable... The prosaic sound of a car, bouncing and crunching up the rough track to the cottage.

Rosemary and I looked at each other.

"Norman?" she hazarded, scrambling worriedly to her feet. "But it *can't* be Norman, he *never* comes! And at this time of night, too! Oh dear, I wonder what can have happened...?" By this time she had reached the window, and she parted the curtains just as the mysterious vehicle screeched to a halt outside the gate. All I could see, from where I sat, was the triangle of darkness between the parted curtains, and Rosemary's broad back, rigid with disbelief and dismay.

Then, she turned on me.

"Lois!" she hissed. "How *could* you...!"

I didn't ask her what she meant. Not after all these years.

"I didn't! Of course I didn't! What do you take me for?" I retorted, and I don't doubt that by now my face was almost as white as hers.

For, of course, she did not need to tell me who it was who had arrived. Not after nearly half a century of this sort of thing. Besides, who else was there who slammed a car door as if slapping down an invasion from Mars? Who else would announce her arrival by yelling "Yoo-hoo!" into the midnight air, and bashing open the garden gate with a hat-box, so that latch and socket hurtled together into the night?

"Oops—sorry!" said Cissie, for perhaps the fifty-thousandth time in our joint lives; and she blundered forward towards the light, like an untidy grey moth. For by now we had got the front door open, and lamplight was pouring down the garden path, lighting up her round, radiant face and her halo of wild grey curls, all a-glitter with drops of rain.

"You naughty things! Fancy not *telling* me!" she reproached us, as she surged through the lighted doorway, dumping her luggage to left and right. It was, as always, like a one-man army of occupation. Always, she manages to fill any situation so totally with herself, and her belongings, and her eagerness, that there simply isn't *room* for anyone else's point of view. It's not selfishness, exactly; it's more like being a walking takeover bid, with no control over one's operations.

"A real, live ghost! Isn't it thrilling!" she babbled, as we edged her into the firelit room. "Oh, but you *should* have told me! You *know* how I love this sort of thing...!"

On and on she chattered, in her loud, eager, unstoppable voice... and this, too, we recognised as part of her technique of infiltration. By the time her victims have managed to get a word in edgeways, their first fine fury has already begun to wilt... the cutting-edge of their protests has been blunted... their sense of outrage has become blurred. And anyway, by that time she is *there*. Inescapably, irreversibly, *there*!

Well, what can you do? By the time Rosemary and I got a chance to put a word in, Cissie already had her coat off, her luggage spilling on to the floor, and a glass of red wine in her hand. There she was, reclining in the big easy chair (mine), the firelight playing on her face, exactly as if she had lived in the place for years.

"But, Cissie, how did you find *out*?" was the nearest, somehow, that we could get to a reproof; and she laughed her big, merry laugh, and the bright wine sloshed perilously in her raised glass.

"Simple, you poor Watsons!" she declared. "You see, I happened to be phoning Josie, and Josie happened to mention that Mary had said that Phyllis had told her that she'd heard from Ruth, and..."

See what I mean? You can't win. You might as well try to dodge the Recording Angel himself.

"And when I heard about the ghost, then of course I just *had* to come!" she went on. "It sounded just *too* fascinating! You see, it just happens that at the moment I know a good deal about ghosts, because..."

Well, of course she did. It was her knowing a good deal about Classical Greek architecture last spring that had kept her arguing with the guide on the Parthenon for so long that the coach went off without us. And it was precisely because she'd boned-up so assiduously on rare Alpine plants that she'd broken her leg trying to reach one of them a couple of years ago, and we had to call out the Mountain Rescue for her. The rest of us had thought it was just a daisy.

"Yes, well, we don't even know yet that there *is* a ghost," said Rosemary, dampingly; but not dampingly enough, evidently, for we spent the rest of the evening—and indeed far into the small hours—trying to dissuade Cissie from putting into practice, then and there, various uncomfortable and hazardous methods of ghost-hunting of which she had recently informed herself—methods which ranged from fixing a tape-recorder on the thatched roof, to ourselves lying all night in the churchyard, keeping our minds a blank.

By two o'clock, our minds were blank anyway—well, Rosemary's and mine were—and we could think about nothing but bed. Here, though, there were new obstacles to be overcome, for not only was Cissie's arrival unexpected and unprepared-for, but she insisted on being put in the Haunted Room. If it *was* haunted—anyway, the room that was coldest, dampest, and most uncomfortable, and therefore entitled her (well, what can you do?) to the only functioning oil-heater, and more than her share of the blankets.

"Of course, I shan't *sleep!*" she promised (as if this was some sort of special treat for me and Rosemary). "I shall be keeping vigil all night long! And tomorrow night, darlings, as soon as the moon rises, we must each take a white willow-twig, and pace in silent procession through the garden..."

We nodded, simply because we were too sleepy to argue; but beyond the circle of lamplight, Rosemary and I exchanged glances of undiluted negativism. I mean, apart from anything else, you'd have to be crazy to embark on any project which depended for its success on Cissie's not falling over something.

But we did agree, without too much reluctance, to her further suggestion that tomorrow morning we should call on the Vicar and ask him if we might look through the Parish archives. Even Cissie, we guardedly surmised, could hardly wreck a call on a vicar.

But the next morning, guess what? Cissie was laid up with lumbago, stiff as a board, and unable even to get out of bed, let alone go visiting.

"Oh dear—Oh, please don't bother!" she kept saying, as we ran around with hot-water bottles and extra pillows. "Oh dear, I do so hate to be a nuisance!"

We hated her to be a nuisance, too, but we just managed not to say so; and after a bit our efforts, combined with her own determination not to miss the fun (yes, she was still counting it fun)—after a bit, all this succeeded in loosening her up sufficiently to let her get out of bed and on to her feet; and at once her spirits rocketed sky-high. She decided, gleefully, that her affliction was a supernatural one, consequent on sleeping in the haunted room.

"Damp sheets, more likely!" said Rosemary, witheringly. "If people *will* turn up unexpectedly like this..."

But Cissie is unsquashable. *Damp sheets?* When the alternative was the ghost of a lady who'd died two hundred years ago? Cissie has never been one to rest content with a likely explanation if there is an *un*likely one to hand.

"I know what I'm talking about!" she retorted. "I know more about this sort of thing than either of you. I'm a Sensitive, you see. I only discovered it just recently, but it seems I'm one of those people with a sort of sixth sense when it comes to the supernatural. It makes me more *vulnerable*, of course, to this sort of thing—look at my bad back—but it also makes me more *aware*. I can *sense* things. Do you know, the moment I walked into this room last night, I could tell that it was haunted! I could feel the... Ouch!"

Her back had caught her again; all that gesticulating while she talked had been a mistake. However, between us we got her straightened up once more, and even managed to help her down the stairs—though I must say it wasn't long before we were both wishing we'd left well alone—if I may put it so uncharitably. For Cissie, up, was far, far more nuisance than Cissie in bed. In bed, her good intentions could harm no one; but once up and about, there seemed no limit to the trouble she could cause in the name of "helping". Trying to lift pans from shelves above her head; trying to rake out cinders without bending, and setting the hearth-brush on fire in the process; trying to fetch paraffin in cans too heavy for her to lift, and slopping it all over the floor. Rosemary and I seemed to be forever clearing up after her, or trying to un-crick her from some position she'd got stuck in for some maddening, altruistic reason.

Disturbingly, she seemed to get worse as the day went on, not better. The stiffness increased, and by afternoon she looked blue with cold, and was scarcely able to move. But nothing would induce her to let us call a doctor, or put her to bed.

"What, and miss all the fun?" she protested, through numbed lips. "Don't you realise that this freezing cold is *significant*? It's the chilling of the air that you always get before the coming of an apparition…!"

By now, it was quite hard to make out what she was saying, so hoarse had her voice become, and so stiff her lips; but you could still hear the excitement and triumph in her croaked exhortations:

"Isn't it thrilling! This is the Chill of Death, you know, darlings! It's the warning that the dead person is now about to appear! Oh, I'm so thrilled! Any moment now, and we're going to know the truth…!"

We did, too. A loud knocking sounded on the cottage door, and Rosemary ran to answer it. From where I stood, in the living-room doorway, I could see her framed against the winter twilight—already the short December afternoon was nearly at an end. Beyond her, I glimpsed the uniforms of policemen, heard their solemn voices.

"'Miss Cecily Curtis?'—Cissie? Yes, of course we know her!" I heard Rosemary saying, in a frightened voice; and then came the two deeper voices, grave and sympathetic.

I could hardly hear their words from where I was standing, yet somehow the story wasn't difficult to follow. It was almost as if, in some queer way, I'd known all along. How last night, at about 10.30 p.m., a Miss Cecily Curtis had skidded while driving—too fast—along the dyke road, and had plunged, car and all, into deep water. The body had only been recovered and identified this morning.

As I say, I did not really need to hear the men's actual words. Already the picture was in my mind, the picture which has never left it: the picture of Cissie, all lit up with curiosity and excitement, belting through the rain and dark to be in on the fun. Nothing would keep her away, not even death itself…

A little sound in the room behind me roused me from my state of shock, and I turned to see Cissie smiling that annoying smile of hers, for the very last time. It's maddened us for years, the plucky way she smiles in the face of whatever adversity she's got us all into.

"You see?" she said, a trifle smugly, "I've been dead ever since last night—it's no wonder I've been feeling so awful!"—and with a triumphant little toss of her head she turned, fell over her dressing-gown cord, and was gone.

Yes, gone. We never saw her again. The object they carried in, wet and dripping from the marsh, seemed to be nothing to do with her at all.

We never discovered whether the cottage had been haunted all along; but it's haunted now, all right. I don't suppose Rosemary will go down there much any more—certainly, we will never go ghost-hunting there again. Apart from anything else, we are too scared. There is so much that might go wrong. It was different in the old days, when we could play just any wild escapade we liked, confident that whatever went wrong would merely be the fault of our idiotic, infuriating, impossible, irreplaceable friend.

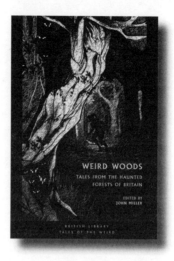

*But foliage surrounded him, branches blocked the
way; the trees stood close and still; and the sun dipped
that moment behind a great black cloud. The entire
wood turned dark and silent. It watched him.*

Woods play a crucial and recurring role in horror, fantasy, the gothic and the weird. They are places in which strange things happen, where it is easy to lose your way. Supernatural creatures thrive in the thickets. Trees reach into underworlds of pagan myth and magic. Forests are full of ghosts.

Lining the path through this realm of folklore and fear are twelve stories from across Britain, telling tales of whispering voices and maddening sights from deep in the Yorkshire Dales to the ancient hills of Gwent and the eerie quiet of the forests of Dartmoor. Immerse yourself in this collection of classic tales celebrating the enduring power of our natural spaces to enthral and terrorise our senses.

ALSO AVAILABLE

There was a faint rustling sound, like some small silk thing
blown in a gentle breeze. He sat up straight, stark and
scared, and a small wooden voice spoke in the stillness.
'Pa-pa,' it said, with a break between the syllables.

From living dolls to spirits wandering in search of solace or vengeance, the ghostly youth is one of the most enduring phenomena of supernatural fiction, its roots stretching back into the realms of folklore and superstition. In this spine-tingling new collection Jen Baker gathers a selection of the most chilling hauntings and encounters with ghostly children, expertly paired with notes and extracts from the folklore and legends which inspired them.

Reviving obscure stories from Victorian periodicals alongside nail-biting episodes from master storytellers such as Elizabeth Gaskell, M. R. James and Margery Lawrence, this is a collection by turns enchanting, moving and thoroughly frightening.

ALSO AVAILABLE

Where the indescribable thrills of music and the arts, piercing early psychology and terrifying supernatural beings find their meeting place, so dwell the startlingly original weird tales of Vernon Lee.

In this collection, fiction expert Mike Ashley selects the writer's eeriest dark fantasies: stories which blend the shocking, the sentimental, the beautiful and the unnerving into an atmosphere and style still unmatched in the field of supernatural writing.

From the modernised folktales "Marsyas in Flanders" and "The Legend of Madame Krasinska" to ingenious psychological hauntings such as "A Phantom Lover" and "A Wicked Voice", Lee's captivating voice rings out just as distinctively now as in her Fin-de-Siècle heyday.

… and then the music was so loud, so beautiful that I couldn't think of anything else. I was completely lost to the music, enveloped by melody which was part of Pan.

In 1894, Arthur Machen's landmark novella *The Great God Pan* was published, sparking the sinister resurgence of the pagan goat god. Writers of the late-nineteenth to mid-twentieth centuries, such as Oscar Wilde, E. M. Forster and Margery Lawrence, took the god's rebellious influence as inspiration to spin beguiling tales of social norms turned upside down and ancient ecological forces compelling their protagonists to ecstatic heights or bizarre dooms.

Assembling ten tales and six poems—along with Machen's novella—from the boom years of Pan-centric literature, this new collection revels in themes of queer awakening, transgression against societal bonds and the bewitching power of the wild as it explores a rapturous and culturally significant chapter in the history of weird fiction.